Brideen

The Journeys of a Famine Daughter

Kathleen McDonnell

AOS Publishing, 2025
Copyright © 2025 Kathleen McDonnell

ISBN: 978-1-998662-60-9

Cover Design: Meredith Lindsay

Visit AOS Publishing's website:
www.aospublishing.com

Author's website:
www.kathleenmcdonnell.com

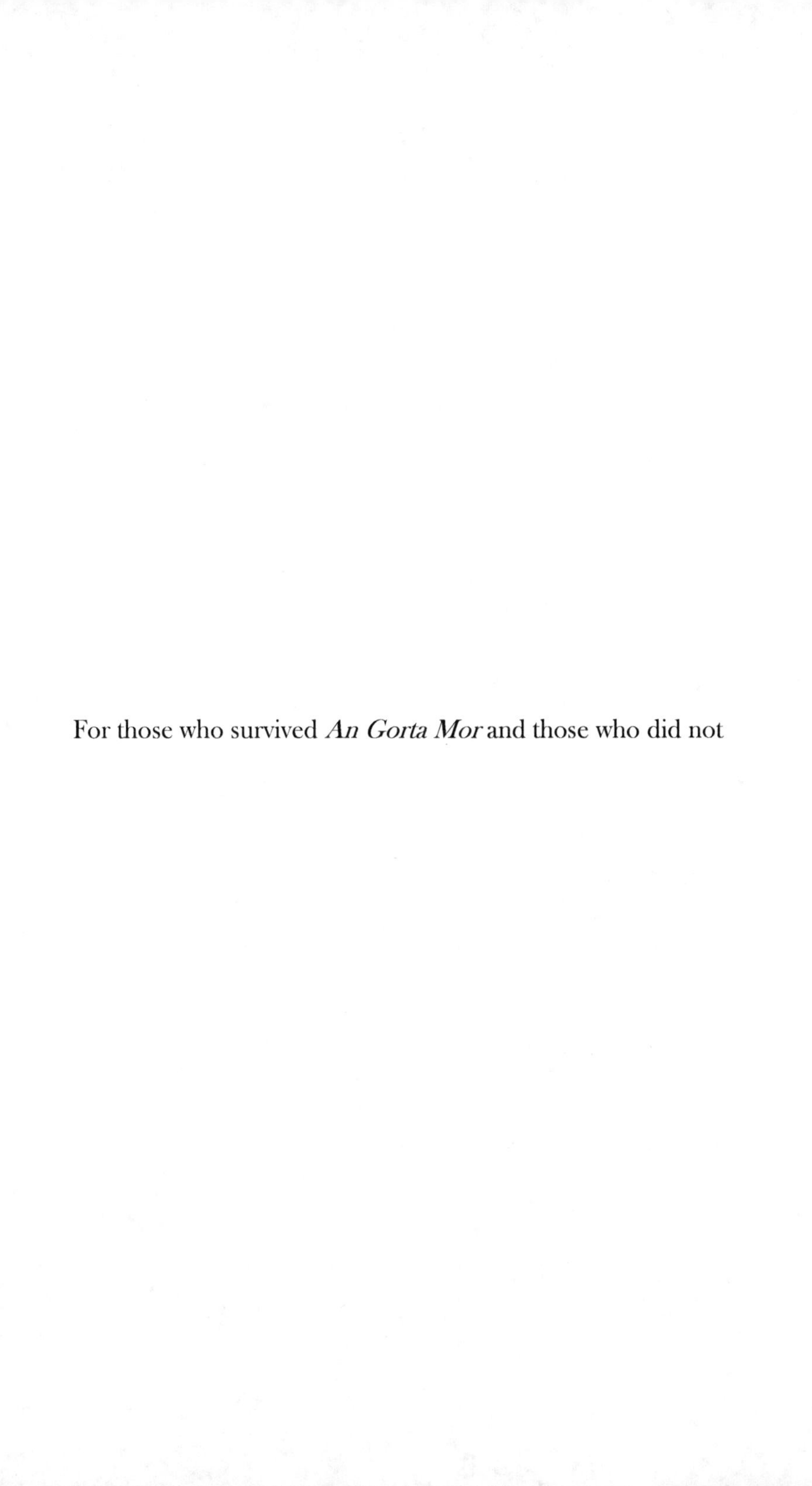

For those who survived *An Gorta Mor* and those who did not

Contents

PART 1: County Mayo, 1839-47

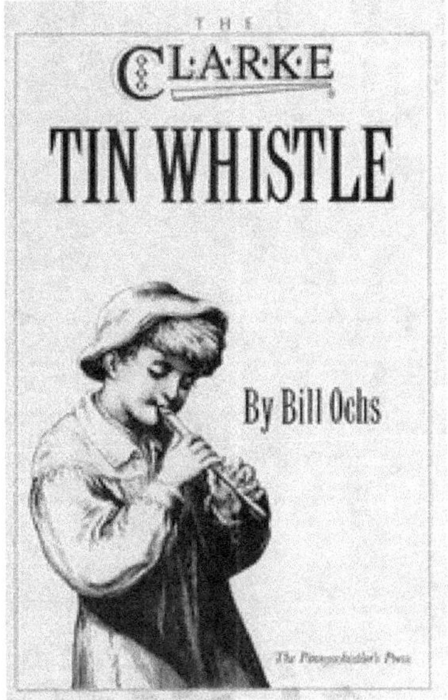

Cover image from The Bill Ochs Tin Whistle Handbook (2019)
with thanks to Margaret Vetare

Prologue: January 6, 1839

"A Most Awful Calamity"

Comparing it with all similar visitations in these latitudes, of which there exists any record, we would say that, for (the violence of the hurricane, and deplorable effects which followed, as well as for its extensive sweep, embracing as it did the whole island in its destructive career), it remains not only without a parallel, but leaves faraway in the distance all that ever occurred in Ireland before... Every part of Ireland—every field, every town, every village in Ireland has felt its dire effects, from Galway to Dublin—from the Giant's Causeway to Valencia. It has been, we repeat, the most awful calamity with which a people were afflicted.

-- Dublin Evening Post 12 January 1839

It was the sixth day of January, Twelfth Night, the Feast of the Epiphany, *Nollaig na mBan,* which some call "Women's Christmas" and others "Little Christmas". The days leading up to that night were a time of signs and wonders. And the first of those signs was the seals.

All along the coast of Mayo, people reported that a great number of seals had come out of the water and settled on the rocks along the shore. It was common enough to see a seal or two on dry land, but never in such numbers. Elsewhere were sighted huge flocks of starlings flying up and down, crows screeching, and crowds of sheep huddled in the fields. The skies were illuminated by bright red streaks, dazzling beams of the Northern Lights. The country people often took occurrences such as these as signs of a coming storm. But there was only a light dusting of snow, covering the ground like a warm blanket.

The day, a Sunday, began well enough. The children were out enjoying themselves in the snow. Indoors all was flutter and bustle, for this was Little Christmas, and everybody was looking forward to the evening's festivities. Around mid-day, the weather became unseasonably warm and humid. The temperature soared, melting all the snow within hours. An unearthly silence came over the land, a stillness so quiet and calm that the flame of a candle burned in the open air without the faintest flicker, and voices in ordinary speaking tones floated between farmhouses more than a mile apart. Toward evening, a warm wind arose, balmy and mild, first caressing the coast, then gathering in strength. The people felt uneasy, so they went to tighten things, especially the hay and the stacks of oats. The men of the house had to go out and put props up against them so they would not be taken with the storm. All the people sat at their fires and thought everything was all right when they had the hay and oats secured, but it was not.

The wind changed and rose to gale force around bedtime; by midnight it blossomed into a hurricane. There was a rumbling noise, like thunder followed by a blast of wind that swept forward like a tornado. Houses shook so that glass and delph were thrown from shelves. Towns and cities were enveloped in darkness and people became frantic, fleeing their homes or sheltering in fields as their dwellings crumbled.

As the wind swept in from the Atlantic, it howled like a banshee. For long hours, the storm raged. Slates were ripped off and chimneys came tumbling down, causing whole towns to blaze. Terrified people sheltered indoors for fear of falling masonry and slates. There was little rain, but where it fell, the force of the raindrops broke panes of glass, however small. Men, women, and children knelt and prayed in the flickering light of turf fires and rush candles.

Those who were in bed got up quickly and dressed themselves. Many ran out into the fields and gardens. Some had a lucky escape, for soon afterwards the house they had fled from was leveled to the ground. Most of the houses were thatched, and when the roof was blown off, the wind came in and sparks were blown all over the house, causing it to catch fire. Many houses were burnt to the ground.

People caught outside had to crawl on their hands and knees. They were not able to hear each other talking over the howling of the wind, and had to communicate in sign language. Such was the ferocity of the howling wind, an awful booming like the deep, continuous groan of thunder. Many thought that the strong winds heralded the end of the world, foretold in superstition to happen on *Oíche Nollaig na mBan.* People began to say the Rosary, praying for the storm to be over.

Thousands of trees were felled, many cattle were killed, and pigs were seen bounding through the air. The River Shannon burst its banks and little could be heard over the din of the high winds. The storm reached Dublin around midnight, where upwards of forty houses were levelled, hundreds were damaged or left open to the elements, and nearly five thousand dwellings lost part of their roofs. Many other towns and cities were devastated, including Galway, Birr, and Portlaoise. As if at the storm's capricious whim, other places escaped almost unscathed, including Cork City and Drogheda.

But the people in Connaught suffered the most, especially the towns and villages of Mayo, who took the full brunt of the savage wind. In Castlebar, the Church of Ireland steeple was blown down almost at once; the wind was so strong it knocked the roof off the wake-house, and the mourners had to take the corpse to a newly-built house in the district until it was buried. The chimneys were blown off the roofs of the houses, and the people went up on the roofs themselves to try and stop the thatch from flying. But the embers from the turf fires in their hearths set the thatch on fire.

The months before that had been very bad, so many people had not gathered in the hay. It was scattered all around the fields, blown to and fro in the haggards. The oats were in reeks in the fields, and they were carried away by the wind.

One man went up onto the roof of his house to keep it from falling in on him. He put his shoulder against the rafter and thought that no matter what kind of wind would come, it would not blow away the house. He said in a loud voice, "Try your best, God!" A mighty big breeze came then and knocked the house and all the stables and barns down. It also blew away the man and killed him.

The waves drove the seawaters inland, carrying the spray and foam for miles and poisoning the lakes, rivers, and wells with sea salt for weeks afterward. Fish were found on hills and mountainsides, while salt stuck to trees and fencing many miles from the nearest shore. Boats were smashed to pieces. The bodies of fourteen men were washed ashore near Ballina, and six vessels laden with grain were sunk. Near Roundstone, a three-hundred-tonne ship, the *Andrew Nugent*, survived two days at sea at the height of the storm. The people on shore lit fires to guide the ship safely to anchor. But as night fell, the boat was swept onto the rocks, and the captain, the pilot, and the fourteen-strong crew perished within sight of the shore.

Those who lived through the horror of that night never forgot it, and were left with a terrible fear of even the slightest wind. Some thought it was God punishing them for their sins. Others thought that the end of the world was at hand. Many blamed it on the *sidhe gaoithe*, fairies who could stir up a whirlwind. Tales of *Oíche na gaoithe móire* were told along the west coast for many generations. But the one told most often was the story of the Miracle of the Butter-Churn Child.

It happened in Ballyhean, in the barony of Carra, County of Mayo. She was but a small child at that time and had only just begun to crawl. The wind that night caused the family cottage to shake so violently that it knocked over the butter churn standing in the corner. To shield herself from the wind's terrible howl, the child crawled into the churn, and did not hear the family as they prepared to leave the cottage. They called her name, they looked everywhere, but they could not find her and feared that she had been blown into the sea by the storm. They took refuge in a neighbouring house, at daybreak returning to their roofless, wrecked home. When they went inside they heard a noise coming from the butter-churn. They looked inside and were astonished at the sight of the lost child, alive, breathing, her arms wrapped around the plunger.

Her name was Bridget Sweeney.

Chapter 1: SAMHAIN

I have but one wish under heaven, and that is for the liberty and prosperity of Ireland. I am for leaving England to the English, Scotland to the Scotch; but we must have Ireland for the Irish. If there is anyone here who is for the Union, let him say so. Is there anybody here for the Repeal? [Cries of "All, all!"]... Let any man run around the horizon with his eye, and tell me if created nature ever produced anything so green and so lovely, so undulating, so teeming with production. The richest harvests that any land can produce are those reaped in Ireland; and then here are the sweetest meadows, the greenest fields, the loftiest mountains, the purest streams, the noblest rivers, the most capacious harbors—and her water power is equal to turn the machinery of the whole world. O my friends, it is a country worth fighting for—it is a country worth dying for... Stand by me—join with me—I will say be obedient to me, and Ireland shall be free.

-- Excerpts from a speech given by
Daniel O'Connell at Mullaghmast in September, 1843

* * *

"Briddy, the praties! They're rolling all over the place!"

Bridget Sweeney looked down at her feet. She was annoyed at Manus, but he was right. The basket she was lugging was much too large for her five-year-old body. It was tipping side to side as she walked, and the fist-sized brown knobs were tumbling out of it. It was the bringing-in time, and she wanted to work alongside the rest of the family to get the potato crop into the pits and buried for the winter. One or another of her older brothers nudged her aside as they trudged through the lazy beds, which made her feel even more like she was in the way, a bother to everyone.

She bent down to pick up the fallen praties and put them back in the basket. But before she could finish refilling, another of her brothers, Mikeen, came along and swiped it away.

"The size of you can barely pick it up. I'll get it, Briddy."

She'd asked the family to start calling her Brideen. She'd heard there was a girl named Bridget over in Islandeady who was called that, and she decided it sounded more grown-up than Briddy. But her brothers laughed and told her it sounded stuck-up, even though the family nickname for her own brother Michael was Mikeen. She decided she didn't care what they called her. In her own mind, she would be Brideen.

Brideen looked along the rows of lazy beds and saw just how many more there were to bring in. There were so many, what her Mam called *an barr iomarca oibre*, a crop so abundant that there wouldn't be enough room in the pits for them all. But Mam always followed that with *buíochas le Dia,* thanks be to God, because she'd lived through so many times when the crop was sparse. Brideen dimly recalled the winter when she was three, when the store in the pits ran out. Mam and Da had given her their praties to eat, because she was the smallest. But Brideen felt bad, knowing the rest of the family was so hungry.

Thoughts of hunger drew her gaze to a place many miles to the west, where the sharp peak of Croagh Patrick loomed over the landscape. It was well known in Mayo that many centuries ago, Saint Patrick had fasted for forty days on that mountaintop. People knew, of course, that an ordinary person who ate nothing for forty days would almost surely starve to death. But this was one of the many miracles worked by Saint Patrick in his lifetime. While on the mountain he chased away the demon birds with his bell, and when he finally descended, he drove all the snakes in Ireland into Lough Corra. In recognition of his saintliness, God promised Saint Patrick that He would spare Ireland from the torments of the Last Judgement. Brideen wasn't sure just what would happen at the Last Judgement, but she was glad it hadn't yet come to pass, and that when it did come, the people in her world would be protected.

There was a pilgrimage that happened every year on Reek Sunday, when hundreds of people would climb to the top of Croagh Patrick. This past July Brideen had asked to go, but her parents said she was still too little.

"It's a hard slog for a little one," Da had said. "You'd be falling behind. You stay here with Mam and Ciaran and we'll see about next year."

Brideen wasn't all that sorry to wait another year. Even from a distance, the mountain looked so forbidding. Still, she was eager to one day find out for herself what it was like up there on the summit, looking out over the green fields of Mayo with the waves of the vast ocean lapping at its shores.

* * *

They lived in a cottage of two rooms, under a thatched roof that her father and brothers had assembled from scraws and rushes and reeds. In the bigger room was an open fireplace, a hob with a hole for the ashes, and a crane suspending the ever-boiling kettle over the flames. A salt box was hung from a nail near the fire to keep the salt dry, next to which stood the bastible, a cast-iron pot oven. On the wall opposite the fireplace was a dresser with shelves holding the milk jugs, and on top a pincer-like holder held a clutch of rushes dipped in fat, to burn when light was needed. At the bottom was an opening where oftentimes sat a clocking hen, and next to it was a settle-bed that functioned as a bench by day. The entire floor of the smaller room was taken up by mats of straw bedding and a wooden ladder up to the sleeping-loft.

The cow usually stayed outside by the doorway, unless the weather was nasty. But there was no way to keep the pig out of the cottage for any length of time. Mam often said she'd rather it was the reverse, the placid cow inside and the restless pig outside. But

Brideen didn't mind. As long as she knew it couldn't get up into the loft where she slept, she enjoyed the pig's antics.

As on most nights, they were eleven around the table—Da, Mam and the children: Manus, the oldest, whom Mam was sure would enter the priesthood, maybe at St. Patrick's down in Tipperary; Máirín, who was about to be betrothed any day now; Siobhan, about whom they all wondered if she might, like Manus, join the sisterhood; then Seamus, Sean Brian, Mikeen, Liam— whom Mam called her four *grasradh*—then Brideen and Ciaran, the youngest.

There were only a couple of three-legged stools, so Brideen and Liam shared one, while Mam took the other for herself and Ciaran, who was not long out of babyhood. The rest took turns standing or sitting on the settle bench. Tonight the meal was praties, of course, with a dish of salt at each end of the table. It wasn't the kind of special night when they might have a bit of bacon. But Brideen was pleasantly surprised when Mam put out a bowl of buttermilk to dip the praties in.

There was usually lots of chatter, but tonight Da was holding court, as he often did, about politics and his hero, the Liberator, Daniel O'Connell, who'd held a mass meeting in County Meath a fortnight earlier. Da learned about it, as he did most political developments, at Walsh's pub, where stories from the newspapers were read aloud.

"There was a huge crowd at the Hill of Tara on the feast of the Assumption. Almost a million people, they said!"

"What's a million, Da?"

"More than you or anyone can count, my girl. They said it took O'Connell's carriage two hours to proceed through the throng. And there was a harp player in the carriage with him!"

Da told them that O'Connell had declared 1843 the year of Repeal for the Act of Union, the law passed in 1800 that took away Ireland's right to self-government and put it under British rule. The whole of the Liberator's public life was dedicated to building and leading the Repeal movement, which was overwhelmingly supported by the Catholic population of Ireland.

"There's going to be another meeting, even bigger, in Dublin in early October," Da said. "I am going to go."

"That's near three days' walk, Da!"

"You've never been that far from Mayo!"

Then Manus spoke up.

"Better watch out for yourself. What if they send troops to break it up?"

Brideen was taken aback by his words, but before she could ask about it, Da waved away his concern.

"The Liberator himself said the time is coming when we will have to choose to live as slaves, or to die as freemen. I know which it will be for me."

* * *

"Gobshites!"

As they all made their way to the crossroads, Brideen grew more and more annoyed. Her brothers kept jumping at one another and trying to pull off the masks that Siobhan had made for them. They were pretending to be ghosts of bodies buried at the crossroads, who supposedly were people who'd taken their own lives and were now burning in Hell. She'd overheard Mam talking about that once, dismissing it as an old legend.

"That's completely daft! There are no bodies buried at the crossroads."

The feast of Samhain was still days away, and here they were, acting like it was going to be some kind of lark! Brideen looked at Liam, who was only a year older than she was. She could tell he was scared by the way he startled every time one of the older boys shouted "Boo!" but he wasn't about to let them know that. Nor could Brideen let on either, for she knew it would lead to merciless teasing. But she had her own fears about that soon-to-come night, and she didn't want to think about it until she had to.

Samhain was the night of the living and the dead, when the souls of the departed were able to pass through the veil into the world of the living. Who knew which one you might meet? Who knew which of the evil spirits might come and try to steal your soul? The *Dullahan,* the *Puca,* the *Leanan Sidhe.* Or Stingy Jack, the blacksmith who roamed the earth, carrying a lantern lit by an ember from hell. In some ways he was the one that scared Brideen the most—he'd managed to trick the devil himself! Unlike the other spirits, Stingy Jack looked like an ordinary mortal. So how would you know if some fellow carrying a lantern wasn't him? Yes, people wore costumes and masks to disguise themselves and avoid harm. But how did you know a mask would work? Mam, at least, took Samhain seriously, saying you must never throw water out the door on this night, because you might drench the spirits and make them angry.

Still, there was much to look forward to in the coming days, for Samhain was All Hallows' Eve, and there would be celebrations on the Feast of All Saints and All Souls' Day. In the early morning they would set out for Mass at the Abbey at *Baile an Tobair.* Much of the ancient building had been laid waste two hundred years earlier by Oliver Cromwell, "that bastard Ironsides," as Da called him. But the grounds were still beautiful, with gardens lovingly tended by the monks. Mass would be held in the small chapel, but the high walls of the Abbey still stood, and Mam said she heard that a restoration of the roof would be commenced soon.

The next day would be Brideen's favorite. The night before, Mam would prepare the dough for the *Bairín Breac,* the speckled loaf dotted with raisins, the kind of treat they only got to eat on that one night of the year. She always made an extra loaf to share with less fortunate neighbors. But the best part was the secret treasures to be found baked into the bread that foretold the future. Finding a matchstick was good luck for winning an argument, a coin meant you'd be wealthy. A pea or a piece of cloth were things nobody wished to find, since they signified bad luck or a life of poverty. The real prize was a ring, which foretold that the finder would soon be married. Brideen wondered if Mam had rigged it so that Máirín would find the ring, since she was certain that her eldest daughter would soon be betrothed to Brendan Burke.

At bedtime they would say prayers for the souls suffering in Purgatory, and leave some soda bread or remains of the speckled loaf out for the departed ancestors, who would be visiting on All Souls' Night. The thought of those spirits didn't distress Brideen, for she knew that the ancestors were friendly spirits who would not cause harm. Mam said the falling leaves were the souls of the dearly departed.

"When a leaf falls on your head, that's one of your ancestors, and you must always say a prayer for them."

When they arrived at the crossroads, games were already going on among the young people. One group of girls were gathered around a bucket, watching as each one took turns dropping gobs of grey molten lead that hardened into different shapes in the cold water. As each one was fished out of the bucket, the girls shouted out which work tool it looked like, foretelling her future husband's trade or profession.

"Ah, Mo's got a spade. You'll for sure be marrying a farmer now."

The girls giggled as they looked in Brendan Burke's direction.

Seeing her sister blush, Brideen had a sudden inkling about why her brothers were carrying on like fools. The presence of so many girls was making them nervous! They might have to dance with one of them! Why being around girls made them so skittish Brideen had no idea, but she saw it as an opportunity to tease them back. But the music started before she had a chance to say anything.

Brideen watched as Brendan Burke approached her sister, and the two of them joined hands for the set dance. The tune was

An Giolla Ruadh, "The Red-Haired Boy", one of her favorites. As she observed the musicians, she paid close attention to their movements, to how they played their instruments. She couldn't imagine how their hands moved so quickly, with such accuracy and smoothness. Two of them were familiar faces, fellows from nearby villages—Junior Gallagher on the fiddle and Enda McMahon working the bellows of the *bosca ceoil*. She didn't know the third one, younger than the other two, who was playing a tin whistle. As usual with reel tunes, the musicians sped up the tempo with each round through the melody, thrilling the dancers, the crowd, and Brideen herself. She felt a powerful longing to become one of the musicians playing this music, but it seemed like something that could never happen. Both Junior and Enda had been tutored by uncles who were acknowledged musicians in their villages. Brideen's family were all good singers, but none of them played an instrument.

She was distracted by a shout from her brother Liam. She looked in the direction he was pointing. Down the road the figure of a man was approaching.

It was Da!

Cries of excitement rose up from the crowd at the crossroads. Everyone knew that Tom Sweeney had gone to Dublin for the big Repeal rally. They all clustered around him, eager to hear his account of the massive event. But his first words stunned them.

"It was all for nothing, thanks to the cowards at Dublin Castle!"

Da told the crowd that the day before the rally, the government in Dublin had issued a proclamation banning the meeting. O'Connell immediately called off the rally and sent messengers on horseback to turn back the thousands of marchers about to converge on Clontarf, just north of the city. Many of the protesters, Da among them, refused to believe the news and made their way into Clontarf anyway. There they were met by troops of armed soldiers. The platform for the rally had already been dismantled. The marchers were devastated.

"Once again, Dublin Castle decided to appease the Protestants rather than stand up for Ireland," Da said. "There were some who wanted to take up arms against them, but the Liberator has always stood against the use of violence in our struggle."

There was silence as the magnitude of Da's words sunk in. Then a voice rang out from the crowd.

"So that's it? You just left?"

Brideen recognized the voice—it was Manus, her eldest brother.

"Yes! We did what our leader wanted, to prevent loss of life. If we'd stayed it would surely have ended in slaughter."

"That's some revolution your man O'Connell's got going there."

There was a note of disdain in Manus' voice that shocked Brideen. Before Da could react he went on.

"What if the Rebel Priest had done the same? Manus Sweeney, my namesake, who gave his life for Ireland? What if he had taken the coward's way out?"

Da exploded.

"Cowards? How dare you! At this very moment the Liberator is being held in Kilmainham Gaol for sedition. He is a hero!"

Siobhan, who was standing near Manus, tugged at his sleeve and shook her head, pleading with her brother to come away and say no more. Then some boys broke in with the familiar rebel chant:

> *Up the long ladder and down the short rope!*
> *To hell with King Billy and God bless the pope!*
> *If that doesn't do, we'll tear him in two*
> *And send him to Hell with his red, white and blue!"*

A hubbub rippled through the crowd and Manus, on the verge of joining in the chant, pulled away from his sister. But before he could begin there were shouts for the dancing to resume, which broke the tension in the air. The crowd drifted back to the crossroad and the musicians started tuning up their instruments.

Brideen stayed behind, worried that Da was still angry. But the resum ption of the music seemed to soften his mood as well. He turned to Brideen and pulled something out of the pack on his back.

"Look, my girl, I brought you something."

He handed her a slender metal tube, black, with holes punched in it. It was a tin whistle, a bit shorter and thinner than the one the fellow in the band was playing.

"See here?" Da pointed to a string of letters on the side of the tube. "That says who made it, someone named Clarke. One of the marchers in Clontarf got it when he was over in England working on the canals. He played tunes on it while we marched to the platform, but when the soldiers chased us away, it fell out of his pocket and afterwards I couldn't find him. The sound of it put me in mind of the Big Wind, that night we thought we'd lost you."

Brideen had many times heard the story of how she was found in the butter churn that night, but it was usually told with an almost jovial air. There was a quiver of emotion in Da's voice right now. *We thought we'd lost you...* He shook his head lightly, as if chasing out the thought, and turned toward the musicians.

"See that fella over there," he told Brideen. "He can show you how to play it."

Brideen shook her head. "I don't know him, Da."

"That's silly. He'll be glad to show you. Musicians always want to share what they know so that more people will learn to play."

"He'll say my hands are too small."

"They'll grow! See, they're just finishing up a tune. Let's go over and talk to him."

Before she could object further, he was on his way toward the dance square. She held back, mortified, as her father accosted the whistle player just as he was lifting the instrument to his lips. The young man turned in the direction Da was pointing and smiled when he saw the black tin tube in her hand.

"Come on over, girlie." Her father waved eagerly at her. "He's a nice fella. Name's Gabriel."

Shyly, she approached the two men.

"So you want to learn to play that whistle, is it?"

Without daring to meet his gaze, Brideen nodded.

"Can you come to market day in Castlebar?"

"Oh, yes," said Da. "We go all the time."

"Come to the stalls near the linen hall, and bring your whistle. I'll show you a tune or two."

"Really?" She was suddenly excited. "Will you teach me *An Giolla Ruadh*?"

Gabriel laughed.

"Oh, I don't think you'll be playing a tune like that right off. But sure, you'll get to it. As long as you practice. Can you do that?"

She nodded eagerly.

"Yes, I will!"

The *bosca ceoil* player called over to him.

"Gabriel, would ye mind using that clab of yours for something other than talking?"

As Brideen watched Gabriel walk back toward the dancers, worried thoughts crept into her mind.

Would he really be at the market? Would he keep his promise to teach her?

And a note of hopelessness, as she listened to the fluid notes waft through the evening air:

How would she ever learn to play a real tune like that?

Chapter 2: THE MISSION

The island is still in a very primitive condition, and though slowly changing for the better, yet the old order of things lingers on. Fifty-two years ago the late Sir William Wilde thus describes the customs of these primitive people: "There are several villages in Achill, particularly those of Keem and Keele, where the huts of the inhabitants are all circular or oval, and built for the most part of round, water-washed stones, collected from the beach, and arranged without lime or any other cement, exactly as we have reason to believe that the habitations of the ancient Firbolgs were constructed. During the spring the entire population of several of the villages we allude to in Achill close their winter dwellings, tie their infant children on their backs, carry with them their loys (spades) and some carry potatoes, with a few pots and cooking-utensils—drive their cattle before them, and migrate into the hills, where they find fresh pastures for their flocks; and there they build rude huts and summer-houses of sods and wattles, called booleys, and then cultivate and sow with corn a few fertile spots in the neighbouring valleys. They thus remain for about two months of the spring and early summer, till the corn is sown; their stock of provisions being exhausted, and the pasture consumed by their cattle, they return to the shore, and eke out a miserable, precarious existence by fishing.

-- Wood-Martin, W.G. "The Rude Stone Monuments of Ireland. On Certain Rude Stone Monuments in the Island of Achill (Continued)." *The Journal of the Royal Historical and Archaeological Association of Ireland* Fourth 8.75 (1888): 368.

The road to Achill was littered over with pebbles and shards of limestone. But Brideen could hardly feel them. For the first time in her young life, she was wearing a pair of shoes on her feet. And not just woolen slippers, but real leather brogues that Mam had bought at Castlebar Market. She almost never bought clothing there, and Brid knew the brogues must have cost a lot. Mam had also insisted that she wear one of her older sisters' gowns over her *leine*. It was a bit big on Brideen, but it was linen with a pretty pattern. Mam said she had to look presentable for the school. To Brideen, it felt almost like she was a lady living in a Big House.

And the best part was the brogues. They felt strange on her feet, but it was a joy to walk without having to avoid the shards. It was exhausting enough just trying to keep pace with Sean Brian, who was ahead of her on the path.

She called out to her brother.

"Can't we stop and rest?"

"Not yet."

"Why not?"

"We just left."

"Did not. That was hours ago."

"Well, there's a lot more hours of walking before we get to Achill."

"What do you mean, hours?"

He turned back with a look of annoyance.

"You know we won't get there 'till sometime tomorrow."

She couldn't pretend she didn't know. Behind them, Croagh Patrick was still plainly visible, so they'd hardly come any distance at all. Once again she'd missed out on the Reek Sunday climb this year. The weather had been terrible that day, and no one in the family had gone. She was secretly glad. This wasn't even a climb, and it was hard enough.

But then she reminded herself that she'd done this walk many times before, with joy and anticipation. They were on their way to Achill! Beautiful, wild Achill Island, where she'd spent summers ever since she was a baby. Achill, where Da was born, where her Sweeney cousins were everywhere—Pollranny, Dooagh, all over the Island. The Sweeneys were a highly-respected family in Achill, not least because of Father Manus Sweeney, the famed Rebel Priest.

It was nearly half a century ago, but the memory of the Year of the French was still fierce among the people of Mayo. In 1798, inspired by democratic revolutions in France and America, armed rebellions against British rule had risen up all over Ireland. In parts of the country, especially in County Wexford, the Society of United Irishmen won some early victories. But that success was short-lived once the government militia and yeomanry were joined by reinforcements from the British army. Disheartened by a series of defeats, the last best hope for the uprising was the arrival of a thousand French troops to support the rebels. On August twenty-second, three French ships landed near Killala in north Mayo, and the battle for control of the west of Ireland began.

Father Manus Sweeney played a crucial role in the Mayo campaign. He'd studied for the priesthood in France and acted as both intermediary and interpreter between the French battalion under General Humbert and the three thousand inexperienced Irish soldiers armed only with pikes and pitchforks. Remarkably, the combined troops achieved success in freeing the towns of Killala and Ballina, then headed south and managed to take the city of Castlebar, proclaiming the newly-liberated region the Republic of Connaught. But the French and Irish forces were not enough to hold back the British. The rebellion was soon crushed and most of the rebels executed. Father Sweeney managed to escape capture for months, hiding out in various places in Mayo. But the Rebel Priest was ultimately betrayed by a fellow cleric, who informed the British of his whereabouts.

Father Manus Sweeney was hanged in the Market Square in Newport in June 1799.

Thomas Sweeney, Brideen's Da, was only a baby then, but he'd grown up on tales of Father Sweeney's martyrdom for the Irish freedom struggle. He left Achill as a young man, but named his first child Manus, after the Rebel Priest. Da had come to live at

Ballyhean when he married Mam, who had no brothers to inherit the family's lands. So Brideen's *Seanathair*, Mam's father, gifted his son-in-law a portion of his rundale plot on the estate owned by Richard Bingham, Lord Lucan.

Though the family home was in Ballyhean, the Sweeneys returned to Achill every summer to spend time with Da's people. Brideen always looked forward to the time in Achill, and this past summer she had passed a milestone of girlhood, spending weeks living in the Booley Huts with her older sisters and cousins. It was the young women's job to look after the herds, which mostly consisted of milking the cows for butter and cheese, which every few days had to be transferred to the main households around Keem. There were also other, grislier tasks like drawing blood from a cattle's neck for pudding, using an ax called a *tuagh chuisle*. The older girls went about the task matter-of-factly, but Brideen was relieved to be told she wasn't ready to learn how to use it.

They spent the whole time in Achill out-of-doors, and once the day's work was done, the fun began. In North Mayo daylight lasted well into the evening, and the booley girls spent the long, golden hours laughing and telling stories. To Brideen there was something magical about being in a society of women and girls, not that that was always the case. Sometimes the young men would arrive, ostensibly to move heavy timber or repair the booley huts. But they'd stay well into the evening, flirting with the booley girls, which often grew into something more. Achill was where Máirín, Brideen's eldest sister, was first courted by Brendan Burke.

But the best were the musical times, especially the set dances, when one of the cousins played a small squeezebox from Germany. She'd acquired it from one of the *Lucht Siúil*, the Travellers or Walking People, who did without homes, instead camping by roadsides in their horse-drawn wagons. The squeezeboxes were becoming popular for playing jigs and reels, and the Irish had taken to calling them *bean chairdín,* or "woman's accordion".

Brideen was still too shy to play her tin whistle in front of anyone, but her aunt Mary, a renowned singer, was often called on to sing old ballads. She had an extensive repertoire of songs, some considered unsuitable for polite company. Brideen's favorite was *Bean Phaidin,* about a jealous woman who wanted to break the legs of the wife of Phaidin, the man she lusted after. There was another song that shocked Brideen when she heard Mary sing it: *Weile Waile,* about an old woman living in the woods who, in the course of the song, stabs her baby in the heart with a penknife and gets hauled away to jail, where she's hanged by the neck until dead. Aunt Mary sang it in a jaunty style, and the other girls loved singing the refrain with her.

It was Brideen's first summer away from her family. It was always sad when booleying time came to an end. But there would be no booleying on this trip. They were headed not for Keem but for Dugort, a village on the other side of the Island, where there was a school Brideen was going to attend, and she was apprehensive.

Da's sisters had told them all about the Mission school, with new buildings and the children dressed in nice clothes.

"It's the finest thing ever seen in Achill," Mary informed them. "And she'll even learn a bit of English."

"Why should she learn English?" Manus burst out. "What's wrong with our Irish tongue?"

"It's a good thing to learn another language," Mam said.

"Not the language of our oppressors, it isn't," said Manus.

"They speak English in America," countered Da. "There's a great world beyond Ireland! Do you know who's visiting from America at this very moment, right here on our shores?"

"I know that your Liberator's another one that doesn't speak our language."

"Frederick Douglass, the great leader of the movement to abolish slavery. He spoke at a meeting in Dublin at the invitation of Daniel O'Connell, himself a fierce opponent of slavery."

The two of them continued to trade barbs, but Brideen was relieved that it didn't rise to shouting. Lately Manus had been more contentious than ever, saying things she didn't understand, things that made Da mad. A few days ago he had even been short with Brideen herself, when she'd noticed something poking out of one of his jacket pockets. It was a short strip of cloth, bright green in colour. With her brother's back to her, she playfully reached over and tugged on it. She was startled to feel the sharp slap of Manus' hand on hers.

"Leave that alone!" he hissed, stuffing the green ribbon back in his pocket.

"I'm sorry, Manus. I just wanted to see what it was."

"It's none of your business."

Manus walked away, glowering. Sometimes he got annoyed with his little sister, but it was rare for him to be truly angry.

Now Mam spoke up to end the men's bickering.

"She'll learn English or something else useful, but she's going to Achill. It'll be one less mouth to feed."

Brideen knew what Mam said had something to do with the praties. She often spoke about the bad crop that happened a couple of years ago. But this was different. There was something wrong with them, something happening now.

* * *

The disease presents the same appearance as that of last year, except that decomposition is taking place much more rapidly, so much so that we fear a great part of the crop is already lost. Several farmers in the neighbourhood of this town sent early potatoes to the market which, when sold, appeared sound, but on being boiled were unfit for food.

-- Mayo *Constitution*, August 4, 1846

Brideen thought back to the day, a few weeks earlier, when her sister Máirín came running into the house. She'd just gone out to fetch some more potatoes from the pit for dinner.

"They've all turned black."

"What's turned black?"

"The praties. When I pick them up they're all soft and mushy and black inside."

"Ah, shut your gob," Da said.

"It's true! Come see for yourself."

"Stop being foolish, child," Mam said. "Just bring in the praties like you're supposed to."

"No! I don't want to touch them!"

The older children, used to Máirín's histrionics, laughed. Mam threw the girl a look of exasperation as she went out the doorway. Moments later they heard a scream, followed by a curse. Mam almost never cursed, and Brideen feared that she'd fallen and hurt herself. But she was on her feet, standing over the bushel.

"They were fine when I brought them in earlier."

"It's the wet rot!"

"That was down in Tipperary," Da scoffed. "The praties here in Mayo are fine."

They looked in the pit and were relieved to find that what was left of last year's crop looked normal. Máirín admitted that instead of taking them from the pit, she'd grabbed some from a bushel of spuds dug up earlier that day.

"Don't put them in with the good ones," Mam said. "They might be cursed."

At this point in the summer, the stores from last season had nearly run out and they'd begun to eat the new crop, which normally they'd store in the pit for later. But now all the good ones were from last year's crop. As each new round of potatoes came in, they looked fine, to the Sweeneys' relief. But after just a few hours, their texture began to change, turning into a black slop.

The same thing kept happening, and they began to hear similar reports from all over Mayo. Not every farm was affected. Some had perfectly good potatoes. It seemed to be striking certain areas, certain plots.

People agonized over what to do about the wet rot. Some said the whole crop should be turned back into the soil. Others argued that would only ruin the soil for the next crop. There were the usual explanations—God's punishment for sin, the work of evil *sidhe*—and no end of stranger theories: The rot was caused by guano from seabirds, by vapors from volcanoes emanating from the center of the earth, and so on.

The deeper, mostly-whispered fear was this: Would there be enough to get through the coming winter? What would they do for seed potatoes next season?

Now, trudging wearily along the pebble-strewn road, all Brideen could think of was eating praties with some butter and a little milk. It would leave a nice, warm, filled-up feeling in her stomach. She was angry that Mam hadn't packed more for the trip. She knew she shouldn't blame her mother. It wasn't her fault if the praties were spoiling. But how was she supposed to walk all the way to Achill without enough to eat?

They walked 'till well past dark, until she was so weary she couldn't take another step.

She yelled at Sean Brian through angry tears.

"I'm not going any farther! I can't! I don't care if we make it to Achill."

She fell on the ground, crying.

"Don't, Briddy. You'll soil your nice dress."

"I don't care. I don't even want to go to that school. I want to stay home with you and Mam and Da and ..."

"I know, little sister. I'm tired, too."

He covered her over with his jacket. They both drifted off to sleep.

* * *

This memorable island, the scene of the greatest attempts at seductive and coerced perversion that have disgraced even Ireland. Achill, the memorable scene of the exploits of Nangle, the soul-buyer, has now, we grieve to say it, become scarcely less remarkable for the miserable condition of its population. Money has indeed been poured into Achill. The propagators of perversion pay handsomely, and we learn from thence, of a date so late as Friday last, that 'Nothing is given of all the money that comes from England, and elsewhere, for the relief of the poor of Achill, except what is given in exchange for consciences. Nangle has doubled his donations in amount, but no one gets anything whatever that does not go to the Protestant school and conform to the Protestant formula.' In short, it is given at the Protestant clergyman's discretion, and it is at his discretion to starve poor Catholics into Protestantism, or, failing that, to let them starve.

    -- From *The Tablet*, a Catholic newspaper, June 5, 1847.

At first, Brideen found the food strange.

Not that it was bad. It just wasn't what she was used to. There was soup at every meal, a broth with carrots and cabbage, vegetables she sometimes had at home. There was often turnip as well, which some folks liked better than potatoes. Her family thought that was a ridiculous notion. Turnips were way too watery. It took potatoes to fill a person up. Yet here at the mission the meals seldom included praties, and people here didn't even grow them much. Brideen had noticed there were none of the lazy beds so abundant around the cottages back home. Instead, seasonal workers called tattie-hokers travelled to Scotland in the early fall to pick them. At least here there wasn't endless talk about wet rot.

But strangest of all to Brideen were the dark, crusty loaves that were the focus of every meal. She knew about this dark bread that was made from different grains, but she'd never tasted it, and was pretty sure that no one back home had any idea how to make it. As much as she missed having potatoes, she found eating bread a tolerable way to fill her belly. And there were a few pleasant surprises, like the presence of small pieces of meat in the soup. At home they only had meat on rare occasions. As for fish, she had tasted salt herring before, but here there were many kinds of fish, which she liked even though she had no idea what they were called. At times she saw women on the beach gutting fish, or hauling seaweed from the shore in great bundles. Here on Achill there was a whole different way of life from her inland village back home.

It was a few months since she'd come to Achill. When they first arrived, she and Sean Brian made their way to Aunt Mary's, where they spent a few hours with their cousins. She was sorry when Aunt Mary said it was time to move on, that it was still an hour's walk to the other end of the Island. They arrived at the Mission after dark, where the woman at the gate denied Sean Brian entry, supposedly because he wasn't enrolled at the school. "She's my sister," he tried to explain, but the woman shook her head and said something in English that they didn't understand. As Brideen watched her brother head off down the road she felt a desperate desire to run after him, but the woman shut the gate and continued her impenetrable harangue. That night, Brideen cried herself to sleep.

She wasn't prepared for the astounding sight that awaited her in the daylight next morning: A great dark cone of rock looming over the buildings and the nearby beach. For a few moments she thought it was Croagh Patrick, that she was back home, that she must have dreamt the long walk to Achill. But no. Achill had its own imposing mountain, called Slievemore.

Over the next few days, she became familiar with the place that would be her temporary home. The Colony, as the Mission settlement was called, was quite large, taking up the bulk of the town of Dugort. It consisted of the school, a mill, a hospital, shops, and other buildings arranged around a square, at the centre of which was a hotel named after the nearby mountain. Rows of well-tended gardens surrounded the hotel, and beyond it was a large house which served as the residence of the Colony's director, the Reverend Edward Nangle and his family. Still farther out were the farm fields and pastures that provided the Colony's subsistence. And over it all loomed the great Slievemore.

The building where Brideen slept housed large dormitory-style rooms with rows of sleeping platforms covered with straw. It was called "the orphanage," which Brideen found curious because she herself was not an orphan, and she didn't think most of the other children at the school were, either. So far she'd learned a bit of sewing and had even managed to pick up a few words and phrases in English, which was easier than she thought it would be. It turned out that many of the teachers at the Mission, including Reverend Nangle himself, had learned enough Irish to communicate with the students. In the course of a day, Brideen would often hear sentences in English that were immediately repeated in Irish. She thought her brother Manus would approve when she would tell him later on at home. But she wouldn't let on to him how proud she felt when she was able to respond to a question in English. She wanted to be accepted by these people who spoke English and wore clothes that were much nicer than hers. She almost wished she could *be* one of them, a sentiment Manus would definitely not approve of.

Much about the place was strange to her. She wondered why it was called a "mission". There wasn't a big church where everyone went to Sunday Mass, like in Castlebar. Instead they had what they called "services" in the big hall, where they sang hymns and listened to readings from the Bible. Brideen had heard some of the stories about Moses and David and Goliath, but she hadn't realized the Bible was an actual book. The priest—whom they called the minister—read from a thick black book, with lots of pages edged in gold ribbon. And there was more than one Bible at the mission. Brideen saw a woman reading one. She must have been saying the words silently to herself, because the woman's lips weren't even moving. As for the hymns, Brideen found most of them stilted and hard to sing. A few had pretty melodies, but none that stirred her like the tunes she learned from Gabriel, especially the slow airs like *An Buachaillín Bán,* "The Dear Irish Boy".

Looking back, she still found it hard to believe how far she'd come since that day at the Castlebar Market. Gabriel was there, at a table outside the Linen Hall, as he'd promised he'd be. In between dealing with customers, he showed her where to put her fingers to play notes on her tin whistle. She'd found it difficult at first, but he reassured her that her fingers would grow, just as her father had said. Da took her to the next market day, and the one after that, so that Gabriel could show her more fingerings and start teaching her simple tunes, like *Fáinne Geal an Lae,* "The Dawning of the Day". A few times Brideen was heartbroken when he wasn't there. But he always showed up the next market day.

As the months went on, her skill on the whistle grew, and in time she was able to figure out many of the familiar tunes by ear. When she told Gabriel she was going away for a while and would have to miss some lessons, he smiled and told her not to worry.

"I can tell already you're of the *pór.*"

"What's that mean?" she asked.

"You're one of the people that's got the music in you. Now you've got the touch, and you won't lose it. There's not much more I can teach you anyway. Just keep playing. Every day, if you can."

"I will."

She left the market that day, her cheeks burning with a mixture of embarrassment and delight. Gabriel said that she was one of the *pór,* that she had the music in her. And he'd said it like he truly meant it.

By the time she got to Achill, she had several tunes she could play fairly well. She was still working on *An Giolla Ruadh.* It was a reel, with a lot of notes, and she still couldn't play it at the speed needed for dancing. She found it easier to play slower tunes and airs, but she was determined to get good enough to play for dances. Jigs were not as fast as reels, but had a trickier rhythm. She resolved to learn "Haste to the Wedding," the jig played when her sister Máirín got married to Brendan Burke. By the next time there was a wedding, she'd have it ready.

* * *

The first few days at the Mission were a flurry of new people and situations, and she had no thought of trying to play. Then things calmed down, and one day after school she got out the whistle. Seeing it, the girl in the cot next to her shook her head.

"What's wrong?" Brideen asked.

"They don't like music here."

They don't like music? It was one of the strangest statements Brideen had ever heard, but before she could even react, the girl added a qualifier.

"At least not that kind of dancing music."

Brideen couldn't imagine what kind of problem the people here could have with dancing music. But it was time for supper, and she had no chance to ask the girl what she meant. She decided it was better to be discreet. From then on, whenever she had free time, she played outside, in the trees out back of the orphanage, to avoid drawing attention from the Mission staff.

There were days when the Colony served as the distribution site for Indian meal to the poor. People from all over Achill came, filling the square to overflowing. It was on one of those days that the reality of life outside the Colony, which living here had mostly shielded her from, came home to her. So many people looked gaunt and stooped, with hunger in their eyes. Even the children looked listless and unsmiling. She felt bad that she had plenty to eat and wished she could do something to help them. <u>Then it hit her:</u> She could give them music. She went to the dormitory and got her whistle.

She decided to try a lovely waltz by the great Turlough O'Carolan, called *Si Bheag, Sí Mhór*. She played slowly, hoping to avoid mistakes, but stumbled on wrong notes several times. Still, she was amazed to see that people stopped to listen. When she finished the tune, people smiled and nodded and a couple of them came up and asked for another tune. She figured she should do one she knew really well, so launched into *Fáinne Geal an Lae,* the first tune she'd learned from Gabriel. It got an even more enthusiastic response because it was so familiar to everyone.

Savoring the applause, Brideen noticed someone walking out of the crowd—a well-dressed lady, clearly not from Achill. She walked up to where Brideen stood and said something in English to her. Brideen couldn't understand, but could tell from the warmth in her eyes that the woman had enjoyed her playing. Then the woman tried a bit of Irish, stumbling over a word then repeating it.

"Alainn, alainn," she said.

It took a moment for Brideen to realize that the woman was saying that her playing was "beautiful." Her praise and the attentiveness of the crowd gave Brideen a moment of deep happiness. But seeing the terrible hunger here brought back her worries about everyone back home. Things were hard everywhere. But surely the Sweeney family wasn't as badly off as these poor people on Achill.

* * *

It was early October. The days were growing shorter, the nights cooler, and Brideen was looking forward to Samhain. It would mark a full year since Da had returned from Dublin with her tin whistle. When she brought up the subject with the other girls, though, her expectations were quickly shattered.

"Oh, they don't do any of that here."

"What do you mean? It's Samhain. It's the biggest night of the year."

"Not here at the mission, it isn't."

"Why not?"

"Reverend Nangle forbids it."

"Because it's pagan," added another girl.

Pagan. It was a word Brideen had never heard before. When she asked, it didn't seem like the others knew what it meant, even the girl who'd spoken the word. But they had a vague idea that it had to do with the head of the Mission's belief that all such revelry was against the Protestant religion. In any case, it was clear that this year, at least, there would be no Samhain for her to look forward to.

Later, just as they were bedding down, an older woman came into the room. One of the girls recognized her as an assistant to Reverend Nangle, and for a few moments they were frozen in fear. Were they all in trouble? Had someone reported that they'd been talking about "pagan" things? There was relief when the woman pointed to Brideen and informed her that someone had come to see her, a young man. At the gate, they'd had trouble understanding his Irish, but they thought he might be her brother.

"Come with me," the woman said. Brideen followed her into the cool night air.

Sean Brian was waiting at the gate.

She looked at him in astonishment.

"Go get your things," he said. "We're going to Aunt Mary's."

"Aunt Mary's? Why?"

"Because you're going home tomorrow."

"Home?"

She could see her brother was in no mood to explain further. She went inside, made a rushed, truncated farewell to the girls in the dormitory, and came back out with her small pack.

Things would be clearer when they got to Aunt Mary's. She'd get to see her cousins again. And maybe she'd get to go to Samhain after all.

Chapter 3: CROWBARS

The rice and Indian meal, both of which are excellent articles of food were cooked in such a manner that, in most cases, they were actually unhealthy, and in all case unpalatable; and the difficulty if possible was increased by giving it out uncooked, for the starving ones in the towns had no fuel and they could not keep up a fire to stew it for hours, and many of them ate it raw. The Indian meal! Who shall attempt a description of this frightful formidable? By some it was stirred in cold water with a stick, then put quite dry upon a griddle. Others make what they call 'stirabout'. This was done by first steeping in cold water, then pouring it into a pot, and immediately after it became so thick that it could not be stirred, neither would it cook in the least. They were actually afraid to take it in many cases, fearing the English intended to kill them.

-- From *Annals of the Famine in Ireland in 1847, 1848 and 1849*
by Asenath Nicholson, New York: 1851

As Brideen swallowed the coarse mixture from the bowl, she felt like gagging. She'd been back for three days and there'd been nothing to eat but this awful mush made from Indian corn called "stirabout".

She pushed away the bowl.

"I can't eat any more of this. I hate it!"

"Well, if you're not hungry..."

"I am hungry! At the Mission we had soup."

"Yes, that's what they gave you so you'd stray from the one true church."

"They never said anything about religion!"

"They didn't need to. The free soup did it for them."

Brideen held her tongue. There was no use arguing with Mam. The word had spread through the villages of south Mayo that Reverend Nangle was practicing "souperism", that his Mission was feeding the people on the condition that they convert to Protestantism. There were some who argued that the Mission was doing good, rescuing so many poor children from hunger. And anyway, what choice did starving people have? But it didn't matter. When word reached Ballyhean that Father McHale, the Archbishop of Tuam himself, had forbidden Catholics from sending their children to the Mission school, Mam's mind was made up. She sent Sean Brian to fetch Brideen

She almost wished she'd never been to Achill. It made it that much harder to be here, back in this crowded two-room cottage. At times she imagined herself back at the mission, feeling the warm, full-belly sensation she had there. She was ashamed of her family, of their poverty, and she was ashamed of herself for feeling it.

They'd been waiting for the new crop to come in. Even though Mam had said they'd have to put up some in store, at least they'd know the time of hunger would soon be over. But now it was clear that the wet rot was back. It was no use digging them up. They were all black, and the store in the pit was gone. Their pig was gone, too. They'd had to sell it to get the yellow meal. Da said they could have gotten the meal for free but for the quarter-acre clause, and their plot was a bit larger than that. Some neighbors were giving up their plots so they could qualify for relief, but her parents were adamantly opposed.

* * *

Viewing, as I have done in gloomy silence, the very many blood-freezing scenes that have passed before my eyes, and also expecting that a fraternal feeling would induce some more competent person to stand forward and expose to the public those horrifying facts which are occurring daily in this parish... Famine and its dire consequences—fever and dysentery—are committing more ravages and carrying to a premature grave more victims this season than the last by a proportion of four to one. And lest I might be supposed to exaggerate, I will mention the names and concomitant facts.

First, appears in the gloomy catalogue of deaths from starvation, Widow Gavan of Carrowcastle, and four children, all of whom died in a lonely hut, and it could not be ascertained how long they had been dead before discovery. It is most probable that they were some weeks, for this reason, that they were in a state of decomposition when found.

John Goldin, from Garrane, and four children died from same cause—one of whom, a girl of twenty years, was removed from the house when dead by a sister of hers, thrown on a heap of stones some distance from the village, and left there several days.

Mrs. James Clarke, of Tawnaghaknaff, also died of want and was carried coffinless by her husband, suspended by a rope from his shoulder. At every pace he moved, the head and knees came in contact; this caused profuse bleeding. Her blood was seen in streams along the roads and fields he passed through.

There is another woman name of Gavin, and daughter, in the townland of Murroa, who died of real want, are now stretched lifeless corpses in a deserted house for the last fourteen days, could not be buried for want of coffins or persons sufficiently courageous to remove them. It is reported that both are disfigured by rats.

Brideenget Carney, of Toueoane, and five children belonging to James Heston, also two children of Honoria Browne of Raslevin; Honour Browne of Treenabantree, and four children. This poor woman was discharged from the poorhouse, she and her children in fever, without any provision; the consequence was that she and her family died of want.

I hope you will not consider that it is due to any neglect that we retarded the return of the number of deaths in the parishes to which I am curate. Notwithstanding the strict inquiry I have made, I could not ascertain the exact number. To enumerate all the deaths from starvation, and the horrifying facts accompanying them, would be an endless task.

-- Extracts of a letter from Rev. P.J. O'Connor, C.C. to the *Weekly Register*, Bohola, May, 1848

This time it started with an argument about Lord Lucan.

Brideen wanted to shut her ears. She couldn't stand it anymore. She was hungry, always hungry, and being still and quiet made the gnawing in her gut easier to bear. But with Da and Manus, it seemed to be the opposite—hunger was driving their fury.

"They call him the Exterminator. He's going to clear all his lands."

"Why would Lucan do such a foolish thing?"

"He says small farms are no good—he wants to put all his land together into big farms. He says he refuses to support people who'll never be anything but paupers. To him we're nothing but vermin. He wants to wipe out half the population of Mayo."

"Listen to yourself," said Da. "You're talking nonsense."

"Am I?" Manus shot back. "Forty houses levelled in one day in Ballinrobe? In Glenisland people had to take refuge in the ditches. Lucan's men forbade anyone from giving them shelter on pain of themselves getting evicted. In one house there were people dying of cholera and they pulled the cabin down right over their heads. A winnowing sheet was placed over their bodies as they lay on the ground. The priest had to administer the Sacrament for the dying in the open air, in torrents of rain coming down."

"I just don't believe it. He can't just be throwing them all out."

"That's exactly what he's doing. He's got brigades who come in the night and pull down the cabins with crowbars."

"But we have leases. Your Mam's family has been on this land since long before you were born."

"Our leases are worthless. They make us pay all our rents together, and if some can't, we all get turned out. One of these nights those Crowbars will show up here."

"That's ridiculous. I don't believe it."

"Just because we've been here for generations doesn't mean he'll let us stay," Mam broke in.

Brideen was surprised to hear Mam's voice, and Da himself was taken aback. She usually kept her thoughts to herself, rarely openly challenging Da with more than a brief word. But this time, uncharacteristically, she had more to say.

"What are we going to do, Tom? It might be time for us to be making plans."

"What do you mean, making plans?"

"For how we're going to stay alive. Our stores are empty. People are leaving Ireland."

"Oh, so we're supposed to book one of those ships to Amerikay? With what money?"

"Someone's got to have a thought for the future," Manus said. "Instead of living in a dream world, waiting for something to happen."

Now Da tore into Manus in fury.

"I know what you've been up to these nights. Running with those Ribbonmen."

"What about them?"

"They engage in thievery and lawbreaking."

"Laws that are evil must be broken. People are desperate. They're starving and the Ribbonmen are taking it from those that have plenty."

"I've heard reports of convoys of grain being attacked and robbed."

"You want to know who's doing the looting? Priests!"

"That's not true."

"It is so. Two priests broke into the grain store in Turlough and stole four cartloads. They did it to feed their parishioners."

"You've been taking part in these raids, then?"

"Taking part! I was in Castlebar for the burning of Lucan in effigy! He galloped in on his great black horse, shouting, 'I'll evict the lot of you!' If we'd known he was coming, he would have been murdered on the spot."

"So that's it, now. You'll be party to the mortal sin of murder?"

"With those willing to stand up to the likes of Lucan. Yes, if I have to. We'll do what it takes to make Ireland free. You're always saying that's what you want."

"Not at the price of murder on my immortal soul."

Manus took a deep breath before he spoke again.

"It's come time for me to leave this house."

"You'll go back to the seminary?" Mam said.

"No, Mam," he replied. "I'm going to follow the ideals of my namesake. I'll be no Priest but I will live as a Rebel."

They watched in silence as he stuffed a few things into a pack, lifted it onto his shoulder, and headed for the door of the cabin.

"Don't do this, Manus," Mam cried in anguish. "For the love of God, don't leave us."

"It's better this way, Mam. I'll be one less mouth to feed."

"I'll never see you again, I know it!"

She threw herself upon her son. He tried to shake her loose but she locked him in a tight embrace. For a few moments, all resistance left him and he clutched at his mother, sobbing. Then, recovering himself, he threw her off and walked out of the cottage, leaving her on the floor and the rest of them watching in disbelief.

Suddenly Brideen remembered the time back before Achill, when she'd asked Manus about the green ribbon in his pocket, and he got cross with her, stuffing it down where she couldn't see it.

Now she understood what it was. Even then, he was already a Ribbon Man.

* * *

I well remember the famine of 46 and 47. I was working for Lord Lucan in them years. As soon as the arrears of those who could not pay amounted to the years rent of the townland, they were all turned out; the houses were pulled down and the land and the poor peoples crops were sometimes ploughed up by his lordships bullocks... I saw a good many bad acts. A woman in fever was lying on the floorin a bed of straw, and they took the bedclothes, straw and all, and pulled them out the door... I did as many as twenty a day, sometimes for the six days of the week without ceasing... First we did not like the work, but after some time we got so accustomed to it we had no feeling... As soon as we arrived at the scene of our labours we ate a feed of brown bread and went to work. We levelled all day until night set in. We lodged in the house; slept on the floors in hay we got in the poor peoples haggards, or in the poor peoples beds; when we got up in the morning at the dawn we cooked our breakfasts and ate them; threw the houses and went on to the next village. We kept up that work for the greater part of four days, and then started for home without leaving a house standing... There is nothing I dread more when I am called before my God than that I belonged to the cursed Crowbar Brigade.

-- Excerpts from "Tale of the Crowbar Brigade as related by an active recruit of the period" published in the Connaught *Telegraph,* August 21, 1880

It was Siobhan who awakened first. She was always the lightest sleeper.

Brideen and Siobhan were snuggled together in the settle bed, while Mam and Da and Ciaran were on the big straw mat. The four boys were up in the loft, and their moans and snorts of irritation could be heard below.

"What was that?"

"Go back to sleep," Mikeen growled.

"But I hear something."

Siobhan was right. There were voices—men's voices—in the distance, growing louder and louder.

Most of the family was awake now.

"Thomas Sweeney!" a voice called out.

"Who is it? Who's there?"

"We have come to take possession of this dwelling."

Now the voices were just outside the cabin. Then a heavy pounding, over and over, and finally a long metal rod with a curved end, like a goose's neck or a pig's snout, burst through the thatch above their heads.

Brideen had never seen anything like it before. But as one after another rod poked through, she knew what they were.

Crowbars.

Her brothers in the loft yelled at the top of their lungs as a man's face peered through the thatch. Brideen lay frozen with fear until Siobhan grabbed her by the hair and yanked hard.

"Come on!" They raced out of the cabin and saw four men wielding crowbars, bashing them against the outside walls. Amid the chaos, Brideen clung to her mother, who was clutching a screaming Ciaran. Da and her brothers struggled to beat back the men with sticks and pieces of brick, while Siobhan pounded their backs and pulled on their shirts to get them from the walls.

"Stop!" came a gruff voice from behind them. In the dim light they could make out a line of uniformed men with weapons.

"Any resistance will be met with maximum force."

Then another, familiar voice from the Crowbar men.

"Better do as they say, Tom. They're perfectly capable of butchering you if ye don't."

It was Padraig Walsh, addressing Da by his name. Padraig ran a nearby pub in Drimloughra.

"Paddy Walsh! What are you doing here?"

Siobhan spoke up in a small voice.

"He's with them, Da."

Da looked at him uncomprehendingly.

"Is that true, Paddy?"

"Lucan will turn me out too if I don't do his business. You heard what they've done in Aughadrina. I have no choice, Tom."

The head of the crowbar crew spoke up.

"Let's finish this job, boys. Time for the battering ram."

They came forward with a long tree mounted on a wagon and began to bang on the walls.

Mam tried to block them.

"At least leave us the walls so we can set up a *scalpeen*!"

"There's nothing I can do."

"Then a curse upon you, Padraig Walsh !" she cried.

There was nothing for them to do but watch, in a daze, as the walls of the cottage became a pile of rubble. One of the crowbar men set a stick afire, about to set the pile of thatch ablaze.

"No!"

As Mam rushed forward, screaming, one of the soldiers blocked her way.

"You've been warned not to interfere."

"Don't burn it. Please! It's all we have left."

Padraig nudged closer to the brigade foreman.

"Can't we just leave them their things? The walls are down, that's all that's required, isn't it?"

The foreman paused for a moment, then threw down the torch and stamped it out.

"Mother o'God, how I hate this work."

"As do we all," Padraig said.

This led to shouts from the family.

"Then why do it at all?"

"How can you live with yourself?"

Da tried to calm them down.

"He's only trying to help. It'll be all right. Let's go down the road to the McNultys' for the night. We'll come back and retrieve them tomorrow."

The soldier overheard.

"Don't try it. You'll just be turned away."

"What?"

"Lord Lucan has warned all his tenants not to extend the evictees so much as a single night's shelter. Go to the workhouse in Castlebar."

"The only reason to go to the workhouse is to get a decent burial. A curse on the lot of you!" Mam shouted as they left.

They wandered around in shock for a while.

"What do we do now, Da?"

"Should we go to the workhouse?"

Mam reacted with fury.

"And let them split up our family? No!"

"You heard him. We may not have any choice. Don't worry, *mo stór*," said Da. "We'll only stay a few days. Then we'll go to my people in Achill."

"How do you know they'll take us in? How do you even know they're all right?

"I don't," Da replied. "But Lucan has no tenants in Achill. One of the boys can go on ahead and send word that we're coming."

Mam was adamant but Siobhan prevailed upon her, too. All three of Brideen's older brothers volunteered to leave right away for Achill.

"You'll never make it. You'll drop dead on the road without food in your stomachs. First we'll go to Castlebar. We'll carry some of our things and try to sell them, so we can get food."

Da was relieved to see Mam relent. He said they should set out right away, so they'd arrive in the morning and have a better chance of being admitted.

"What about our things?" said Siobhan. "Are we just going to leave them here?"

Mikeen, Seamus, and Liam spoke up at once, saying they would carry it all.

They quickly picked through the rubble. The dresser and the ladder had been smashed by the crowbars, but both the settle bed and iron pot were intact. Brideen spied a dusky metal tube. Her whistle! She'd almost forgotten about it. With all the trials since coming back from Achill, she'd hardly played it, and was glad to see it wasn't even bent.

The first light of dawn was breaking as they set off, Brideen clutching her tin whistle.

Chapter 4: TO SLIGO

The impression made upon me by this short tour can never be effaced. Bad as were my expectations, the reality far exceeded them. There is a prevailing idea in England that the newspaper accounts are exaggerated. Particular cases may or may not be coloured, but no colouring can deepen the blackness of the truth; the evil is one that defies exaggeration. When we entered a village our first question was how many deaths? "The hunger is upon us" was everywhere the cry. The town of Westport was itself a strange and fearful sight, like what we read of in beleaguered cities. Its streets crowded with gaunt wanderers, sauntering to and fro with hopeless air and hunger-struck look--a mob of starved, almost naked women around the poor-house clamouring for soup tickets. The survivors were like walking skeletons--the men gaunt and haggard, stamped with the livid mark of hunger; the children crying with pain; the women in some of the cabins too weak to stand. When there before I had seen cows at almost every cabin, and there were besides many sheep and pigs owned in the village. But now the sheep were all gone--all the cows, all the poultry killed--only one pig left; the very dogs which had barked at me before had disappeared--no potatoes; no oats.

As we went along our wonder was not that the people died, but that they lived.

-- From Distress in Ireland, Narrative of William Edward Forster's visit in Ireland from the 18th to the 20th of 1st month, 1847, *London, The Society of Friends, 1847*

I hold in my hands a list of twenty-seven villages which have been pulled down and destroyed. They once contained happy homesteads but now there is not a vestige of them to be found. I can name some of them. The village of Aughadrina contained about seventy houses, but now no trace of it remains, and the land

*on which that and other villages were built is now employed in
feeding Lord Lucan's bullocks.*

-- Lord Frederick Cavendish, quoted in the London *Weekly
Chronicle*, August 4, 1850

"It's all gone."

They'd heard about the mass evictions in Aughadrina. But
even after they'd walked far beyond the town, Da kept repeating
the phrase over and over. It was as if he couldn't believe his eyes,
and only by repeating the phrase over and over could his mind
come to terms with the reality: the village of Aughadrina once
existed, right here, on this spot about an hour's walk from the
ruins of their cottage. But now it was gone. Vanished. There was
no rubble, no markings in the ground, almost no evidence that
there had been dwellings there, with families and their patches of
praties.

A couple of other people were walking around the grounds.
Da called out to them.

"What happened here?"

"Evicted—every last one of them."

"But how'd it all get plowed under?"

"Lucan's men said he's going to put his horse barns here."

As for Mam, she kept saying the names of the families she
knew there: the Heneghans, the Murrays, the Morans. Where had
they gone? Where were they now? Had Shelagh Moran gone to
her parents in Ballina? Maybe down to her sister's at Spiddal? It
was as if Mam was desperate to come up with a plausible
explanation...

It was upsetting for Brideen to witness her parents' shock.
She herself had only a dim recollection of the few times she'd
been to Aughadrina. She was relieved when they left the site. She
wanted time for them to just be together, without all the talk of
disaster.

But it wasn't to be. A couple of miles outside of Castlebar they began to see the bodies, lining both sides of the roadside, some so fresh and lifelike it wasn't clear if they were dead or not. It was an awful sight, but her curiosity kept getting the better of her. Who was this woman, that child? How had they come to be lying here, dead, on the cold ground? Wasn't someone coming to get them? To bury them?

"Don't look," Mikeen told her. "Just keep walking."

The closer they got to Castlebar, the more bodies they saw. Finally they arrived at the outskirts of the town, and a feeling of dread came over them as they spied in the distance the forbidding grey stone walls of the Castlebar Union—the workhouse. They had to go through the centre of the town to reach it, where a market was set up for people trying to sell items of furniture and clothing. Sean Brian suggested they set up to sell the items they'd carried from Ballyhean, but Mam shook her head.

"We don't know but what we'll still need them. In any case, if we arrive at the workhouse with money, they'll just take it away.

As they headed in the direction of the grey building, they heard the sound of breaking glass. A man was lobbing stones at a window on one of the town buildings, blasting a hole in one of them. Hearing the commotion, a couple of constables came running, but as they approached, the man didn't even try to evade them.

"Come and get me," he called to the constables. "At least in gaol I'll get a meal."

As they walked, Siobhan remarked on the fact that since they'd entered the town they'd been spared the sight of more dead bodies. Da said it was because the town officials had cleared them.

"To take them to be buried?" asked Brideen.

"If they can find coffins for them," Da replied.

It was only as they got closer to the workhouse that Brideen understood what he meant. There were a few unburied corpses, but for most, an attempt had been made to bury them in shallow, barely covered graves.

Finally they got to the far outskirts of Castlebar where the workhouse stood on the bare and treeless land, looking half-fortress and half-prison. They had heard about the stone walls of great thickness, about the immense wards with wooden platforms where the paupers lay on straw bundles. But it turned out that even that meagre comfort would be denied them. There was a sign on the gate, which none of them could read. But they knew what it said even before a voice shouted from the other side of the high grey walls.

"The workhouse is closed."

"Closed? How can that be?"

"Bankruptcy. Closed months ago by order of Lord Lucan and the Board of Guardians."

"But people are dying. What are we to do?"

"Go to Swinford."

"How do we know it'll be open?"

"You won't know until you get there. If it's closed, go on to Sligo."

Another voice broke in.

"If you don't want your family to starve to death ye better leave Ireland."

"What, to America? We don't have money for the passage."

"Half a crown'll get ye from Sligo to Liverpool."

"Liverpool?"

"In England you'll get fed. And there's real work. Not like here, building crumbling roads."

"What do we do, Da?"

"Do we go to the workhouse in Swinford?"

"I guess we'll have to," he said.

Mam exploded.

"We'll go to no workhouse! *Casain na Marbh.* I'd rather die in a bog hole!"

"We have no choice, Mam. There's nowhere else to go."

"Yes, there is."

"What? England?"

"You heard what he said. We'll get fed there."

A fierce argument commenced between Mam and Da. Brideen had never seen such anger between them. When her parents had arguments, her older siblings usually managed to smooth things over with a joke. But this time they were frightened into silence.

At one point Mam turned away and started to pull on the wagon.

"Where are you going?"

"To sell these things so we can get to Sligo."

Da realized it was useless to continue the argument. Mam's mind was set on getting to Sligo. They went back to the square and set up in the street with other sellers. Several people came by to inspect what they had. One offered to buy the iron pot for sixpence, but Mam waved him off.

"Away with ye! It's worth at least a shilling."

"Whatever you say," the man said as he started off. "Beggars can't be choosers."

"We're no beggars!" Mam shouted after him.

They sat for hours, but had no more takers. It was getting late in the day. Da said they should get some rest and try tomorrow. They found a sheltered spot near some cabins and prepared to bed down for the night. There was a man leaning against the doorway of one of the cabins. Da approached to let him know of their presence, but thought better of it.

Sometime before dawn they awoke to screams from the nearby cabin. Someone inside had opened the door to find a body falling limp onto the doorstep. It was the corpse of the man they'd seen leaning there the night before.

"He must've died during the night."

Mam told them to go back to sleep until daylight. But Brideen couldn't get the thought of the dead man in the doorway out of her mind. How can a person die standing up? What if Mam died during the night? Or Da? She'd never known a time when she feared that her parents could not take care of her, could not make things right for her and her siblings. As she drifted off, she had a nightmare in which the lifeless, emaciated body rose up from the doorstep and stood silently, looking at her.

* * *

I can recollect being awakened in the early morning by a strange noise, like the croaking or chattering of many birds. Some of the voices were hoarse and almost extinguished by the faintness of famine; and on looking out of the window I recollect seeing the garden and the field in front of the house completely darkened by a population of men women and children, squatting in rags; uncovered skeleton limbs protruding everywhere from their wretched clothing, and clamorous though faint voices uplifted for food and in pathetic remonstrance against the inevitable delay in providing what was given them from the house every morning. I recollect too, when walking through the lanes and villages, the strange morbid famine smell in the air, the sign of approaching death, even in those who were still dragging out a wretched existence...As a young girl, I had no conception of the full meaning of the misery I saw around me, yet it printed itself upon my brain and memory.

    -- Josephine Butler, recollecting a visit to Ireland in 1847, "Our Christianity Tested by the Irish Question," London, T. Fish Unwin Publisher, 1887

When they went back to the marketplace in the morning, Mam lifted Ciaran in her arms and walked out into the center of the square. She sat down on the ground and put the child on her lap, holding him almost like a baby, though he was nearly four. She called out to the passers-by, wailing in a pitiful voice:

"Alms! Alms for me and my child."

It was a shock to Brideen, to see her strong, decisive mother take on the demeanor of a beggar so convincingly. It was like she had become another person altogether. Brideen cringed as she saw a couple of women approaching. One was younger, near Siobhan's age. They were both simply dressed, clearly not destitute. Brideen had seen ladies like this before, in Castlebar and at the Westport Market. Someone told her they were called Quakers, and that they helped people in need. Their dresses made Brideen think of the pretty one Mam had bought her to wear to the Achill Mission. It was long gone now, probably lying in the rubble of their cottage.

Mam cried out more insistently as the two ladies passed. Why was she acting this way? Was she just pretending, or was her true desperation showing through? Brideen couldn't tell, but her cheeks burned with shame. And now it was affecting Ciaran, who was crying and trying to wriggle out of his mother's grasp.

The younger of the two women bent down to comfort Ciaran, and offered him a biscuit.

"I'm sorry I am not able to give more," she said in Irish. "There are so many in need here."

Meanwhile, the older lady walked over to Brideen, who turned away in embarrassment. She said something in English and gestured to her companion.

"She says she remembers you," the younger one told Brideen. "You're the girl who played the tin whistle at the dispensary in Achill."

Brideen was startled at the mention of the place. She swung around to face the woman, and recognized the fine lady who had complimented her playing that day.

As the older lady spoke in English, her companion repeated her words in Irish.

"Your playing was lovely. Do you still have your whistle?"

Brideen nodded, showed it to her.

"You don't have the strength to play it now, do you?"

Brideen shook her head.

"Why aren't you at the Mission?"

Brideen could barely talk. "My parents..."

"I know," said the lady. "They wanted you to renounce your religion. For myself, I do not approve of popery, but it was un-Christian for them to do that. What will you and your family do?"

Brideen explained that her father wanted to go to the workhouse in Swinford but her mother wanted to go to Liverpool.

The lady took a coin out of her bag and bent down to press it into Brideen's hand.

"Don't go to the workhouse. Give this to your mother. It'll pay the passage for all of you."

Brideen looked at the coin, almost mesmerized by its appearance. She knew such things existed, that people were able to obtain things in exchange for coins. But she'd never actually seen one.

"Now go get your strength back, so you can play your pretty whistle again."

The two women went on their way and Brideen ran to show the coin to the others. When she handed it to her father, he was momentarily dumbstruck.

"What is it, Da?"

"It's a crown piece!"

"Is that a lot?" asked Liam.

"You've no idea, lad!" Da replied.

Brideen spoke up.

"The Quaker lady said it would be enough for us to go to Liverpool."

"But why did that lady give you a crown?" Mam asked. "Do you know her?"

Brideen started to explain how the Quaker lady had heard her play her whistle in Achill, but the others were so overcome with excitement they barely listened. They clamored to buy food with the coin, but Mam said they had to save most of it for the passage. She gave it to Siobhan and sent her in search of some bread. Siobhan soon emerged from a nearby bakehouse with two dark loaves.

"I told her I could pay, but I don't think she believed me. She just handed me the loaves and said, 'God be with you, child'."

"God really is with us today," said Mam. "We'll need all of that crown for the passage."

Mam broke off pieces of the loaves and they tore into them. It was the first substantial food they had eaten in days. Brideen remembered how strange she found the bread at the Achill Mission. Eating it now was a different kind of strangeness, a sensation of warmth and fullness in her stomach that she'd almost forgotten was possible. She immediately wanted more, but Mam said they had to save the rest.

"We'll need it for the strength to walk to Sligo."

"But I'm still so hungry," said Brideen.

"We all are," was the reply.

"But I'm the one the lady gave the coin to." Brideen immediately regretted her words, knowing full well what Mam's response would be.

"Oh, so you think you deserve more, is it?"

"No," Brideen mumbled, embarrassed.

While they sat eating, a boy walked through the public square hawking newspapers.

"*Tá sé marbh! Tá sé marbh!*" he cried out over and over.

Clearly someone famous had died. Da rushed over to ask who it was. At the boy's reply, he let out a cry of agony and fell on the ground, weeping. Brideen had never seen Da cry. It was a terrifying sight.

What happened? Who was it that died, to bring Da such grief?

* * *

The most remarkable man of the age, Daniel O'Connell, died at Genoa on Saturday the fifteenth. He rendered his last sigh with the calm of an infant who falls off to sleep. He requested that his heart – that heart which always beat for the cause of religion and liberty—should be taken to Rome, and that noble heart has been embalmed and encased in a silver urn. His body will be transported to his native mountains, to remain there to the day of resurrection. Let us hope and pray for Ireland, let us hope and pray for Daniel O'Connell, this great servant of God, because he was a servant of man, a great and sincere apostle for liberty.

-- From Bucks Gazette, Saturday, May 29, 1847

Da was inconsolable. Any resistance he harbored about going to Liverpool vanished with news of the Liberator's death. As they made their way to Sligo, he would periodically collapse to his knees and weep, as he had back in Castlebar.

"*Mo chroí briste.* Ireland is broken. My country is no more."

Then he would fall silent again.

A few hours into the walk, they came upon a cluster of cottages. There was no one around, and the cabins appeared empty. Having rarely ventured this far beyond Castlebar, they did not know the name of this village, but there was no sign that the inhabitants had been forcibly evicted, as in Ballyhean and Aughadrinagh. So where had everyone gone?

"Maybe we can sleep in one of the cottages," Sean Brian said. "Keep us dry if it rains."

Mam immediately slapped down the idea.

"You don't know what's in them. There could be... fever."

They could tell that she'd held back from using the word that was really in her mind: "corpses".

As they set out the next morning, Siobhan stopped abruptly.

"What was that?"

They all listened to what sounded like a low moan coming from one of the cabins. She headed in the direction of the sound, with Liam trotting after her.

"Is someone there?"

A weak voice, a woman's, responded from inside the cabin, but her words were indistinct.

Siobhan poked her head inside the open doorway.

"Hello?"

"Help us. Please."

Mam shouted at them from behind.

"Get away from there!"

Now both Liam and Siobhan had stepped partway inside the door.

"Siobhan! Liam!" she shouted again. "Get back here now!"

A moment later the two of them emerged and returned to Mam and the others.

"There's a mother and four kids in there," Siobhan reported. "The father's dead."

"What's the matter with you? They've got the fever!"

"She wants us to help her get to St. Ciaran's Well. She says he turned one sack of oats into four sacks. And once there was a giant salmon there that fed a hundred people."

"The woman has lost her mind. We can't go drag some lunatic along with us."

"But there's no one around to help them, Mam. All they've got to eat is some nettles."

"Can we give them a bit of our bread?" Liam added.

"No, child! It's all we've got to get us to Sligo."

"But we can't just leave them here!"

"There's nothing to be done! We can't save them. It's ourselves we must save."

Mam was right. They all knew it. Brideen remembered how horrified Mam was when she heard about mothers who abandoned their children to starvation. To Mam, such behavior was utterly beyond all understanding. She was determined that, no matter what, her family would survive, and they knew that the sheer force of Mam's will was what had gotten them this far.

The dying woman was right about the Holy Well. It was just up the road, tucked under a large rock with offerings of coins and rosaries scattered around it. But there were no giant fish or sacks of oats.

Little Ciaran, who by now was so weak he rarely spoke, tugged at Mam's skirt as he held up an acorn he'd found on the ground.

"An offering to your patron saint? Go on, little one. It's all we've got."

Brideen thought of her tin whistle. It was something of value that could be left at the Holy Well. But she silently begged for St. Ciaran's forgiveness, and said nothing as her little brother placed the empty shell among the offerings.

The walk should have taken them no more than two days. But they walked so slowly, weak from hunger, that they were still more than a day away from Sligo. They passed some work crews, hired to build new roads so they could collect relief. The work was so poorly done that many were crumbling as soon as they were completed. Some of the roads simply ended, left abandoned and unfinished.

By now they had become numb to the sight of bodies lying along the roads. Brideen made sure not to look at them, to keep them from taking hold in her mind, like the man in the doorway at Castlebar, the standing corpse in her dream.

As they drew closer to the city, they realized they were part of a great movement of paupers. Thousands had already gone on to Liverpool, carrying nothing with them except fever. The destitute and starving were pouring into the industrial towns of England like an avalanche. Some arrived there with the intention of emigrating to Canada, to Australia, and especially to the United States, But for the most part, those were the ones who had relatives and friends already established, who could help them with money for their passage.

At the port in Sligo they heard stories of 'coffin ships', vessels in which the emigrants were packed together in the hold, resulting in many dead of fever on arrival. It made them almost grateful that they couldn't afford passage to America; for now, their interest was in getting fed, not emigrating. They heard about a small paddle steamer, the *Londonderry,* on which the passengers could ride above-deck instead of being crammed in the hold. They managed to secure passage on the next day's sailing. It cost them everything they had left, but it was worth it. Upon payment, crewmembers distributed small rations of bread.

They spent the night outside near the quay, along with dozens of others booked on the *Londonderry.* The following morning they joined the throng at the base of the ramp, waiting their turn to board. Mam mounted first, with Ciaran in her arms, followed by Siobhan, Brideen, Sean Brian, Mikeen, and Liam. But as Seamus and Da approached the ramp, the bosun stepped forward. He blocked their way, saying something in English.

Da was taken aback.

"Is he saying we can't board?"

One of the crew translated the bosun's words into Irish.

"He says you only paid for eight. There's ten of you."

"We were told a half crown would cover all of us."

The crewman relayed Da's words to the bosun, who just shook his head. The sailor turned back to Da with an apologetic shrug, saying there was nothing more he could do.

Da tried again to get the bosun to reconsider, but Seamus stopped him.

"I'll stay behind, Da. Maybe he'll take one more."

Mam shouted from the top of the ramp.

"You'll do no such thing."

"It'll be easier, Mam. He's old, he's the father, they'll let him on."

"It's all of us or none!"

"No, it's not, Mam. I'm not going. No matter what you say. I'm not going."

The whole family looked at him, dumbstruck.

"What do you mean, you're not going?" Mam demanded.

"I'm staying in Ireland. I'm going to find Manus."

"Find Manus? What are you on about? The divil's got into you."

"I know where he is. Where *they* are. I'm going to fight for Ireland at my brother's side."

She knew who he meant by 'they'. They all did. Seamus was going to join the Ribbonmen. Had he made a promise to Manus? Had he planned to do this all along? There was no way to know. But they could see there was no use arguing. His mind was made up. In his determination and stubbornness, it was as if he himself had become Manus.

Seamus turned to the crewman who was interpreting for the bosun.

"Tell him I'm staying behind. But my brothers and sisters need their father. You have a father, don't you? Please. Let my father come aboard. Now."

As they watched the bosun listen to Seamus' words in English they could see he was inwardly shaken, torn about what to do.

Then Brideen broke the silence.

"Tell him I have something for payment!"

Everyone looked at her in astonishment.

"Ye do?" the crewman practically shouted.

"Yes! It's come all the way from London."

She took her whistle out of a sack slung over her shoulder and held it out to him.

"What's that?" he started to ask, but the bosun had already stepped forward and took it from Brideen's hands.

"I know what it is. It makes music," he said in English. "Can you play this?" He'd asked Brideen directly, without the interpreter, but she seemed to understand, and nodded fiercely. He held the whistle back toward her.

She grasped the cylinder and lifted it to her lips. At first it made almost no sound, as she had so little breath. But when she tried a second time, a solid note rang out. She began to breathe as deeply as she could, until she could feel the melody of *Si Bheag, Sí Mhór* flow in and out of her body.

Her family watched in astonishment. They knew she could play; they'd heard her play a little, but not whole tunes. Even Da had no idea that she'd mastered entire melodies, much less one of the most beloved airs in all of Ireland.

As Brideen played, all activity on the ship and in the vicinity came to a halt. Silence reigned. When she'd blown the final notes of the air, she lowered the whistle and began to hold it out toward the captain. But the captain paid her no mind. He was quietly weeping, and when he finally took note of her gesture, he shook his head and lightly waved the whistle away with his hand.

"Go on. Get on board. The lot of you."

Da mounted the ramp and wrapped his arms around Mam, surrounded by his children. Brideen tucked her whistle back into the sack, embraced her little brother, and said a silent prayer of thanks to Saint Ciaran. She was right not to leave the whistle at the Holy Well. She'd saved it for the better offering.

As the paddles of the *Londonderry* began to churn and thrust the vessel out into the water, Seamus stood on the quay, waving. Brideen called out to her brother.

"We'll see you when we come back to Ireland. We'll all be together again."

Of course they would. Of course they'd return to Ireland. After all, she still hadn't had the chance to experience what it was like to look out from the summit of Croagh Patrick.

A meeting of the magistrates was held yesterday, at reception of the pauper immigrants. As much as twenty thousand pounds of the ratepayers' money will probably be expended in addition to what has already been spent. After laying out seven thousand pounds in erecting sheds already, the Poor Law Commissioners very coolly write down requiring us to erect more.., The number of immigrants from Ireland since the Ist January, is about 150,000, of whom about 46,000 have emigrated. A few have wandered away; but 102,564 are believed to be still in this town. During the last four weeks only, no fewer than 45,216 have been landed here and most of them have applied for relief. In the same period last year, the immigrants applying for relief were only 1,824.

-- Liverpool *Mercury*, Tuesday, May 4, 1847

PART II: The Black Country, Wednesbury, England, 1847-58

A hurrier and two thrusters heaving a cart full of coal through a mine.
Image from *The White Slaves of England* by John C. Cobden, 1853.

Chapter 4: MINERS and NAILERS

The Black Country. The name is eminently descriptive, for blackness everywhere prevails. The ground is black, the atmosphere is black, and the underground is honey-combed by mining galleries stretching in utter blackness for many a league... The roaring fires are seen for miles around, pouring their fierce, throbbing flames like volcanoes. Then a hundred chimneys of iron-works display their blazing crests, or sheafs of fiery tongues. Then the dull gleam of heaps of roasting ironstone makes you fancy that the old globe itself is here smouldering away. Overhead dense clouds of smoke reflect a lurid light rolling fitfully before the wind while the hissing and rushing of steam, the clang and clatter of machinery, the roaring blasts and the shock of ponderous hammer-strokes, all intensified by the presence of night complete an effect that amazes alike the eye and the ear... By day you hear the same noises and see the fires divested of their nightly terrors, yet find it difficult to believe that a scene of so much havoc and seeming confusion represents prosperous industry and one of the most important departments of British trade.

-- from *All Round the Wrekin* by Walter White. London: Chapman and Hall, 1860

Brideen took up the iron rod, blazing hot at the tip, and began pounding it with the mallet, making the splinters shave off bit by bit. Normally she didn't like working at the forge, but today she was alone in the back cottage, and was enjoying the solitude. At least there was only the sound of one hammer—her own—rather than the cacophony of multiple mallets. There was a slight breeze blowing through the one window, which lessened the intense heat of the burning coals.

She placed the rod back in the forge and pumped the bellows, setting the coals ablaze and bringing the tip of the rod to an intense glow. She went through the same motions several times, heating the rod, then dipping it in the bucket of water to cool it. She was careful with the tongs to keep the blazing tip far from her body. When she decided the point was sufficiently sharp, she lifted it over to the back table and inserted it into the header. She resumed pounding, no longer with brute force but maneuvering to flatten the protruding tip. Finally she lifted it with the tongs again and dunked it in the bucket of water, watching the cooling steam rise up.

She'd noticed that some of the fellows tended to be a bit reckless and oftentimes burned themselves. Brideen had learned to be more careful. When she first started working as a nailer, she sometimes rushed, trying to keep up with the other, more experienced workers. Then one day one of the other women, Mary Lydon, suggested she slow down.

"What're you rushing for? To make a few pence more? It's all going to your man Conner anyway."

She meant Roger Conner, whose nailworks it was, and in whose cottage Brideen, Mary, and a dozen other workers lived.

She ran her finger over the nail head, still warm to the touch. It was smooth. A fine nail. She couldn't help wanting to do a good job of it. Besides, Roger would be pleased, and not berate her as he did when she first arrived at the Conners'. She reminded herself that making nails was better than hauling coal through the narrow passage in the mine.

She started work on another nail, savoring the quiet and solitude. But soon thoughts began to crowd into her mind, memories of all that had happened in the two years since they left Ireland. Many things she was just as happy to not to remember.

* * *

Suffocation on Board the Steamer Londonderry!

It is seldom that we are called on to notice a more fearful catastrophe than what has taken place on board the Londonderry steamer. The account of the appalling occurrence will, we are sure, be universally read with feelings of horror. The circumstances of the case are briefly these: - A steamer sails from Sligo to Liverpool in the afternoon, with about 170 steerage passengers on board – chiefly emigrants going to their intended port of embarkation. The steamer, which also carries a number of cattle and sheep, proceeds on her way; but as the night approaches, the wind begins to blow more fiercely, and the sea to rise. At this season of the year, and in a sea so exposed as the Irish Channel, this was no strange occurrence. With her decks crowded with passengers and cattle, the captain and crew find it difficult properly to attend to the safety of the ship; and we do not wonder at it. A crowded deck must inevitably hamper the operations of the seamen.

The question arises – how are the passengers to be disposed of? With the captain and mate, the subject does not receive a second thought. With abundance of accommodation in the spacious cabin (there being only three cabin passengers), they compel the helpless passengers, resisting and struggling it may be, to descend into the only steerage accommodation the vessel afforded – a small room, some 18 feet long, 10 or 12 feet wide, and about 7 feet high. Into such a small space, which would not accommodate beyond 40, even were the ventilation attended to, upwards of three times that number are recklessly forced. Not the slightest precaution is taken to secure a supply of fresh air to the poor creatures thus huddled together. The idea that free ventilation was indispensable seems not to have struck any of those in charge. Nay, as appears from the evidence, the smallest chance of a supply of fresh air being conveyed to the steerage is cut off by the hatchway being closed; and to keep all fast, a tarpaulin nailed over it.

The shrieks and groans of the unfortunate creatures, though no doubt loud, frequent, and prolonged, while strength remained, are unheard or unheeded by the crew. At last one of the passengers, more fortunate than the rest, succeeds in forcing his way through the companion, and informs the mate of the awful calamity that was consummating. Measures are immediately taken to afford relief, - but too late. By this time (need we wonder at the result), 72 human beings had been literally suffocated. More than one-half of those who had entered the steerage alive and well, are now dead! It is melancholy to reflect on the sufferings which must have been endured in this horrid hole – of the struggles of the victims to secure relief – of their trampling, tearing, and crushing each other – and of their agonized ravings in the closing scene of the fearful tragedy.

-- Dundee Courier 13 December 1848

"That could have been us," Siobhan said.

By the time the news of the wreck reached them, the Sweeneys were safely ensconced near Wolverhampton. It had been months since they disembarked the steamer at Liverpool and began the trek to the Black Country, where they were told there would be work for the whole family in the coal mines. But with the news of the catastrophe on the *Londonderry*, the very same vessel that had carried them from Sligo, the terrible memory of that passage came hurtling back into Brideen's mind. She had never felt terror like she had in the hold of the *Londonderry*, not even when the crowbar brigade ripped into the house in Ballyhean, nor at the sight of the corpse standing in the doorway in Castlebar. The screaming winds, the churning waves shooting water all around them, Mam and the other women saying the Viaticum prayers because they were all about to die, Mam was sure of it and so Brideen was, too.

And yet somehow the storm grew weaker and the water stopped rushing over them. The crew had been getting ready to seal the opening with a tarpaulin, as they did on the later voyage, which was how the passengers in the hold had suffocated. When they stepped off the ship at Liverpool it was a miraculous rescue, a joyful release, a nightmare ended. But when the news came of the latest tragedy, it was like it was happening all over again. What if the crew had managed to seal off the opening on their voyage? What would they have found in the morning?

That could have been us.

* * *

Wednesbury consists of one long street, along the turnpike road, with many lateral ones branching into courts and alleys, inhabited by the working classes. There is no drainage worth the name, no scavengers or system of cleansing, and the supply of water very scarce and indifferent. There are no pipes, a few pumps, and the wells are often bad. The people complain much, and have to carry water near a mile, or to buy at a halfpenny for three cans. The workhouse of the town has very bad water in the well, and they are obliged to fetch it for washing or drinking several times a day. The courts, alleys, and small streets are unpaved or ill paved, full of stagnant puddles, privies with open vaults, pigsties, etc.; there is, in fact, no care taken on these points, and the greatest neglect appears.
-- from the 2nd Report of the Commissioners on the Enquiry of the Health of Towns, London, 1845

The town of Wednesbury is situated in the midst of the mining district of South Staffordshire, a district remarkable in connection with the immigration of the Irish into England. In no other large town in Great Britain, except Liverpool, Manchester or London, will one be so struck with the large proportion the Irish form of the population, and in no part of England is the Irish language so prevalent. In the ordinary conversation of social and business intercourse, it is the language between the exiles; it is spoken not only in their homes, but at their work and in the street. The Irish located here are chiefly from the poorest parts of the west of Ireland. Imagine such a people thrown suddenly among the

English population – could two elements more antagonistic come together? To complete the antagonism, the Irishman's language is to them a foreign tongue, his religion is in their eyes a jibe and a reproach. Everything tends to place him in the position of the bondsman and the serf. Throughout all England our poor people are found filling this position – hewers of wood and drawers of water; but in this locality their occupation is of the most slavish kind, and their social position the lowest that can be found.
-- from "An Irish Colony in England," *The Nation*, Vol. 16, No. 2, 1856

When the Sweeneys disembarked from the *Londonderry*, they really did receive British government relief in Liverpool. They could scarcely believe it was real when they saw what awaited them: A meal of milk, potatoes, and a couple of loaves of bread. It was barely enough but by now they were used to hunger, and Mam doled it out carefully to last through the two days' walk.

They were instructed to go to a town near Birmingham, where there were many emigrants from Ireland. They found the prospect of finding a whole Irish community in Wednesbury "almost too good to be true," as Da put it. But sure enough, within hours of arriving, they met people from Mayo, Roscommon, Galway—a few they already knew, many others with familiar names. Da wondered if he might even find some of his people from Achill there. They were overjoyed that they could speak their own language and needn't worry about learning English—at least not yet.

Wednesbury or "Wedgebury" as the locals called it, was a bigger, more bustling town than they were used to. The only place in Mayo that was comparable was Castlebar, and Brideen had only been there a handful of times. As they approached the town they could see in the distance the vast Lloyd's Colliery near Hob's Hole. There were the iron works, the hot blast of the furnaces, the foundry where the iron ore was smelted to produce pig iron, where innumerable items were cast: Iron for buildings and bridges, parts for steam engines, wheels and axles for the railways. The site also contained large quantities of clay, which was used to produce bricks and tiles. And the foundation of it all was the mine, where thousands of men, women, and children worked endless hours, digging out the coal that powered the steam engines for all this new, imposing industry.

They'd never seen anything so vast and intimidating, and the idea of going through that narrow entrance and down underground to work for hours a day was unimaginable. But there would be no more relief from the English government, no other prospects for work that would allow them to eat. There was nothing else to be done but to do it.

* * *

I have been three weeks in the pit. I hurry with my brother. I don't like it, but my father can't keep me without going. It's such hard work. It tires my back. I think it will continue to tire me after I become more accustomed to it. I go down the shaft at half past five and stop a bit, and then we begin... They use me well at pit, they don't beat me or call me but I'd rather be at school than at the pit. I can't read.

-- Matilda Carr, Age 12

I am 19 years old. I was between nine and ten when I first went in the pit. I trapped for three or four years at first but have hurried since. I go down between five and six in the morning and I come up generally around five in the evening. It depends on what the hurrier gets how much we have to hurry. I have ever been much tired from my work.

-- Mary Shaw

I am not 17 yet. I have been in the pit seven years. I have been four years hurrying. It does not tire me to hurry now. I did tire me when I was little. I like going to the pit, but I would rather go to service. I don't like the confinement.

-- Hannah Clarkson

-- From interviews conducted in Yorkshire, contained in the
Report of the Royal Commission on Children's Employment
(Mines), vol. XV, 1842

The deaths in mines and on the pit-banks are as follows:
Fell down the shaft: 13 (under 13)); 16 (age 13-18); 31 (18 and
older)
Fell down the shaft from rope breaking: 1 (under 13); 2 (18 and
older)
Drowned in the mines: 1 (under 13); 3 (18 and older)
Fall of stones, coal and rubbish: 14 (under 13); 14 (age 13-18); 69
(18 and older)
Injuries in coal-pits, the nature of which is not specified: 6 (under
13); 3 (age13-18); 32 (18 and older)
Explosion of gas: 13 (under 13); 18 (age 13-18); 49 (18 and older)
Suffocation by choke-damp: 2 (age 13-18); 6 (18 and older)
-- from the Report of the Royal Commission on Children's
Employment (Mines), vol. XV, 1842

The whole family worked underground, except for Ciaran,
who was too young, and Mam, who looked after him and
prepared their meals. Every job had a name, and a very specific
function. Mikeen and Sean Brian were hewers, working down at
the seam, mining the coal with sharp picks and other hand tools.
Siobhan worked as their getter, shovelling the coal into the tubs,
often working on her knees. Da worked as a hurrier, harnessed to
a tub and pulling it through the narrow roadways. Liam was his
thruster, pushing the tub from behind with his hands, sometimes
with the top of his head. They would both have to crawl on hands
and knees, since the tunnels were less than a foot high. The tubs
of coal sometimes weighed a thousand pounds or more.

Brideen was a trapper. She was just old enough to work
legally, under a law passed by the British Parliament in 1842. It
was her job to open and close the trap doors that allowed fresh air

to flow through the mine. She had to sit in total darkness for up to twelve hours at a time, waiting to let the coal tub through the door. It was not hard work but it could be dangerous, especially if she fell asleep.

They found a house to rent on the Old Park Road, right near the colliery. They worked every day, starting before dawn and finishing after dusk, except for Sundays, when they went to the mission house for Mass, said by Father George Montgomery. He was the priest who had become a central figure to the Irish emigrants of Wednesbury, who were largely ignored, if not openly scorned, by the English Catholic hierarchy. Father Montgomery had established the temporary mission with his own resources, and had begun the process of building a new church, despite opposition from Protestants, who threatened to buy the land and tear it down.

There was one other day off granted to the colliery workers, and that was the Fair held for the Feast of Saint Bartholomew in August. It was the high point of the year, near the end of the Sweeneys' first year in Wednesbury, and they were excited to be part of it. Brideen in particular had a plan. She'd continued to play her whistle on Sundays, and was learning a new tune called "Willie O'Winsbury". It was a waltz-tune, the kind of long ballad beloved by the English, about a king's daughter who falls in love with a commoner named Willie. The king is outraged, but relents when he meets Willie and decides he's worthy of his daughter's hand, so grants the couple gifts of gold and land. Brideen had overheard some people discussing whether the song was actually about Wednesbury itself, in the olden times. The lyrics were in English, of course, but she was determined to play the tune for the people of the town.

The day of the fair, Brideen positioned herself at the edge of the crowd, a bit removed from the noisiest part of the square. As she began to play, some fairgoers clustered around her to listen.

Then a man nearby with a handbarrow became agitated and began to speak loudly to the crowd. Brideen couldn't understand a word of what he was saying, but he kept pointing at her whistle as if he was about to seize it. She stopped playing and clutched the instrument to her chest.

One of the listeners came over to Brideen, a fellow from Mayo who'd been living in Wednesbury for a few years and understood some English.

"Don't worry," he told Brideen. "This fellow isn't going to take your whistle, he just wants to look at it."

She lifted it off her chest but held on to the mouthpiece, reluctant to let go of it entirely. The man with the handbarrow pointed to the inscription on the whistle and once again talked excitedly, directing his words to the Mayo fellow, who again turned to Brideen.

"This man's name is Robert Clarke. He says he's the fellow what made your whistle. That's his name on the side of it. See?"

It took Brideen a few moments to comprehend what he was saying. She glanced over at the man's cart, which was loaded with sheets of black metal and tools. In one corner of the cart was a clutch of tin whistles. She'd never thought before of someone actually making a whistle, or of how it was made. But working in the colliery she'd seen how metal was forged, and now she understood. This man was a maker of whistles, and it was he who'd made this very one.

The Mayo fellow and the man with the handbarrow kept talking effusively.

"Mr. Clarke wants to know where you got this," he said to Brideen.

"My Da got it from a man in Dublin."

As he listened to the translation, Clarke seemed to know exactly what Brideen was talking about. He explained that once he'd made a certain number of whistles, he'd set off on a walk from his home in Coney Weston to the West Midlands, pushing his tools and materials in his handbarrow. On the way he stopped at village markets and sold the "megs", as he called them, for a ha'penny. He remembered selling one to a man from Dublin, who'd come to the West Midlands for work digging the canals. He figured that might be how one of his whistles got to Ireland.

"I've ne'er heard one played so well as you. You must keep on playing so people will know about my whistles. Tell them it's made by Robert Clarke of Coney Weston!"

Brideen was almost giddy with excitement. She couldn't wait to tell Da and the rest of the family that she'd met the man who made her whistle, and that he'd praised her playing.

* * *

With this abrupt height the Black Country here terminates, and Vulcan leaves the fields to Ceres. We look across to Barr Beacon, one of the note-worthy hills of the neighbourhood, from the top of which you can survey the delightful sylvan region of Sutton park and Chase. Therein are large clear lakes, cascades, miles of wood, forest glades, stately trees, and tangled covert, bold wooded eminences, grassy levels and uplands, and great slopes roughened and beautified by fern and gorse. It charms the rambler by wildness, and the chance of losing his way in the thickets, and rewards the antiquary by sight of some furlongs of a Roman road - Icknield Street, along which he may pace undisturbed.

-- from *All Round the Wrekin* by Walter White. London: Chapman and Hall, 1860

They decided to mark the end of their first year in Wednesbury with a ramble in the countryside. It was a Sunday in October and the weather was mild and clear. It had been a hard time in the colliery, especially for Da, who seemed to be developing a chronic cough. People told him it was from the coal dust, that he should get out of the mine and find some other work. But it was what he knew how to do, and he wanted to stay on working with his sons and daughters. They heard the potato crop back in Mayo had somewhat recovered, but there wasn't enough to feed the people. Many were still dying of starvation. But for the Sweeney family, the nightmare of the famine was over. Their strength was coming back. They had food to eat.

They decided to end their ramble with a climb up Barr Beacon, a hill just outside of Walsall, north of Wednesbury. It was an easy walk up to the top, so they weren't expecting the remarkable sight that greeted them, as the dark sprawl of the Black Country was replaced by a gorgeous landscape of trees, greenery, and small lakes.

"Look!" Brideen shouted, exulting in the sight below. "You just turn around and it's like the whole world changes from black to green!"

"It looks like Mayo down there, doesn't it, Da?" added Mikeen.

They all turned to look at Da, who was barely able to speak because he was wiping tears from his eyes. With all the trials they had been through, leaving Ireland had been the hardest thing for him.

"Let us offer thanks to God and Our Lady for saving us from starvation and bringing us to this beautiful spot," said Mam.

They bowed their heads and said three Hail Marys and a Glory Be. Brideen was surprised to see tears in Mam's eyes as well. Da was the sentimental one. She was always the strong one. After the prayers, she went to hug her mother.

"Don't worry, Mam. God will protect us."

Chapter 6: THE FEVER

Well, the epidemic fiend answered the invitation, and in 1848 cholera again appeared in our midst. The disease lasted in this country from October, 1848 to December, 1849. This district was attacked late in the season, and murky Bilston again ran rapidly to the front of this dreadful race with a record of 605 deaths; while on the other side of us, West Bromwich with a clearer atmosphere, had only 21 deaths. At Wednesbury 212 deaths were registered, although our Board of Surveyors were fairly energetic in remedial measures. For the reception of cholera patients they erected a Hospital of wooden huts on Monway-field, to the left of the Moxley Road just beyond the site of the present railway bridge.

-- from The Wednesbury Papers by Frederick William
Hackwood, 1884

When Bonker the undertaker arrived, Siobhan sent him away without even asking Da, who was too distraught to speak.

Nobody seemed to know what his given name was. Everyone just called him "Bonker" Turner. He went around town with a pet goose, an old bird that followed him everywhere with the fidelity of a trusty dog. He was employed to collect the dead into coffins, which were really just boards knocked together, and transport them in a horse-drawn wagon from the hospital huts and residences. He then hauled the load up Church Hill, depositing the coffins into a huge grave that had been dug on the north side of St. Bartholomew's church. There the rector delivered the rites at a safe distance from the excavation—Protestant rites, they were, since at that time there was no Catholic parish in Wednesbury. Of course there were deaths among the more prominent residents of the town as well, but reluctant to have their dead tossed into the mass grave, they took care of their own, as the Sweeneys intended to.

When Bonker hesitated, Siobhan wondered if he was just holding out for his allowance of brandy.

"Ye sure?" he said. "Ye could catch the fever."

Like many in Wednesbury, he had enough of a smattering of Irish to understand and make himself understood. Siobhan told him that they'd already been living with Sean Brian, who was recovering from it, so they knew the precautions, and the funeral mass was to be held outside so no one else would be infected.

"Well, then, you needn't worry about drawing the curtains neither."

Siobhan smarted at his little joke. Normally all curtains in the house would be drawn except for the one nearest the body to allow a clear pathway to heaven. For the same reason, all the mourners wore dark clothing to avoid drawing the notice of any spirits that might be lurking in the shadows. At least outside the candles could be properly placed at the head and foot, along with a pair of shoes to aid the journey to the next world.

Then the wails of the keening women would begin, bidding the soul of the departed to spend seven days in the grave before ascending to the glories of heaven. "*Seacht lán reilic Padh-ruig agus tomba Ghriosd go bheannachtaibh le h-anam na marbh!*"

How could it be that she, who kept them out of the workhouse, who kept them away from that fever cabin, who kept them alive all the way to Sligo... how could it be that it was she who was now gone?

Mam was one of the last to die in the outbreak.

* * *

Gabhaigi i leith, a dha Mhuire, go gcaoine sibh mo ghrá gea,
Ochóne is ochóne ó
Ceard atá le caoineadh ágainn mura gcaoinimid a chriámha,
Ochóne is ochóne ó

(Come to me, you two Marys, and keen with me, Alas, alas
What have we to keen without his bones? Alas, alas)
     -- *Caoineadh Na Tri Mhuire* (Lament of the Three Marys)

Her heart was full of rage.

God took Mam but not Sean Brian. Why? They'd both caught the fever, but Sean Brian still lived. Why? He was just a brother, but she was Mam!

These were evil thoughts. She knew God could hear them, but she couldn't help it. Why Mam? Mam was the one she needed! Mam was the one she couldn't live without! Why?

Now she must move away from Da and the rest, to go live with strangers. She had no family now. It was gone. Broken. Dashed to nothingness, like waves on the shore.

The wake had been well-attended, though it was more subdued than back home. Not as much drinking, and no raucous singing, just sad ones like *Uirimh Mhic Fhinin Dhubh,* the lament for Black Finn, sung by Paddy Durkan. When he was finished, his sister Maeve called out to Brideen.

"How 'bout you play your pretty whistle for your Mam?" Brideen had been dreading that someone would ask for the whistle, and she couldn't bear to.

One of the other women spoke up.

"G'wan with ye, she can't play the whistle. Her heart is too heavy. Leave the child be."

In the short time they'd been in the Black Country they'd come to know many people who'd come from Mayo and Roscommon, and much of that was because of Mam. She'd always had a gift for connecting with people. Back home she seemed to know every family within twenty miles in every direction from Ballyhean. Now all the families she'd met here came flooding to the wake—the Walshes and the Durkans from Ballina, the O'Briens and the Burkes from Kitimagh, and the McDonnells from Oughaval near Westport. It was Mary McDonnell who'd come to her aid about not playing her whistle, and Brideen went over to express her gratitude.

But just then one of the men started up singing *Caoineadh Na Tri Mhuire,* "The Lament of the Three Marys", and Brideen was overcome, feeling her body might shatter from grief. She stumbled forward, falling between Mary McDonnell and her son Sean. Though not much bigger than Brideen, he managed to catch her before she hit the ground, then lifted her into his mother's arms. Brideen burrowed into Mary's bosom like a newly-born stoat, and sobbed until her tears ran dry. When she finally lifted her head it was Sean's face she saw first. She could see in his eyes a deep sympathy, as if in her agony he could feel the unimaginable loss of his own, living mother. Speaking barely above a whisper, he expressed sorrow for her loss.

"*Ar dhéis Dé go raibh a anam dílís*"

* * *

The whole village resounds with the strokes, and each cottage has its little forge occupying the place of the wash-house. We look into one after another and see none but women at work, three or four together, assisted in some instances by a boy or girl. The fire is in common; and one after another giving a pull at the bellows, each woman heats the ends of two slender iron rods, withdraws the first, and by a few hammer-strokes fashions and cuts off the nail, thrusts the end into the fire, and takes out the second rod, and gets a nail from that in the same way. So the work goes merrily on; the rods growing shorter, and the heap of nails larger. "It ain't work as pays for men," answers one of the women in reply to my inquiry.

-- from *All Round the Wrekin* by Walter White, London, 1860

Mam was gone to Heaven and was now with the angels. That was the message they sent to their eldest sister, Máirín. They'd received the joyful news that she was still living, as were Brendan, her husband, and their three children. There had been a fourth, a baby daughter, who died of fever during the hunger times. They'd gone to stay in the Swinford workhouse, but, horrible as it was, it was the workhouse that saved them.

Letters to Ireland took weeks, but Siobhan found a neighbor who could write a letter, so at least they could let Máirín know about Mam's passing. What was truly distressing was that they had no way of contacting Manus and Seamus to tell them that their mother was gone. And now they were faced with the unbearable prospect of a return to unrelenting hunger. Even before anything was spoken, Brideen knew that much of the burden of relieving their situation would fall to her.

For some time Da had had the cough, but once he started bringing up black bits of sputum, there was no way he could go back into the mine. Siobhan would have to leave the mine, too, to take care of him and cook for them all. Sean Brian was still recovering his strength from the bout of fever. That left Liam and Mikeen still working in the mine, and their wages alone couldn't sustain the family. Ciaran would soon be old enough to replace her as trapper. But the thought of her little brother languishing in that dark passage was too painful to contemplate. It had to be put off for as long as possible.

So when Roger Conner approached them about work in the nail shed, there was no question which of the Sweeneys would take up the offer. It meant Brideen would have to go live in the cottage on Dudley Street, even though it already housed four different families under one roof. Roger Conner and his wife, Mary, had two young children, Thomas and baby Edward. Roger's sisters Honor and Margaret lived there too along with their mother, also named Margaret. The other lodgers were John and Bridget Welch and their son Anthony, Peter and Mary Lyden and their son Patrick, and Peter and Catharine Mealy. In the mornings the men went off to work in the mine, except for Roger, who oversaw the women and children working at the forge in the back shed. Only Roger's mother and infant son were relieved of the harsh, unrelenting work of nail-making.

Brideen would of course rather have stayed with her own family, but she didn't really have a choice: Working in the nail shed came with room and board as well as wages, which were vital to her family's subsistence. She was able to visit home on Sundays and sometimes in the evenings, since Dudley was only a couple of streets over from her family's cottage. But it was a lonely life for Brideen, the only one among the nailers who had no spouse or relative living there. What made it worse was the fact that she just didn't like Roger Conner or his family.

The Conners hailed from County Roscommon, and had only been in the Black Country a year longer than the Sweeneys. When the families first became acquainted, Ma had wondered how Roger had become a nail master in so short a time. There were some whispers among the Irish in Wednesbury that he'd gotten the shop by underhanded means. But Da would only hear expressions of gratitude that Roger had come to their aid by hiring Brideen. Margaret and Honor often pointed out how lucky Brideen was that their brother had "rescued" her from working in the mine. Soon after she moved to Dudley Street, Brideen learned that the Conners had collected relief in Roscommon, even before the second potato blight struck in 1846. That only cemented her disdain for them. The Sweeneys had never applied for famine relief—a point about which Mam had been especially proud.

Still, there was no denying that things were better for the Sweeney family. With her room and board taken care of, they had enough to eat and even her meagre wages were a help. With the Conners acting like they were her betters, Brideen decided the way to show them up was to become an expert at nailmaking. Over time she did just that, and gradually gained a grudging respect from Roger. Things got even better when Mikeen started courting Margaret Conner, and it dawned on the sisters that Brideen might well become their sister-in-law, a family member.

As the mourners at the wake had assured her, the pain of Mam's passing lessened over time. There were even brief periods when Brideen forgot about her. But these times were always followed by a renewal of sorrow on top of the sting of guilt. She resolved to mourn her mother for the rest of her days. Mam must never be forgotten.

* * *

I always love to walk about in the villages of the nail-makers. The clinking of hundreds of their little hammers supply the arias to the great concerts and oratorios of mechanical industry. They are poorly-paid and have to work long and hard to earn bread in competition with machinery. Indeed, it shows the superabundance and exigencies of labour that nails should be made at all by hand at this late day of mechanical improvements. But thousands of families in this district have inherited the trade from several generations of their ancestors, and they are born to it, apparently with a physical conformation to the work. Then thousands of cottages are equally conformed to it in their structure. For each has a little shop room attached to it generally under the same roof. Thus the whole business becomes a domestic industry or house employment for the family, and frequently every member, male or female, young or old, has his or her rod in the fire all the day long and often far into the night. Although they earn but little, they earn it at home, and the whole social operation and aspect of their industry is rather interesting. These little house- shops are scattered far and wide over the district, sometimes in little villages and hamlets, but often on high and breezy hills and behind the hedges of green and rural lanes. So they in the majority of cases really make comfortable little homes for honest and contented labourers.

-- from *Walks in the Black Country and its Green Border-land,* by
Elihu Burritt, London: 1868

"Justice for nailers!"

It was the last thing Brideen could have imagined herself doing, marching in a mass procession of nail workers. But here she was, with the Welches, the Lydens, and other Wednesbury nailers, walking the twelve miles to Halesowen to join the burgeoning strike there. From there they would head farther south to Bromsgrove, where nail workers from all over the Black Country would take a stand against cuts in their wages.

Their departure was difficult. Roger was furious and told them not to bother coming back to work. After two years in his shop, Brideen had become familiar with his moods and tantrums, and she could tell he was genuinely shocked that his own crew stood up to him. And he was anxious about his own future. The entire industry was changing, as more and more nails were being made by machines in factories. In an effort to compete, the cottage nail masters cut back on their workers' already meagre wages. Many Black Country workers retaliated by taking their nails to sell at Tommy shops, where they were further exploited by middle-men known as "foggers". The foggers paid prices well below the going rate, often in currency that could only be used in the Tommy shops, and cheated the nailers by short-weighing their scales. One way or the other, the nailers ended up on the losing end. Periodically the workers would rise up against the foggers and nail masters, resulting in periods of strife and rioting, with an ever-present threat of violence.

Brideen and the others in the Conner nail cottage knew that Roger was far from the worst of the nail masters. They worked long hours and were paid poorly, but were treated fairly well as members of the household. They weren't surprised that Roger's own family members didn't join them on the march to Halesowen. Although it seemed to Brideen that Margaret wanted to go, she held back to avoid her brother's wrath. She longed for something better than making nails for the rest of her life.

As the little group left the Dudley Street shop, Brideen felt energized. But as the walk progressed, she felt a nagging fear set in. What in the name of God was she on about, defying her employer and walking away from one of the few sources of income the Sweeneys had? She didn't dare tell Da what she was doing. As much as he'd support the justice of their cause, he'd be even more anxious about the loss of her wages. As they joined the larger group on the road to Halesowen, Brideen resolved to be brave as she listened to the older workers talk about the last big strike. Ten years earlier, several thousand workers from all the nailing districts had gathered at a mass meeting. The nail masters had agreed to hear their demands and negotiate. Instead, the nailers were met by a troop of cavalry with sabres drawn. They put up fierce resistance, with some of the nailers using their hammers as clubs. But the following day the cavalry was reinforced by troops and artillery brought in from other counties, resulting in arrests, injuries, and some deaths. In the end the nailers were forced to disperse without achieving any of their wage goals.

Oh, you nailmakers all that day remember well,
The last strike of which this tale I tell,
How cold and hungry we that heavy day,
To Bromsgrove Town did take our toilsome way,
And these nail forgers, miserable souls,
Will not forget the givers of the cause,
Nailmasters are hard-hearted viles,
And the way we took was 13 miles.

Oh, the slaves abroad in the sugar cane,
Find plenty to help and pity their pain,
But the slaves at home in the mine or fire,
Have plenty to pity but none to admire,
Now, I wish I could see all nail dealers,
Draw such a load as did we poor nailers,

And see such punishment and such smarts,
That it might soften their hard stoney hearts.
           -- Anon., written on the occasion of the nailers'
           strike in 1842

Listening to the stories, Brideen felt a mixture of outrage and fear. After spending two years of her life making nails, she knew in the core of her being that their demands were just. She was coming to a whole new understanding of her Da's love for Daniel O'Connell and his quest for justice for the Irish nation. She felt new stirrings, a longing to be part of a bigger fight for justice for herself and her fellow nailers. But what if this march was met with the same response as the one ten years ago? What if she got caught up in a riot?

In the end, none of them got a chance to find out. Word came that a severe winter storm had struck the Bromsgrove area, and heavy snow had forced the marchers to turn back less than a mile out of Halesowen. The groups from the Black Country, including Wednesbury, ended up doing the same.

Among the nailers, there was bitter disappointment, and Brideen was surprised at how strong her own reaction was. Once again, the nailers' efforts had been thwarted. And what was in store for Brideen herself? The Welches and the Lydens were going to ask Conner to take them back, and she had little choice but to do the same. It was clear from the older workers' stories that nothing would change. Everyone knew that things would only get worse. The whole industry was passing into oblivion as the big factories took over. Sooner or later Roger Conner would have to close his own shop.

What was she going to do? Become a chainmaker, like many nailers did? She was older now, she had some skills, she was employable. Could she find some kind of factory job in Birmingham? No matter what, she had to keep making an income for the family. Da still couldn't go back to the mine. Nor would

Sean Brian, who'd started to drink too much during his recovery from fever, and was well on his way to becoming an utter wastrel. Siobhan had long been courted by Martin Duffy, but he was growing impatient with her frequent postponements of the wedding because of worries about who would take care of Da and Sean Brian. Brideen knew she should do her part, so her sister could have a life like other women her age.

She had to keep bringing in money. She had to. But how?

Chapter 7: FACTORY GIRL

Some large establishments employ hundreds of women and girls, whose appearance is such that a visitor from Lancashire remarked to his Birmingham friend,"Why, your factory girls look like ladies." The making of steel pens depends so much on light stamping-presses and sprightly fingers that it ranks with the most desirable of what is known as "female employments" being neither dirty nor laborious. It is pleasing to pass from room to room of these large works, and see four hundred women and girls, all clean and properly dressed. A girl who knows how to make the most of her time will cut out 300 gross of blanks, more than forty thousand a day, and earn from 12 to 15 shillings a week. The hours of work are from eight to seven.

What becomes of all the steel pens? Birmingham uses up between eight to nine tons of steel a week in pen manufacture. If all have gone well, they emerge with a temper acceptable to writers in all parts of the civilised world. Even in Turkey, for has not Albert Smith recorded that he saw a Musselman selling steel pens in the streets of Constantinople?

-- from *All Round the Wrekin* by Walter White. London: Chapman and Hall, 1860

"Everything depends on wearing a decent dress."

Margaret spoke as if it were all decided, and Brideen knew there was no point in resisting her sister-in-law. Because as of a month ago, that's what they were. Her brother Mikeen and Margaret were married by Father Montgomery on a Sunday morning at the still-unfinished church. The whole Irish community in Wednesbury had turned out, and afterwards the festivities had gone late into the night. Life was still hard, but the joy of having something to celebrate was palpable among the guests. Margaret wore a dress of fine linen with braided embroidery around the bodice. And now she was insisting that Brideen wear that very dress to apply for work at the Hincks and Wells pen factory.

"Margaret, no! It's your wedding dress!"

"You need to look nice to get the job," Margaret insisted. "You can't go in there looking like some dirty nail girl."

For a moment Brideen felt a stab of pain, remembering that Mam had given much the same reason for the new dress she'd worn to Achill.

"You should practice a few English phrases, too," Margaret went on.

"Why? They'll know I'm Irish."

"Sure they will. Speak a bit of English and they'll think you're the better sort of Irish."

Brideen realized Margaret was older and knew more about these things than she did. And she was grateful for the help, for the inevitable had finally arrived. Conner's nail shop was cutting back, and would gradually shut down production in the coming months. The Welches and the Lydens had already been let go. Only family members would remain in the work force, though Roger, prevailed upon by Margaret, kept Brideen on for a while longer.

A few days later she presented herself at the Birmingham factory, wearing a pair of brogues she shared with Siobhan and Margaret's wedding dress, for an interview with one of the foremen. She nodded solemnly as he spoke, then offered up her few practised phrases in English that—she hoped—answered the questions he was putting to her.

"I am a hard worker. I live close by. I will work every day."

She was hired on the spot.

Her first days in the factory were overwhelming. She'd been accustomed to spending her days in a small shack crowded around a single forge with five or six other workers, doing work that involved simple repetition of actions—feeding the fire, applying heat to an iron rod and pounding it into shape. But the factory was vast, cavernous, and the manufacture of steel pens was infinitely more complicated, involving different types of machinery and several stages of assembly. Brideen was assigned to a room full of benches fronted by rows of stamping-presses, where the first stage was completed. The girls took steel ribbons off a roller, placed them on the presses, and through a quick series of adjustments and pulls on the lever, turned out "blanks" that looked almost like steel lace. Some of the girls got very adept at the work and could make as much as fifteen shillings a week. Brideen observed them carefully. As she had back in the nail cottage, she resolved to join the ranks of these expert pressers.

In time she adjusted to her new life. Every morning she rode one of the barges carrying coal and iron down the Old Canal to Birmingham, where she disembarked at the Jewellers' quarter and took the short walk to the Hincks and Wells steel-pen factory. Even for a beginner, the pay was better than at the nail forge. She liked wearing decent, clean clothes, and found an unexpected delight in being with so many other girls and women. Her sisters were a lot older than she was, and at home she was surrounded by brothers. The steel-pen girls were talkative and playful, especially when they gathered in the yard to have tea on their breaks. It reminded her of the time she'd spent with the girls and young women in the booley huts that golden summer in Achill, which now seemed like a distant lifetime ago.

In Wednesbury she was around other Irish speakers all the time, but here she was managing to learn some English. The work was demanding, but it was a pleasant experience leaving the factory every day, clean and not exhausted.

* * *

As I went a-walking one fine summer's morning,
The birds in the bushes did whistle and sing.

The lads and the lasses in couples were sporting,
Going down to the factory their work to begin.
I spied one among them, she was fairer than any,
Her cheeks like the red rose that blooms in the spring
Her hair like the lily that grows in yon valley.
She was only a hard-working factory girl.

I stepped up beside her, more closely to view her,
When on me she cast a proud look of disdain.
Saying "Stand off, young man, my soul's not for stealing,
Although I'm a poor girl, I think it no shame."

"I have land and fine houses adorned with ivory,
I have gold in my pockets and silver as well.
And if you'll go with me, a lady I'll make you
No more need you answer the factory bell."

Oh love and temptation are our ruination,
She said "go find a lady and may you do well.
For I am an orphan with ne'er a relation
And I'll stay a hard working factory girl."
>   -- "The Factory Girl," traditional ballad dating
>   from the late 18th century

One day as she departed the factory in the flood of female workers, Brideen noticed a man standing by the gate. He was clearly a gentleman, dressed in a dark blue waistcoat and wearing the new fashionable hat called a "bowler". To her surprise, he came toward her.

"Good day, lovely lady."

She understood his greeting and nodded hello back.

"Such a fine lady as yourself, you stand out among all these others."

Brideen could only understand bits of words, but she could tell he was paying her a compliment. Which was odd, since many of her co-workers were better dressed than she was. Still, she felt a bit flattered, and smiled appreciatively.

The rest of the crowd went on their way, but he stayed and continued to talk. Now she had little idea of what he was saying. Her understanding of English was improving, but she couldn't keep up with the speed of most conversations. She kept nodding, pretending to understand. She didn't want to reveal her ignorance. She wondered if he could tell that she was Irish.

At one point he reached over and took her arm. He seemed to want her to go somewhere with him, and she began to feel uneasy. She had heard her co-workers talking about men who preyed on young factory girls, talking about their wealth and feigning interest in marriage. This fellow in the bowler hat might be one of those men, and Brideen had no intention of going with him. She tried to disengage his arm, but gently, so he wouldn't be insulted.

She heard a voice behind her.

"*Dia dhuit!*"

A young man was approaching them. Brideen was surprised to hear someone speaking Irish in this part of Birmingham. The gentleman held tight to her arm. He seemed to want to hurry her away. The young man called out again.

"*Fan suas!*"

He was calling on them to stop and wait. She shook her arm hard enough to break the gentleman's grip.

"Bridget Sweeney!"

Brideen had thought the young man looked familiar. It was Mary McDonnell's son, whom she hadn't seen since Mam's funeral more than four years ago.

"Is that you, Sean McDonnell?"

She looked toward the gentleman and was startled to see him hurrying away, without saying a word.

"You've said right," he replied in Irish. "Good thing I got here to chase that fellow off."

"I wasn't going to go with him."

"He had designs on you."

"I know what he was up to! You don't have to tell me."

"He was pulling you off with him. I came along just in time."

"I'd already gotten away from him.

"That's not how it looked to me."

"I was fine. I don't need to be rescued by the likes of you, Sean McDonnell."

"I just happened by on my way from work. When I saw what was happening, I was worried. I thought you might need some help."

"I know. I don't mean to sound ungrateful, really I don't. He did... scare me a bit."

"You've got to watch out for those types. And just so you know, I now go by the name of John."

"You do?

He explained that his workmates here in Birmingham found it easier to pronounce his English name.

"So you speak English now?"

"I know enough to get by."

"I'm trying to learn some, too."

She told him that she'd been let go from Conner's nail shop and was now working at the steel-pen factory.

"What with the big factories taking over, pretty soon there won't be any nail shops left."

"Well, I hate to break it to you, but it's the likes of me that's put you out of the job."

"What do you mean?"

He told her his job was at one of the big metalworks.

"We work the big machines making nuts and bolts... and nails!"

Brideen could only laugh.

"I'm bringing home more now than I ever did from the nail hut. Maybe I should thank you for that, too."

She said she had to go. The barge back to Wednesbury was leaving soon.

"I'm on my way there myself," John said. "To see my mam."

She felt a familiar twinge of jealousy. He was one of the lucky ones who had a mother still living. Then she remembered how he was at her mother's wake, the sympathy in his eyes as he helped her to her feet.

"I see your mum around Wedge, but not you for a long time."

"The family's still there but I'm living here in Birmingham now. Closer to the job. Why don't we ride the barge together?"

"Sure. As long as you think I'm safe to go along with you, John McDonnell."

It took him a moment to absorb the teasing quality in her voice. Then he laughed.

"G'wan away with ye, girl!"

On the barge he talked about life in Birmingham and the groups fighting for workers' rights. He and his mates had been going to meetings led by Feargus O'Connor, a leader who was promoting the idea that every worker should own a piece of land to support himself and his family. O'Connor believed that was the way for them to escape greedy landlords and the oppression of factory work.

"O'Connor's an Irishman, so he knows about land theft."

"You sound like one of those radicals my Da talks about."

"There's a lot of that in Birmingham and I want to be part of it. There's a group called the Political Union. They used to be very powerful in the city, with a Catholic leader, a priest named McDonnell, same as me. The Protestant leaders were afraid he was getting too powerful and got the bishop to transfer him to a church down near Bristol. The older fellows say that it knocked the stuffing out of the movement."

"I've heard of that Father McDonnell," Brideen said. "Da says he was a great friend of Daniel O'Connell, that he brought the Liberator to speak in Birmingham."

"That was back when you and I were just wee ones," John noted. "Some of my mates joke that I'm the secret son of Father McDonnell. They say I should become a priest and take up his work. Which, of course, my mam thinks is a great idea. Every Irish mother wants at least one of her sons to become a priest."

"Is that what you want? To join the priesthood?"

"I've thought about it for a while. But I'm not sure."

* * *

*September 18, 1853. Certificate of Marriage in the District of West Bromwich in the County of Stafford: John McDonald, age 20 years to Bridget Swanwick, age 17 years, married in the St. Michael's Chapel according to the Rites and Ceremonies of the Catholic Church by Thomas Revill. This Marriage was solemnized between us: **X** The mark of John McDonald, **X** The Mark of Bridget Swanwick, in the Presence of **X** The Mark of Margaret Conner.*

-- from the General Register Office, West Bromwich

"Who in the name of God is this Swanwick person?"

It wasn't until months later that Brideen learned that her marriage to John McDonnell had been registered under a name other than her own. The clerk in the Register Office tried to assure her that there was no problem, that it was just a misunderstanding.

"They just didn't hear your name right. If they don't quite understand what a person is saying, sometimes they just write down something more familiar. Swanwick—that's a village down Portsmouth way. Happens all the time with Irish names. Doesn't mean your marriage isn't properly registered."

By now Brideen knew just enough English to understand the clerk, and she was reassured to learn that she wouldn't be considered as "living in sin". Not that it was something she herself believed. God knew her heart, no matter what the priests thought. Still, it was nerve-wracking to find out such an important error had been made. It was hard enough learning spoken English. Was she going to have to learn to read and write it, too?

Of course there wouldn't be much opportunity for learning anything now. With her belly so big with child, she'd soon be leaving the steel-pen factory. She'd known it within days of the wedding, but she was amazed by the number of women who could tell, long before her belly began to show. Even the girls at the factory knew, at least the ones who'd had babies of their own. Though still only seventeen, Brideen was glad to become part of the great sisterhood of Mothers. Though she often felt acutely the absence of the one she wanted most—her Mam.

People liked to comment on their short courtship, compared to Siobhan and Martin Duffy's, making sly jokes about how she and John couldn't wait to be married. She laughed, but she knew it was true. Right from the evening they rode the barge together from Birmingham, she knew her life was profoundly changed.

In fact, it was on those daily trips down the canal that their courtship truly blossomed. The slow-moving barge made a number of stops on the way, which gave them time to be together, to laugh and talk about things. The barge hands often sang as they loaded and unloaded cargo, and one time Brideen was moved to join them in a well-known ribald song. This one had many verses, of which Brideen knew only a few. But she loved the chorus, a melodic, almost wordless lilt, and she urged John to sing along with her on it. He was reluctant at first but when he finally joined in, she was delighted to hear what a deep, full-throated singing voice he had. Brideen herself paused singing to hear him more clearly, which briefly unnerved John. But as soon as the chorus came around again, she resumed singing. The moment their voices slid back together, they grinned at one another in a moment of shared exhilaration, a feeling that something missing had been found, a lost lamb returned to the flock.

The song told a tall tale about a man named Peadar who leaves home in search of work, leaving his pregnant wife Piegin behind. He stays away for more than twenty years, but doesn't realize it, and when he finally returns, he discovers a man in bed with his wife. She insists that the man is his own son, at which point he delivers the song's signature line: *Ach féasóg ar leanbh ní fhaca mé riamh* ("A beard on a baby I have never before seen.") When the chorus came around next time, John was overcome with laughter and struggled to keep singing. Brideen kept going, but she soon collapsed in peals of laughter too. John caught his breath enough to spew out a few words before they both dissolved back into helpless mirth.

"Baby with a beard... Can't get it... out of me head!"

They kept on until their sides aches, then finally grew quiet, watching the ripples of the barge moving through the canal waters. John broke the silence.

"So, do ye still play that whistle?'

Brideen was started by the question.

"My whistle? I... Not so much, since..."

He'd asked the question quite innocently, but right away he saw how it unsettled her.

"Oh, *mo chroi.* I had no notion... You must have sad memories..."

"No, no, it's all right. I know you didn't mean..."s

Mo chroi. He'd used the same term, "my heart," that Peadar called Piegin. She recalled the look of deep caring in his eyes on that wrenching day, and how much it meant to her.

He went on.

"Making music, it's a lovely gift, you know. One day I hope to hear you play again."

As the weeks went by, she found she desired to be with this man—now, soon, as often as possible. She'd heard about feelings such as this. Love, but not the same feeling she had for her Da, her siblings, even Mam, whom she'd loved more than life itself.

She was now enveloped in that state of mind she'd heard people speak of, but never knew for herself. Until now. She was in love.

I ngrá. Thit I ngrá.

Nor was there any doubt that he felt the same about her. He told her later that for him, it began the moment when she asked him about becoming a priest.

"I said I wasn't sure. But I lied. I knew right then my future was you, not the priesthood!"

They were bound, connected, in their hearts and minds, and they both longed to be so in their bodies. But they could not succumb to temptation. In the eyes of God and the Church, it would be a sin to come together before they were married. Still, she knew that many people did so, and that some Catholics found ways to be together without actually committing sin.

As she did with John.

They didn't have much opportunity, given their long days in the factory and John's lodgings over a pub with six of his workmates. After their wedding, he moved to the Sweeney household, where he and his new wife had to share a bed with two of her brothers. It wasn't the best situation for the newlyweds, but it suited Da just fine. He formed an instant bond with his new son-in-law, glad to finally have a family member with whom he could talk about politics and the rights of the working man. Da continued to call him by his Irish name, Sean, but John never corrected him. Brideen's brothers were glad to have him around, too. They loved his humour, and that he knew so much more than they did about the world beyond Wednesbury.

In particular, Da couldn't get enough of John's tales about Feargus O'Connor, the charismatic leader of the radical Chartist movement in Birmingham. A powerful orator at open-air meetings where he addressed thousands of his followers, O'Connor was seen as near to a spiritual son of Da's hero, Daniel O'Connell. Even to the Irish, their surnames were startlingly similar. Like the Liberator, O'Connor had spent time in jail for his views. And the best thing for Da was that, like the Liberator, O'Connor was committed to political change by peaceful means, rather than the violence advocated by Da's own Ribbonmen sons.

* * *

> *The Lion of Freedom is come from his den;*
> *We'll rally around him, again and again;*
> *We'll crown him with laurel, our champion to be;*
> *O'Connor the patriot, for sweet Liberty!*
> *The pride of the people – He's noble and brave;*
> *A terror to typrants, a friend to the slave;*
> *The bright star of Freedom, the noblest of men;*
> *We'll rally around him, again and again.*

-- "The Lion of Freedom"
lyrics by anonymous author, 1841

John and his workmates were fervent supporters of O'Connor's Land Plan, in which factory workers would be granted small plots of land to farm, and landlords would be compelled to grant leases to tenants in perpetuity.

"Then the poor people wouldn't be at the mercy of abusive landowners, like we were back in Ireland!" Da exclaimed when John told him about O'Connor's ideas.

"The Tories say it would undermine the whole notion of private property," said John. "And we say yes! That's the whole point! Land belongs to the people. Owning property is a kind of theft!"

Da roared with laughter.

"Property is theft. I like the sound of that!"

To Brideen and her siblings it was like watching their father come back to life after a long spell of lethargy. After the death of Daniel O'Connell, it was as if Da had given up on life and could no longer see a future for himself, or for Ireland. Now, even his health was starting to improve. The cough persisted but the black sputum was diminishing, though not enough for him to return to the mine, especially at his age, and Brideen was glad to hear no more talk of it. But with the stirrings brought on by the young men's ardor for the Lion of Freedom, he'd begun to speak about another kind of return, one that concerned her.

Da wanted to go back home. To Ireland.

When they left home, they never thought of it as permanent. Even as they stood on the deck as the steamer pulled away from Sligo, Brideen had promised Seamus they'd be coming back someday. But she knew now that was a child's hope. During the seven years the family had been in the Black Country, their lives had changed. In Mayo they'd been turned out of the home they'd lived in all their lives. They were homeless and barely escaped starving to death. Here they had a life—a hard one, yes, but with a roof over their heads and food to eat. They were still—mostly— together as a family. And now Brideen was bringing a new life into the household.

She hadn't told Da what her brothers were hearing in the pubs, from people who had gone back to Mayo and Roscommon: Reports of the emptiness, the eerie quiet, the once-familiar places where no human being could be heard and no living animals could be seen for miles. More than one person said, "Ireland is like a tomb." She knew how prone her compatriots were to exaggeration, but hearing that chilled her to the bone. Returning to Ireland would only be a source of dismay and sorrow for them all. Brideen feared that it would break Da's heart, or drive him to the grave.

She decided to ignore his comments, and hoped he'd forget about it in the excitement over the birth of a new grandchild. And the baby was coming soon, according to Molly Gallagher, the midwife. Brideen learned from other women about the breaking of the waters as the first sign of labor. But Molly said there was something else she should watch out for, that might be an earlier signal. She called it the "bloody show".

"What's that?" Brideen asked.

"Exactly what it says," the midwife replied matter-of-factly. "Ye'll know it when it comes."

She was right. One day, there it was, on her knickers.

She shouted to her husband.

"Go get Molly Gallagher."

"Why?"

"You're asking me why?"

She laughed at the look of shock on John's face.

"As if ye don't know, foolish man!"

* * *

The green pastoral plains, the fruitful valleys, as well as the wild hillsides and the dreary bogs, has equally ceased to be animate with human life. The 'land of song' was no longer tuneful; or if a human sound met the traveller's ear, it was only that of the feeble and despairing wail for the dead. This awful unwonted silence, which during the famine and subsequent years, almost everywhere prevailed, struck more fearfully on their imaginations, as many Irish gentlemen informed me, and gave them a deeper feeling of the desolation with which the country had been visited, than other circumstances which had forced itself upon their attention.

-- from *The Ancient Music of Ireland, Vol. 1* by George Petrie. Dublin: The Society for the Preservation and Publication of the Melodies of Ireland, 1855

"You're saying I can't go to my own child's baptism?"

By now Brideen was almost shouting at Molly Gallagher, who was insisting that she must stay in bed for a few more days.

"But why? I feel fine. I want to go and hold my baby while he receives the sacrament."

"You know you can't go anywhere until you've been properly churched! And if you wait for that, think of what could happen. What if the little one were to take sick and die? He'd have to spend eternity in Limbo!"

There were no rules about how long a woman had to wait after giving birth to be "churched", the term for the special purification blessing. But older women like Molly adhered to the practice of at least ten days of lying-in, which Brideen thought foolish. With so many children, even her own mother hadn't been expected to lie abed all that time. But Brideen knew there was no point arguing; none of the men in the household, including her own husband, would dare defy the midwife. And in truth, she was relieved once her new son was baptized Edward Joseph, after John's father, as was the custom, because it put an end to the fear, ever-present among the Irish, that a baby might die before receiving the sacrament.

Of course, there were other protective rituals that had to be carried out, which had little to do with Catholic teaching. Everyone knew that the greatest danger to newborn infants was the threat of being stolen away by fairies. First-born boys like Edward were especially in danger. As in most households, the fire tongs were placed across his cradle at night, since it was well known that iron repelled fairies. Molly Gallagher added the extra precaution of putting a red cloth over him.

"The color red reminds fairies of blood, and they are known to drink blood to survive."

In such a crowded house, it was easy to keep a constant eye on the baby during daylight hours. Ciaran was especially taken with his little nephew, whom he insisted was really his baby brother.

"So you're saying he's a changeling, are you?" his older brother Liam teased.

"No!" Ciaran was appalled at the thought. "I just like to pretend he's my brother."

With no prompting, Ciaran then decided he was Edward's guardian angel, and hovered around the cradle whenever he was in the house. The real problem came at night, when Sean Brian might be stumbling around the cottage in a drunken stupor, and tip over the cradle.

Though their brother had survived the wave of cholera that had taken their mother, Sean Brian was never the same. During his convalescence he'd started drinking, and never stopped. He kept his stashes of *poitín* in various corners about the house and was always pilfering coins from other family members to go to the distiller. Even more distressing than watching Sean Brian's deterioration was witnessing his acute shame over his weakness. Twice he had tried to stop drinking *poitín,* which triggered terrifying bouts of severe shaking lasting several days, during which he lay awake all night screaming, seeing things that weren't there. It was a living hell for the whole family, and they were almost relieved when he went back to drinking. Da had long ago stopped berating his third-eldest son, realizing he had no control over his demons. It was a source of great pain to Da and the other children.

Edward's birth had introduced a note of joy into a home that was still seeing more than its share of difficulties. Which is why Brideen didn't talk about her own state of mind, the sadness that was enveloping her. It was so hard to give birth to a child without her own mother's love and guidance. It was like a breach in the natural order of things. She loved Edward beyond measure, but every day she ached for Mam. Within a couple of weeks of giving birth, a melancholy settled upon Brideen—deep, all-encompassing, unlike any feeling she'd ever known before. She longed to share with her husband the great sadness that had come upon her.

Tá brón Orm. Tá brón Orm.

But she didn't want to burden him. He was working so hard to support her and the rest of the family, not to mention his own mother. No, it was better to hide herself away, until the anguish lifted. But there were times she feared it would never leave her.

One fine day in early spring, Brideen decided to visit Siobhan, who now lived near Walsall with her family. They'd moved there when her husband Brendan secured work at one of the lock-making factories. As it was a Sunday, John was at home looking after Edward. As she departed Wednesbury, she felt an urge to detour a couple of miles east and take a walk up Barr Beacon. The sadness was beginning to lift, and she hoped that the bracing air would help it. The last time she'd done this walk was just before Mam died, and though she feared that it would stir up painful memories, she felt strongly drawn there. As she began the gradual ascent up the hill, she felt an uncanny sense of Mam's presence for a moment, and it was comforting.

At the high point she gazed down at the green valley, as they'd done that day with Mam. She noticed a figure in the distance, walking in her direction up the other side of the hill. It was a man, and there was something distinctly familiar about his gait. Could it be one of John's workmates, she wondered, taking in some fresher air than the factories of Birmingham? Then she saw that he was carrying a satchel and figured he was a traveller with a destination.

The man kept walking, drawing closer and closer to where Brideen was standing. It was a few moments before she could believe what her eyes seemed to be telling her. But when he came within a few feet of her, she knew.

It was Manus. Her long-lost brother.

"It can't be you, can it?"

He stopped and took a long look. It had been seven years since he'd seen his sister, when she was barely out of childhood. But when she called out, her voice was exactly as he remembered it.

They both ran and flung their arms around one another.

"Manus!"

"Briddy!"

Never had she been so happy to hear that despised nickname!

She had a thousand questions: How did he come to be here in the Black Country? Had he come looking for the family, or was it an accident that they met like this? She couldn't wait to take him back to Wednesbury to meet his little nephew, to see the looks of utter amazement on the faces of her siblings. Even despite their earlier estrangement, she knew Da would be overjoyed to see his eldest son again. But there was one matter that couldn't wait. She had to tell him about Mam. Now.

A shadow came over his face, and she instantly regretted telling him so soon. But it couldn't be helped.

"How?" was all he said.

"The fever. Sean Brian got it too, but he recovered."

"When?"

"She's gone four years now."

Manus drew her to his chest and let out a mighty moan. The words that came out of him weren't only for his own grief, though.

"Oh, little Briddy. Oh, my poor little sister."

The two of them headed back down the hill. Eager to get home quickly, Brideen stopped a carriage on the way to Walsall and asked the driver to get word to her sister: "A miracle has happened! Come to Wednesbury as quickly as you can!" Siobhan arrived with her husband and children within a few hours, and that evening there was a joyful reunion of Sweeneys in the family home. Even the surrounding neighbors came by to share in what was almost a reverse Wake, celebrating the missing lamb returned to the flock.

Later, when the guests left and things quieted down, the Sweeneys began their volley of questions for Manus. Da posed the main one.

"How in the name of heaven did you find us?"

Manus told them it was common knowledge that the Irish who landed at Liverpool either continued the voyage to America or went to the Irish areas of Birmingham and the Black Country to find work.

"I knew you couldn't afford the passage, so I went to Birmingham and asked around among Irish fellows from Mayo. They'd heard about the wedding of one of the steel-pen factory girls and one thing led to another. I was on my way to Wednesbury when I had an urge to walk up that hill and see the lay of the land."

"That's where you saw me!" Brideen exclaimed. "I had the same notion!"

Mikeen laughed.

"'Twas a fairy put the same idea in your heads!"

Da broke in.

"So you knew we'd arrived at Liverpool, then?"

For a moment there was an uneasy silence. Then Manus spoke quietly.

"Yes, I knew. From Seamus."

They erupted simultaneously in shouts of joy.

"Seamus!"

"He found you, then!"

"We didn't know if he would."

"How is he? Where is he?"

A stricken look came over Manus' face.

"We lost him, Da. I lost him. I should never have let him go."

Then he broke down in great heaving sobs. After a time he managed to quiet down and began to tell the story.

"Seamus did indeed find his way to the Ribbon lodge. In Roscommon, you needn't know where. I was so glad to see him, but him being so young, I worried that he didn't have the stomach for what we were doing."

He paused for a moment, unable to continue.

"There was a landlord turning out his tenants. Doesn't matter his name. The authorities still won't put a stop to things, so we do it ourselves. As was our practice, we gathered a large group of men and marched onto his land. We carried pikes, but we had no intention of harming his family or servants. Our only purpose was to deliver retribution on the one who deserved it. Seamus wanted to go along. He'd never been, I shouldn't have let him. Someone had tipped them off that we were coming. One of ours, a Judas. So they were ready for us. Some of them had guns. We had only our pikes. They opened fire, and one of their bullets took him down..."

Overcome again, Manus paused.

"We fled. I carried Seamus on my back, but it was too late. His final resting place is in Mayo, outside Aghamore."

"We must go there," said Da. "You must take me there."

"I can't, Da. I cannot go back to Ireland. Ever again."

"What? What are you saying?"

They fell silent, waiting for Manus to explain.

"But two days after they killed poor Seamus, that landlord dared to go out in the town square. There would be no punishment, no repercussions for him. I always carry a knife on me. Just in case. And one day, there he was. It was a market day. He was bent over a basket of turnips. I came up behind him. He never saw it coming. No one did. Though as I ran off, I saw some in the square who might recognize me. But if that would be my fate... justice had been done.

"I confessed my sin. I did penance. The priest said before he would give me absolution, I must vow to God that I will never kill again. And I did. Now I am wanted for murder. They are looking for me. But my greatest sin was not the killing of an evil landlord. It was my failure to protect my brother. No penance could relieve the guilt of that."

He paused and turned to his father.

"Can you forgive me, Da?"

A quiet grief settled over them, as Da took his eldest son in his arms.

After that night, Da never again spoke of returning to Ireland.

Chapter 8 STAY OR GO?

The Irish are a rude people, subsisting on the produce of their cattle only, and living themselves like beasts, a people that has not yet departed from the primitive habits of pastoral life.
    -- from *Topography of Ireland by* Giraldus Cambrensis, aka
Gerald of Wales, 1187

It is lamentable to find, that this population scarcely ever thinks of anything but eating and drinking when the day's labour is over. The house of the working man is not much inhabited by him. The mine has his days, and the ale-house his evenings. He cares not for his family. The wife may care if she will; but she was brought up in a house of the same kind, and what else can be expected of her. The women in this neighbourhood seldom wear caps. They mostly use a handkerchief tied round their head, and neither in person or manner show much of grace, or attraction. They are early used to carry heavy burdens, and help to load and unload at the mouth of the pit; hence they become coarse and unwieldy, and lose that natural pleasantness, if not gracefulness of appearance, which is common to their sex.
    -- from "Osborne's Guide to the Grand Junction Railway," 1838
quoted in *A History of Wednesbury* by Bev Parker

The Irishman deposits all garbage and filth before his house door here, as he was accustomed to do at home, and so accumulates the pools and dirt-heaps which disfigure the working- people's quarters and poison the air. He builds a pig-sty against the house wall as he did at home, and if he is prevented from doing this, he lets the pig sleep in the room with himself. This new and unnatural method of cattle-raising in cities is wholly of Irish origin. The Irishman loves his pig as the Arab his horse, with the difference that he sells it when it is fat enough to kill. Otherwise, he eats and sleeps with it, his children play with it, ride upon it, roll in the dirt with it, as any one may see a thousand times repeated in all the great towns of England. The filth and comfortlessness that prevail in the houses themselves it is impossible to describe... For when, in almost every great city, a fifth or a quarter of the workers are Irish, or children of Irish parents, who have grown up among Irish filth, no one can wonder if the life, habits, intelligence, moral status — in short, the whole character of the working-class assimilates a great part of the Irish characteristics. On the contrary, it is easy to understand how the degrading position of the English workers, engendered by our modern history, and its immediate consequences, has been still more degraded by the presence of Irish competition.

-- from "Irish Immigration" in *The Condition of the English Working Class* by Friedrich Engels. Leipzig, 1845

* * *

"They say we are pigs. How can we live in a land where we are so hated?"

It was an endless subject of discussion in the Sweeney household. Stay in England or go to America? It was almost ten years since they'd left Mayo. Ten years since they'd narrowly escaped death from starvation. They never stopped thanking God and the Blessed Virgin Mary for sparing their lives and bringing them to a place of safety. After a time, nestled in the bosom of the Irish community, the Black Country almost began to feel like home, But that was only because they were able to ignore the larger society, and the low esteem it held them in. Back in Ireland, the disdain of the Anglo-Irish ascendancy for their poorer countrymen was a familiar and longstanding state of affairs. But here in England, the hatred they experienced was of a different order. And it was getting worse.

Galvanized by the militant Orange order, a Protestant preacher named William Murphy had been publicly denouncing

Catholics and what he called "popery". There was consternation that a man with that name could stir up such hatred of his own countrymen. But Murphy's fiery speeches ended in angry marches through the Irish quarter of Birmingham, and people feared it was only a matter of time before things erupted in violence.

"It's terrible for children to grow up surrounded by such hate," Da said. "As long as we live here, we are living in the land of the enemy."

Having relinquished his dream of going back to Ireland, Da's hopes were now fixed on going to the United States. But privately, his children doubted that he could manage such a long sea voyage in his state of health. Siobhan, especially, was firm in the belief that Da should live out his days in England, with her and her family. She and Brendan had no desire to go to America, nor did Mikeen and Margaret, who now had three children. The two youngest Sweeney brothers, Liam and Ciaran, could go to America. But Sean Brian was a lost cause.

As for Manus, his situation was complicated. He wanted to leave England, but with the constabulary in aggressive pursuit, it was safer for him to stay put for now. And lately he'd found a sense of purpose, and even a measure of redemption, working under the guidance of Father Montgomery. The new church of St. Mary's-on-the-Hill was finally finished, but his ministry among the poor Irish of Birmingham was still all-consuming. The priest enlisted Manus' help in his efforts to halt the fist fights and pub brawls that were a regular feature of Irish life in Wednesbury, a task that suited the onetime terror-monger, now dedicated to a life of peace. His family wondered if Manus himself might end up training for the priesthood. But whether he ever took the vows or not, it seemed to Brideen that her eldest brother was taking the very path that her husband John had rejected in marrying her. And both paths were right in the eyes of God.

Another of Father Montgomery's duties was reading the letters to his illiterate flock from their relatives who had emigrated, which often contained money for a passage to America. The priest did what he could to assist their emigration, and made no secret of the fact to his superiors. He considered the Irish in England a wounded people, strangers in a land that was not their home, and believed the only solution to the woes of the Irish in Birmingham was emigration.

The pressure to emigrate was all around her. But still Brideen was torn. Her second child, named John after his father, had just been born. It had been a blessedly easy birth, and the profound sadness she'd experienced after Edward had not returned. She and John needed to settle their lives, to have a house of their own to raise their growing family. Now that the cost of an ocean crossing was within reach, John was set on going to America. Lately he'd been hearing from his workmates about opportunities in the city of Baltimore.

"The Irish there have found good jobs building the new railway. They've got their own neighborhood, like here in Wednesbury, but with a fine new church named after St. Peter. And there's a school for Catholic children. Our children could learn to read, Brid! And the new railroad's going to go to the western frontier, where there's open land, good land for farming."

Even though Feargus O'Connor was dead and his Land Plan had come to nothing, John's longing to own his own land remained as strong as ever. And there was nothing to keep him here. His own mam, Mary, had died not long after baby John's birth.

Like so many before them, the Sweeney family was on the verge of being riven asunder. Even before the famine, the leaving of home had become an inescapable truth for the Irish people. And, for Brideen, its bitter corollary: The knowledge that she would never see her Da or her siblings again.

* * *

Ye brave Irish heroes, wherever you be
I pray stand a moment and listen to me.
Your sons and your daughters are going away
And thousands are sailing to Amerikay

On the morning of leaving, they move to and fro
Till the trunks are all packed up and ready to go
O the tears from their eyes do fall down like the rain
And the horses are prancing, going off for the train.

And when they reach the station you will hear their last cries
With their handkerchiefs waving and bidding goodbye
O their hearts will be breaking as the ship leaves the shore
Fare thee well, dear old Ireland, we may ne'er see you more

O I pity the mother who brings forth the child
And I pity the father who labors and toils
To care for their children they work night and day
Knowing when they are reared up, they will go away

So good luck to those people and safe may they land
They are leaving their country for a far distant strand
They are leaving old Ireland, no longer can stay
And thousands are sailing to Amerikay

-- "Thousands are Sailing to Amerikay,"
traditional ballad, c.1860-70

As she nursed baby John on the upper deck of the H.M.S. *Pioneer,* Brideen was mesmerized by the vastness of the sky. She'd never gotten to see it from the summit of Croagh Patrick, but here it was now, spanning endlessly over her head.

When she was little, the old people used to talk about how Castlebar was the farthest they'd ever been from home. Now here she was on a ship in the middle of an ocean that seemed to go on forever. She'd had no idea of the enormity of the world. Would they ever reach land? Did land even exist? Would she ever again walk on solid ground?

A tune popped into her head, one of the ones she'd learned from her teacher Gabriel all those years ago. It was called *Amach Ar An Aigéan*, "Out on the Ocean," and although she hadn't played it in a long time, she could feel how the rolls and sways of the melody echoed her experience in that moment.

"Yes, little one!" She said out loud. "We're out on the ocean!"

At the sound of her voice, the baby tore away from her breast and looked up. Brideen laughed at his startled express, and for a moment it almost looked like he was laughing too.

For the first few days out of Liverpool, they'd seen and heard an abundance of birds—the plunging dive of gannets, the nasal whines and caws of kittiwakes. But as the H.M.S *Pioneer* moved farther out to sea, the bird sightings grew fewer and fewer. Now the only sounds on deck were the sloshing of the waves, the creaks and groans of the wooden ship, the grunts of the pigs and goats in cages—all occasionally pierced by the gagging of seasick passengers vomiting into the sea.

Since emigrants weren't allowed to board their ships before the time of sailing, they'd had to spend five nights in Liverpool. They stayed in a rank, overcrowded lodging house overrun with fraudsters known as "runners", who seized emigrants' luggage and charged exorbitant fees to return them. John caught one in the act of cadging one of their bags and threatened to smash his face in, which caused little Edward to burst into screams of fright.

It was only now, in the quiet of night on the water, that the wrenching memories of the departure came rushing back into Brideen's thoughts. Mikeen and Margaret had offered to take in Ciaran, and he decided to stay behind with him. Brideen wasn't prepared for the pain of saying farewell to her darling little brother, but at least she had hope of seeing him again. Not so

Sean Brian. Siobhan was adamant that she didn't want him around her children. Even the workhouse wouldn't take him in his condition. By now it was clear to everyone, even to Sean Brian himself, that he wasn't long for this world. Manus said he'd take him to Father Montgomery's mission at St. Mary's, to keep him from dying alone on the streets of Wednesbury. Later, when the time was right, Manus said he hoped to join them in America.

But the worst was saying good-bye to Da.

"*Go néirí le Dia.* Go with God." was all he could say, in a voice barely above a whisper, as the barge set off down the canal toward Liverpool. Edward seemed to comprehend what was happening. He tugged at his mother's dress, saying *Seanathair* over and over and asking why his grandfather was staying behind on the quay.

Brideen drew comfort from the fact that at least one of the family was emigrating with them: Her next-oldest brother Liam. Since her marriage, he was the brother who'd become closest with her husband, so John was overjoyed when he announced he was coming with them to America. Liam had always been a restless soul, dissatisfied with working in the factories and eager to experience the world beyond the Black Country. He was unmarried. Other than Da and his brothers, there was nothing to keep him here.

* * *

I think it would be rendering a service to humanity, if those who ship so many poor Irish emigrants from Liverpool & c. to this country could be induced to take pains, and examine properly the conditions of the passengers instead of driving them on board ship like so many cattle at the last point of embarkation. I have crossed the ocean many a time and oft, and have since late years acted as Doctor on board of several large American ships bound from Liverpool to New York, and find it absolutely necessary that some sort of reform must be made to better the condition of the poorer classes of emigrants.

From Liverpool each passenger receives weekly 5 lbs. of oatmeal, 2 ½ lbs biscuit, I lb. flour, 2 lbs.rice, ½ lb. sugar, ½ lb. molasses, and 2 ounces of tea. He is obliged to cook it the best way he can in a cook shop 12 feet by 6! This is the cause of so many quarrels and many a poor woman with her children can get but one meal done, and sometimes they get nothing warm for days and nights when a gale of wind is blowing and the sea is mountains high and breaking over the ship in all directions. On such days we have been obliged to go with buckets of water and a bag of biscuits to steerage and feed the passengers to save them from starvation.

-- from "Condition and Care of Emigrants on Board Ship," letter by anonymous writer, *New York Times,* October 15, 1851

The emigrants who had enough money purchased "cabin passage" and slept in private rooms. The vast majority of passengers bought bunks in steerage, also called the 'tween deck for its position between the cabins and the hold. There weren't enough bunks, so the men mostly slept on the floor. It was frequently overcrowded, with poor ventilation.

Brideen managed to avoid getting into arguments with other mothers by preparing food at odd times, when the cook shop wasn't busy. But it meant that John and Edward rarely had a warm meal. In the confined space of the hold, the danger of contagion from typhus or cholera was always there. Back during the famine there were tales of the coffin ships, and they'd thanked God that they weren't on one of them. But now, here was death travelling side-by-side with them. Brideen felt powerless, knowing they'd be on the ship for several more weeks with no way to isolate themselves from sick and dying passengers,

Early in the voyage, Edward walked near a corpse. Her impulse was to shout at him to keep distance from it, but she also wanted to distract his attention, hoping he wouldn't notice the body at all. But she could see that he was already old enough to pretend that he hadn't. He was hoping to spare his mother the worry, but nothing could do that. She was consumed with constant anxiety that her children might fall ill.

One evening several days into the crossing, Brideen thought she heard music. She looked in the direction it was coming from and saw a young fellow playing a fiddle. Leaving the sleeping children with their father, she drew closer and listened intently, trying to identify the jig he was playing. A couple of nearby women griped that the noise would keep their babies awake. The fiddler halted, but some of the other passengers called for him to continue. To bring down the volume he moved toward the stern end of the hold and resumed playing.

She went to find her bag and rifled through it, searching for her whistle. With two babies to care for she'd barely touched it in months. But now, hearing those few notes of the jig stirred in Brideen an urgent desire to play it again. By the time she located the whistle and moved closer to the fiddler, he'd moved on to a different tune. She would have tried to play along with the earlier jig, but this tune was unfamiliar. She stood listening, uncertain what to do. When he finished, he looked over at Brideen and pointed his bow in her direction.

"Have you got a tune there, Miss?"

She was taken aback and almost shook her head, then hesitantly raised the whistle to her lips and began the opening notes of *An Giolla Ruadh,* one of the tunes she'd learned from Gabriel. At first her playing was stilted and uncertain, but soon it began to flow more easily. By the second part of the tune, she noticed the fiddler was playing along with her, and she nodded to show him she was pleased. At the end of the tune, she was thrilled to hear some passengers applauding, which did indeed wake up one of the sleeping babies.

They agreed to play again, but when the fiddler didn't show up the next night she feared he might have been stricken with fever. But he reappeared two nights later, and soon after they began to play, a group of passengers formed a square and started dancing. Brideen and the fiddler ran through several sets of dance tunes, then decided to stop early to avoid waking the babies again.

In the quiet of the hold, it occurred to Brideen that there had been no reports of deaths on the ship for several days running. Maybe the wave of fever had run its course, she thought. Maybe now she could take in the deep joy of making music again and let it dampen down her worries.

Around the fifth week at sea, Brideen woke one morning to excited shouts of "Land ho!" With the children and John, she joined the rush of passengers up onto the deck. Some crew members were pointing at a dark mound, barely visible in the distance.

"There it is!" Someone shouted. "That's America!"

"Where?"

"That's not America!"

"There's nothing there!"

"Yes, there is," said the one of the crew. "An island. We'll be heading 'round it into the bay to get to Baltimore."

"But where is Baltimore? Why can't we see it, too?"

The crewmen laughed.

"Because it's another three days' sail up Chesapeake Bay."

The mood on the ship quickly deflated at the prospect of more days of sailing lay ahead. Still, America was there—a speck on the horizon, but there.

The waiting was almost over.

PART III: Hagerstown, Maryland, 1858-71

Flag of the First Regiment of the 69th Irish Brigade

Chapter 9: WHOSE WAR?

It's by the hush, me boys,
I'm sure that's to hold your noise,
And listen to poor Paddy's narration.
For I was by hunger pressed,
And in poverty distressed,
And I took a thought I'd leave the Irish nation.
So, here's you boys, Now take my advice;
To America I'd have you not be coming,
For there's nothing here but war,
Where the murdering cannons roar,
And I wish I was back home in dear old Erin.
Meself, and a hundred more,
To America sailed o'er,
Our fortunes to be making, we was thinking;
But when we landed in Yankee land,
they shoved a gun into our hand,
Saying, "Paddy, you must go and fight for Lincoln."

-- from "Paddy's Lamentation,"
traditional, circa 1864

* * *

October 5, 1862

My darling Da,

I am writing to you from a place called Hagerstown in the state of Maryland. I hope you received my last letter from the city of Baltimore. It was sent some time ago, and there have been many changes in our lives, which I will recount in this letter. But the most exciting thing is that for the first time I am writing it in my own hand! And in English, too! It has been a very hard thing to learn, and given your respect for all kinds of learning, I know how proud you are of your third daughter, who can now read and write.

Thomas is now nearly three years old. He is a very happy child, more so than his two brothers, who in their young years endured the leaving of their homeland and the rigours of an ocean crossing. I have told Thomas about you and Mam, his beloved *seantuismitheoirí* and his other family back in Ireland, especially of his uncles Seamus and Sean Brian, who now dwell in heaven with their Mam and our blessed Lord.

My other news is of one who will soon be coming to this earth. Yes, Da, another one on the way, another grandchild for you! The birth will not come for some months yet, still John and the boys are excited about it. As for myself, I cannot deny my hope that this one will be a daughter. How I long for the company of a girl in this household, a sentiment Siobhan and my sister-in-law Margaret most surely understand.

Now I will tell you how we came to leave Baltimore. I said in my earlier letter about the prejudice we first encountered here, the people who were against letting in Catholic immigrants, claiming that we wanted to subjugate America under the authority of the Pope. I have since learned that these people call themselves the "Know-Nothings". Can you imagine? Parading your own ignorance like a badge of pride? We learned to ignore their insults, calling us "Micks" and even "monkeys", especially once we'd settled in the Irish neighborhood around St. Peter the Apostle church. The people there welcomed us and assured us that the Know-Nothings did not represent the beliefs of most Americans.

John was fortunate to have steady work in the Baltimore & Ohio rail yards, but as you know, he has long wanted to live on the land again. Since we have been in America he has learned much about a place called Iowa where there is good farmland to be had. We heard that a former parishioner at St. Peter's was seeking to hire a manager for his hardware store in Hagerstown. He wanted a fellow Irishman, with a family who could help run the store. Hagerstown is a growing city and with the B&O (that's what the people here call it) it has become the main rail connection to the western United States. John got it in mind that living there would move us that much closer to Iowa, which lies just beyond the great river called the Mississippi. I don't think either of us understood just how far away that was, how vast this country is. But we asked our pastor, Father McColgan, to write and accept the position for us.

Hagerstown is seventy-five miles from Baltimore, and we were just able to afford the train fare (people here don't walk the kind of distances they do back in Ireland). I was uncertain about leaving our Irish community in St. Peter's parish. There is a Catholic church here, St. Mary's, though the parishioners are mainly German, not many Irish among them. We had formed such strong friendships while in Baltimore, and I deeply miss the loving community in St. Peter's parish. Fortunately, we have not encountered the same anti-Irish sentiment here, maybe because there are too few of us to bother anyone! We do not regret making the move. John is happy running the store, and we both know the merchandise well. Da, can you believe it? Once I made nails in Roger Conner's forge—now I am selling nails in America! And now that I can write, I am keeping the store ledgers, so we don't have to hire help to do it.

Now I must speak briefly of unhappy things, dearest Da. As I'm sure you know by now, the United States is at war with itself. The southern states ("states" are like Ireland's counties) have broken away and formed their own Confederacy in order to keep the Negroes in bondage. The northern states remain loyal to the Union and to President Abraham Lincoln, who intends to free the slaves. We live in the state of Maryland, which is very close to the Confederate states, but is loyal to the Union side, a fact that makes me very glad. This war is a mystery to those of us who have come recently. America, you are supposed to be the land of freedom. So why are you fighting one other? But I know full well that had I to choose, I would choose the side of those who are against slavery.

You used to speak about Daniel O'Connell being an Abolitionist, and I was too young to understand what that meant. But now I see the evil of slavery with my own eyes. Some Negro slaves come to the store on errands for their owners, but not all the Negro people in Hagerstown are slaves, and a few even own property, which I found surprising. There is a Negro man who works for wages at the dry goods store next to ours. His name is Jeremiah, and we have become friendly with him. We laugh because neither of us understands the other's way of speaking English. He plays an instrument called a "banjar" that Edward has become very taken with. Jeremiah has been showing him how to pluck and strum the strings.

I know our beloved Father Montgomery will read this to you, finding the right words in Irish. To write this letter to you, I have asked Sister Nazarius about many words. She is a teacher at St. Mary's school, and has helped me a great deal with my writing. Of course I never learned to write in our native tongue, and since leaving Baltimore I have little reason to speak it. Few of the Irish people here in Hagerstown seem to know much of the language of their birth.

There is so much more I wish to tell you about, but my hand is growing tired and I must attend to the store. We are all doing well in our new home, and John and the boys send their love to you and the rest of the family.

Your loving daughter,

Bridget

* * *

The depot at Hagerstown is a scene of wild activity. Immense stores of all kinds are pouring in for the subsistence of the army; every available foot of space is covered with barrels, bales and boxes.

-- *Harper's Weekly,* October 18, 1862

It had taken Brideen three days to write the letter. It was exhausting, searching for the words she didn't know and finding out how to spell them. What she didn't tell Da was that Sister Nazarius wasn't the only one helping her. Her main teacher was her own son Edward. Every day when Edward and his younger brother John came home from St. Mary's school, they would do their schoolwork beside their mother in the store. John, whom they'd taken to calling Johnny to distinguish him from his father, was still a beginning writer. But Edward had made great progress in English, and more often than not, he was able to find the words she needed. The next day he would take a page of the letter to school with him, and his teacher, Sister Nazarius, would correct the spelling or find a better word. She would then re-write the letter on a clean sheet, which Edward brought back to the store later that day, and reading her own words in finished form helped Brideen learn even more. For the teachers at St. Mary's, it was simply part of their work to teach not only the children in their classrooms, but their parents struggling to learn English at home.

"There is so much more I wish to tell you." She'd written those words to her father, but they weren't quite true. There were things she deliberately kept from him, painful things, like the baby girl who was stillborn just weeks earlier. What purpose could be served by telling him about a grandchild he would never know?

She also didn't say anything about how painful it was to leave the Irish community in Baltimore. After spending nearly two years there, they'd become part of St. Peter's parish, and formed what Brideen thought would be long-term friendships. Having to uproot again, so soon after leaving their homeland, was too much, but it was what John wanted. Iowa had become, in a sense, his promised land, and in his mind this move brought him closer to it. But it also put them right on the doorstep of danger, of a civil war on a scale unimaginable back in Ireland.

At first she'd gone along with her husband's plan. But once it was clear that the move might put her family in harm's way, she grew angry at John. She found herself asking God's forgiveness for the spiteful, accusing thoughts that periodically surged through her mind. But she couldn't help herself. After all they'd been through, why did he add to her anxieties in this way? This war wasn't theirs. She didn't want any part of it.

Then her brother Liam announced his intention to join the fighting, and her rage grew more intense. She was convinced that moving closer to the field of battle had planted the idea in Liam's mind, and it was all John's fault. She knew how distressed Da would be to learn that his seventh son was fighting in a bloody war, and she begged Liam not to enlist. But she knew that it was hopeless, that his natural bent for action would find an outlet, one way or the other.

And now he'd gone to Virginia to enlist in the Irish Brigade, to fight on the side of the Union. The brigade was made up almost entirely of Irish immigrants, and they flew their own green flag with an image of a golden harp. They hadn't been in any battles yet, but the war was growing more intense. Just weeks earlier Confederate troops had marched through Hagerstown on their way to Fredericksburg, a town fifteen miles south. A bloody battle was fought near a place called Antietam Creek. More than two thousand Union soldiers had died there. Rumours were flying that more Confederate attacks were coming any time, that things were going to get worse once President Lincoln issued an official proclamation that would be the ultimate affront to the Confederacy.

She decided it was better for Da not to be told any of that, especially not for him—or anyone—to know of the seething anger she nursed against her own husband.

* * *

That on the first day of January, in the year of our Lord one thousand eight hundred and sixty-three, all persons held as slaves within any State or designated part of a State, the people whereof shall then be in rebellion against the United States, shall be then, thenceforward, and forever free; and the Executive Government of the United States, including the military and naval authority thereof, will recognize and maintain the freedom of such persons, and will do no act or acts to repress such persons, or any of them, in any efforts they may make for their actual freedom. And by virtue of the power, and for the purpose aforesaid, I do order and declare that all persons held as slaves within said designated States, and parts of States, are, and henceforward shall be free; and that the Executive government of the United States, including the military and naval authorities thereof, will recognize and maintain the freedom of said persons.

-- from the Emancipation Proclamation issued January, 1863 by President Abraham Lincoln

The fighting began on the morning of July first, 1863, about thirty miles from Hagerstown, near a town called Gettysburg. Among the regiments was the Sixth-Ninth Infantry, bearing their green-and-gold flag. Early the next morning Brideen rushed to the Lyceum to look at the list of casualties posted on the door.

"Was his name there?" John asked when she got back.

She shook her head.

"Thanks be to God," he said. "On this day, at least, Liam Sweeney is not among the dead."

Fine, she wanted to reply, but what will happen to him tomorrow or the next day or the day after that? But she held her tongue and went out again, to attend to her duties with the women's brigade at Rochester House.

The streets were unusually crowded that day, with townspeople racing from store to store, desperate for news. Hospital tents had been set up outside the Lyceum, ready for the overflow when the sites nearer to the battlefield ran out of beds. But wagons of wounded were already flooding in, and the temporary hospital sites at the Lyceum quickly filled to capacity.

Then word came that a wealthy widow, Frances Kennedy, had given over her estate, Rochester House, to accommodate the overflow of wounded Union Soldiers. She was from a prominent family known for their belief in religious tolerance. Brideen and John were proud that their fellow Irish were such enlightened community leaders, though they later learned that the Kennedys were in fact Presbyterians who originally hailed from Scotland.

With the support of Frances Kennedy, the women of Hagerstown organized a round-the-clock brigade to provide nursing care and supplies of fresh-cooked food to the wounded. Brideen joined them at Rochester House, leaving John to watch the store and care for the children. It was a deeply unsettling sight, walking through the rows of cots with men calling out names of loved ones, moaning in pain, or simply lying unconscious. Most of the medical care had to be provided by the few women who had actual nursing skills. But like most of the local women, Brideen was able to help tend to the less severely wounded, and she naturally adopted the role of comforter for these suffering souls. She was grateful that she had something to offer them in their hour of need. Not only did it distract her from own troubles, but her feelings of sympathy began to soften her heart toward her husband, if only for a time.

Most of the bedded soldiers seemed to grow calmer and more stable, and she realised just how many hours she had been away from her family. It was time to go home for a break. As she prepared to leave, another wagon arrived from Gettysburg with a fresh load of wounded soldiers. Determined to get home for a least a few hours of respite, she exited the gate of Rochester and tried to hurry past the wagon before she could be noticed. Her children needed to see her, and she needed to get away, if only for a short while, from the terrible suffering and death around her.

She passed the open wagon, keeping her gaze straight ahead. One of the men was calling out for his sister. She tried to shut out the voice. It was the sort of cry that arose constantly from the arriving wagons—moans of soldiers in agony, desperate for relief. But it was more typical of them to cry out for their mothers, or for a nurse. Maybe that soldier's mother was too far away to come to his aid, she mused. Then something snapped in her.

Could it be ...?

She rushed back to the wagon. Lying among the wounded was a man able to raise his head just enough for her to see his bloodied face. She reached over a reclining, barely conscious figure lying next to him, to clutch his hand.

"Brid!"

"Is it you, brother? Is it you?"

The wagon resumed its march toward the front door of Rochester House. Brideen walked beside it, clutching Liam's hand the whole way, all thought of returning home now forgotten.

The nurses went about their work of transferring the wounded onto the cots. When they removed the blanket covering Liam, Brideen saw that the bloody marks on his face were minor compared to the pool of blood around his left leg. It was a deep buckshot wound. She held her breath as she watched the nurses remove the bullet and stanch the wound. Within minutes the physician, Dr. Wroe, arrived to examine it and to administer a dose of morphine for pain. He spoke to the nurses in medical terms Brideen could barely understand. But she'd witnessed so many other cases that she understood the crucial information Dr. Wroe was conveying to the nurses: That they need not prepare for amputation of the limb. At least for now.

Brideen wept with relief. Her brother would live. With or without his leg, her brother would live.

Thanks be to God.

Brideen called over to one of her neighbors to carry the news to John: Her brother Liam was at Rochester House, grievously wounded. She would not be coming home, but staying the night at his side.

She crawled onto the cot beside him and cradled his head in her arms until he finally drifted off. Then her own tears of exhaustion began to flow, until she finally fell asleep herself.

* * *

"When Lee crossed the Potomac and entered Pennsylvania, followed by our army, I felt that the great crisis had come. I knew that defeat in a great battle on Northern soil involved the loss of Washington, to be followed perhaps by the intervention of England and France in favor of the Confederacy. I went to my room and got down on my knees in prayer."
-- General Dan Sickles, commander at Gettysburg, quoted in *Intimate Memories of Lincoln* by Rufus Rockwell Wilson, 1903

When Liam woke the next morning, Brideen expected he would still be weak and exhausted. The last thing she expected was that he would want to talk about his experiences of the past few days. But she was wrong. He needed to talk, to communicate what he'd been through, to a person who knew him not as a fellow soldier but someone close to him, who knew his people and where he came from.

"We were two days into it by then, Brid. So many down, so much blood. I couldn't bear it anymore, I wanted to run away. Some did, and can you blame them? We got our orders to march up to a site called Cemetery Hill. Can you believe it, Brid? Cemetery Hill! I was sure we were marching to the very place where we'd meet the end of our days on this earth. But then I saw the priest standing in front of a group of soldiers. They were kneeling and he was making the sign of the cross:

"'In the name of the Father, and of the Son, and of the Holy Spirit.'

"The answer came: 'Amen', and more soldiers came and knelt. And he went on: '*Kyrie, eleison.* Lord, have mercy. *Christe, eleison.*' And the soldiers replied, 'Christ, have mercy.' It was a

Mass, Brid. Father O'Brien saying Mass right there on the battlefield. I could feel my faith flooding back into me. I knew the Lord would be with me, with all of us. I knew this was not my day to die. I ran over and knelt down with the rest.

"It was a sweltering hot day. We were in heavy uniforms and we had no warning that Pickett's men were approaching with heavy artillery. The Rebels had our boys on the run, even as both armies were still arriving. The first two days had been bloody, and everyone was near total exhaustion. Then Pickett's charge met our front lines right at the center of the Union line. Some regiments ran off. But we held our ground. The Sixty-Ninth Irish Brigade. We were the only regiment not to withdraw."

She could barely follow his account, and she knew nothing about battlefield maneuvers. But she could tell how desperately he needed to talk.

"General O'Kane called us together and reminded us what we were fighting for: A Union that had given a million Irish a new chance at life. That put steel in our souls. The Confederates thought they could breach our line of defense and split the Union side in two. When they were only a few dozen yards from the wall, O'Kane ordered us to jump up and open fire. Pickett's men were staggered and thrown into disorder. They fell right there, Brid. Like sheep to the slaughter. Over half our Brigade was killed. Irish blood and Irish bones covered that field. But we drove them off. An Irish general leading a platoon of Irish soldiers, Brid. We drove them off. We saved the Republic."

With that final triumphant phrase, Liam paused, exhaustion finally overtaking him, and fell into a deep sleep. Brideen watched him silently for a few minutes, and came to understand something she hadn't before. This war was about something bigger than her life and all she'd been through. It was about something as fundamental as Ireland's freedom was to her own people. This country had taken her family in when they needed a place to go. She was now a part of it, and the Union cause was beginning to feel like her own.

Chapter 10: THE WAR COMES HOME

Monday, July 6, 1863: "Afternoon. At this moment fighting is going on in our very own town and the balls are whizzing through the streets... Oh God of Heaven, have mercy upon us and deliver us from this terrible war."

-- from the diary of Hagerstown resident Louise Kealhofer, quoted in Historical Marker Database, Maryland Historical Trust

"The cutting and slashing was beyond description; here right before and underneath us the deadly conflict was waged in a hand to hand combat, with the steel blades circling, waving, parrying, thrusting, and cutting, some reflecting the bright sunlight, others crimsoned with human gore; while the discharge of pistols and carbines was terrific, and the smoke through which we now gazed down through and on the scene below, the screams and yells of the wounded and dying, mingled with cheers and commands, the crashing together of the horses and firey flashes of small arms presented a scene such as words cannot portray."

-- account by civilian eyewitness W.W. Jacobs, quoted in Historical Marker Database, Maryland Historical Trust

"Johnny, no! Come back here!"

Brideen's eldest child was the very model of a good son, but her second was the defiant one. Always ready to buck the rules, to push back against outside control. For all the trouble he sometimes caused, Brideen secretly loved those qualities in him. But this was a serious matter. No sooner had she forbade them all to leave the house, there was Johnny scurrying out the door.

"I said get back here this minute!"

"I got to go to the store!" he shouted back to her. "What if Da needs help?"

His voice was momentarily drowned out by the sound of gunfire.

"Do you want to get yourself killed?" Brideen screamed. But he was already out of earshot.

Their home was almost at the edge of Hagerstown, away from the fighting. John had gone to work early that morning. The hardware store was on Baltimore Street, right near the center of town.

The people of Hagerstown were grateful that the bloodbath at Gettysburg was over. But they hadn't bargained for the war landing right on their doorstep.

General Lee's troops, intent on fleeing into the Confederate state of Virginia, were heading toward the Potomac. The Union cavalry, just as determined to prevent them from crossing the river, galloped into Hagerstown, where the two sides clashed at the intersection of Baltimore and South Potomac Streets. From there the fighting spilled into the rest of the town. For more than seven hours, residents could do little but cower in their houses as the constant boom of gunfire reigned outside. For Brideen those hours were pure agony, worrying about her husband and son, not even knowing where they were.

In the late afternoon, the pounding of horses' hooves reached the house, followed by the sound of a bugle.

"They're retreating!"

The rush of horses grew progressively louder, until it felt like the herd was almost on top of them. The children all ran to the front windows to see the Confederate cavalry galloping past the house. All except Brideen, who went to the front door, which opened out to a small landing with several steps leading up to it. They were astonished to see her step out onto the landing.

"No, Mama!"

"The soldiers will see you."

Standing in front of the house in plain sight, Brideen started screaming at the departing cavalry. The children had no idea what she was saying, though the older ones had vague memories of what they'd heard from sailors on the Atlantic crossing. Curses, in Irish, were coming from Brideen's mouth, so fierce and untrammeled she looked like she might explode.

The little ones were crying, begging her to come inside.

"Stop, Mama!"

"They'll shoot you!"

But even the soldiers who were close enough to hear Brideen over the pounding of the horses paid her little mind. The few who looked over in her direction seemed to shrug off her behavior as nothing more than that of a crazy woman.

No shots were fired. The Confederate troops kept on their way until they were out of sight. The boys led Brideen, still shaking with anger, back into the house.

"Burn in hell! All of them! Mother of God, how I hate this war!"

The shouting and rage finally subsided. She broke down in tears, sobbing into Edward's chest. After a few moments she began to calm down, but when her husband and Johnny walked through the front door, she ran to her second son.

"What did I tell you about going out?"

Brideen gave him a hard slap across the face. A stunned silence took hold among the other children. They'd never seen their mother do a thing like that. But before anyone could react, she turned to her husband.

"I wish we'd never come here! We should have stayed in Baltimore. I should never have let you bring us here!"

John was dumbfounded, but somehow he knew not to respond, that at this moment his wife's emotions were beyond her control. He gently shook his head and quietly uttered her name.

"Oh, Brid..."

"What if you hadn't come back? What would I do? What would the children do?"

Her tears started up again as she let him take her in his arms.

"I've been through too much, John. I can't take any more."

"I know, *mo stór*," he murmured. "I know."

* * *

The streets were quiet once again. But more casualties of the war were left in their midst. More bodies to tend to, more wounded to care for. Brideen was relieved to have something to claim her attention. The ferocity of her emotions the previous day still frightened her.

When she went to the hardware store, Edward was already there. Jeremiah was showing him a lick on the banjar.

Of course! Music was what she needed, what they all needed. Now that they'd gotten to know him better, Jeremiah generously let Edward play his banjar whenever he was at the store.

"This boy's getting awful good," he told Brideen. "He knows a bunch of chords now."

Chords, yes! Brideen realized that he could play to accompany the tunes she played on her tin whistle. She'd been so overwhelmed with the war chaos she'd barely taken it out since they'd left Baltimore.

At home, she got out the whistle and they tried a few tunes. The two instruments made a strange combination at first. But Jeremiah had a feel for the rhythms of the jigs and hornpipes, and showed Edward how to adjust the rhythmic strums to the tunes. After a few days, they felt ready to play for other people—"Red-Haired Boy," of course, and a hornpipe, "The Rights of Man," already well-known in America because it was named after a book by Thomas Paine, a hero of the War of Independence from Britain.

After school the next day Edward came to the infirmary and they played as a duo. Edward made a few mistakes but the soldiers didn't care a whit. They were delighted, especially with the fact that the music was being played by such a young person. The whole atmosphere of the sick ward became somehow lighter, and

Brideen was thrilled that a child of hers was taking up a musical instrument. After the first day the soldiers and the other nurses clamored for more. It became the pattern of the sick ward: Edward arriving after school with his banjar, joining his mother on tin whistle.

More fighting occurred the next week, led by the Union Gen. George Armstrong Custer and his Michigan cavalry brigade. Custer's troops rode into town from the east, scattering and capturing stunned Confederates. After finally driving the Confederates out, the war was still raging around them, of course, but to experience even relative peace was a relief for the citizens of Hagerstown. The town was still a Union supply depot and the infirmary at Rochester House was busy with wounded brought from nearby skirmishes.

Business was steady at the hardware store, but Brideen and Edward found time to do their musical interludes on most days. In fact, music had become such a central part of life in the infirmary that they felt a duty to get some playing time in each day. Edward's skill on the banjar was growing with daily playing. At one point a couple of Black soldiers from the regiments on the western front stopped by Rochester House. They were surprised to see a white person—much less a boy of thirteen—with an instrument that in their world was played exclusively by Negroes. Edward explained how he had been taught the basics by a worker at the neighboring store. The soldiers seemed pleased to learn that interest in the banjar was spreading, and they were highly complimentary of Edward's playing.

For Brideen the tunes came to mean far more than they'd imagined when they first started playing together. If it hadn't been for Edward's idea that they play for the patients at Rochester House, she might never have picked up her tin whistle again, so all-encompassing was the stress of building a new life in wartime. She needed the sustenance of the music of her homeland. It fed her soul and made her feel connected to her family back in Ireland in ways she couldn't begin to put into words.

What made it even more gratifying was the emerging interest in music on the part of her third son, Thomas. His next older brother, Johnny, took after his namesake father, watching as he worked and sorted the various mechanical items in stock. It was almost as if Thomas had to choose which brother to take after. He was only nine and was beginning to show the kind of dexterity needed to play a stringed instrument like the banjar. But Brideen recalled that she was even younger when she started playing the tin whistle, and at the time she was convinced that she'd never be any good because her fingers were too short. But children believe that now is forever, and have little concept of the future. Of course it hadn't seemed real to her that her fingers would ever grow long enough to reach and cover the holes. She did wonder, though, if Thomas would be better off learning another instrument, to avoid the discouragement of trying to keep up with Edward.

"He could take up the fiddle," Liam suggested. "There are a lot of fiddlers in the Sixty-Ninth. Paddy O'Flaherty over there is one of the best. He played tunes around the fire every night. Jigs, reels, hornpipes. It kept our spirits up, made us feel like we were back home."

Brideen looked over at the man Liam was pointing to. The whole side of his left shoulder and upper arm had been disfigured by shelling, with only his hand and arm above the wrist relatively unscathed.

"How sad he won't be able to play anymore."

"Oh, he'll figure out a way to bow with what's left of that arm. I've seen fellows bow with one of their feet, I swear it."

Liam was suddenly animated.

"I know what! I'll ask Paddy if he could take a bit of the day to teach Thomas a few things. He had to leave his fiddle back in camp, but I'll bet we could borrow one from somebody in town."

Brideen couldn't imagine how it could be possible for Patrick O'Flaherty, with one arm so damaged, to teach her boy anything. But he agreed immediately when Liam proposed the idea. Word got around, and by dinner that evening, a woman appeared with a fine-looking fiddle in a carrying case. She asked that someone point out the man looking for a fiddle, headed straight over to Johnny, and laid the case at the foot of his bed.

"This was my husband's," she said. "He died at Fredericksburg; it's too painful for me to see it just sitting there, reminding me of his beautiful playing. I thought of selling it, but when I heard about your situation, and the young man you want to teach, I knew that's who my Henry would have wanted it to go to."

Thomas was standing nearby, having stopped by after school to see his mother before heading to the store. Paddy nodded to him to come to the bedside, directed him to open the case and lift out the instrument for everyone to see. It wasn't the kind of rough-hewn wooden fiddle the Irish played, but smooth mahogany, a parlor violin.

"I don't know what to say, ma'am. It's... beautiful."

"How it looks isn't important, young man," she said. "It's how it sounds. Do you want to learn how to make it sing again?"

"Oh, yes I do, ma'am."

Even while Thomas was nodding, Paddy had taken the bow out of the case. He gestured to Thomas to place the fiddle over the bandages on his left shoulder, while he gripped the end of the neck with his fingers. Then he lifted the bow with his right hand and ran it over the strings, sending a ripple of the four notes through the hall. Satisfying himself that the strings were in turn, he launched into a jaunty melody, slowly at first, then gradually picking up speed.

Brideen watched in astonishment.

"It's a miracle he can play so well, in his condition."

"Wait 'til that wound heals, you'll hear him at his best," Liam replied.

"And it's a tune from back home," she continued. "I think it's named after a fellow called Hoban."

"Maybe back in Ireland," Paddy spoke up. "Here they call it 'Waiting for the Federals.'"

"Federals?"

"The Union troops."

Adapting tunes from the home country to fit what's going on over here, Brideen thought. Can't be any harm in that.

When the tune came to an end, Paddy passed the fiddle to Thomas. The boy lifted it to his shoulder, as he'd seen Paddy do, then ran the bow over the top of the strings. On his first few tries, the sound came out scratchy. Paddy shook his head.

"Not so hard. Just press lightly, and make it smooth, back and forth."

Thomas tried again, with a more delicate touch. This time the strings sang rather than scratched.

"That's more like it," said Paddy. "You'll get it in time, boy. For now, what you need to do is thank the lady for her generous gift."

Brideen turned to look for the woman, but she was nowhere to be seen.

"She must have slipped away while you were showing Thomas the bowing."

A soldier called over from his cot by the doorway.

"I saw her leave. She was wiping tears off her face."

"Perhaps it was painful to hear her late husband's fiddle played once again," Brideen said. "Let's take a moment of thanks to God for this lady's wonderful gift."

As she bowed her head, the entire infirmary fell silent.

* * *

Brideen was pregnant again. Word got around the infirmary even before she was showing, which didn't surprise her. Women, especially those who'd given birth themselves, seemed to sense early on when one in their midst was carrying. But one day as she walked by the supply room, the door was slightly open and she overheard some of them chatting.

"Number five? Or is it six?"

"Another mouth to feed."

"Those Irish, they breed like rabbits."

She knew they were talking about her. She'd heard comments like that before, and was usually able to shake them off. But another voice brought her up short.

"Someone should tell her to pay a visit to Mrs. Comstock for some Pennyroyal tea."

Alicia Comstock was known around Hagerstown as the woman who concocted mixtures of herbs that could cause a pregnancy to abort. One of the herbs was called Pennyroyal, a name Brideen remembered because it sounded playful, not like a plant with power to disrupt the body's natural processes.

These women were Protestants. Maybe this was something they could contemplate doing, but they knew full well that such a choice wasn't available to Brideen, that it was forbidden by the Catholic religion. She'd long been aware that many in Hagerstown viewed the Irish with disdain, that their large families kept them poor and ignorant. But she'd never heard it so openly expressed. How could they put it so baldly, to not welcome a child into the world, as she had welcomed each of hers? And yet she couldn't deny that there had been times when it was hard, very hard, when she was nearly overwhelmed. Men had no idea how hard it was, birthing a child, raising a family. What was it like for her mother? Did Mam ever wish that…? It was too disturbing to think about. She had to banish such thoughts from her mind. Each child was a gift frtom God, now and forever.

Later that year, she gave birth to another baby, William, named after her brother Liam, who was nearly recovered from his wounds. And the war came home to Hagerstown again, in a way no one could have anticipated.

* * *

County Hagerstown, July 6, 1864

    I.   In accordance with the instructions of Lt. Genl. Early a levy of $20,000 (twenty-thousand dollars) is made upon the inhabitants of this city. The space of 3(three) hours is allowed for the payment of this sum.

    II.   A requisition is also on order for all goods stores.

    III.   The following items will also be furnished from its merchandise or the hands of citizens' merchandise, viz 1500 suits of clothes, 1500 hats, 1500 shoes or boots, 1500 shirts, 1500 pairs of drawers, 1500 wool jackets.

    IV.   4 (four) hours is allowed for the collection.

The Mayor and City Council is for the execution of these riders. In case of noncompliance, the usual penance will be enforced upon the city.

Jno. McCausland, Brig. Gen'l., Cmd.
    -- from *Follow the Money: The 1864 Confederate Ransom of Hagerstown, Maryland* by Stephen R. Bockmiller, 2014.

When the ransom demands in the letter to Mayor Cook got out, word spread like wildfire through the town. Everyone knew what the "usual penance" would amount to—the sacking and utter destruction of the town by fire.

Some of the townspeople immediately assumed the ransom demand was nothing more than a bluff. The main theatre of the war had moved farther to the south, and the Confederates were steadily losing ground to the Union. Another U.S. election was looming in fall 1864. President Lincoln and his generals were determined that the war would come to an end by then. Yet now, seemingly out of nowhere, Confederate commander McCausland had issued a threat to burn the town down unless he received immediate payment and goods. What could be the purpose of such a bizarre request?

Yes, Hagerstown was a Union supply hub and they needed supplies and money. But that was only part of the reason, some townspeople said. At this point, the Confederacy had few options left. Their strategy came down to simply hanging on, to prolong the hostilities until a new president, one more amenable to Southern-state demands, could take office. But similar burnings had happened in other towns, and Hagerstown was once again occupied by Confederate forces. Who could say they wouldn't act out of sheer vengeance?

Brideen and John were torn. Maryland was a Union state, but the commitment to end slavery was not nearly as strong here as in the more northerly states. Hagerstown itself had a significant number of Confederate supporters, many of whom made no secret of their views on slavery. Living in a place where loyalties were so divided made it difficult to decide what was right for the community as a whole.

But the well-off among the citizenry didn't waste time agonizing or debating what to do. They began to flee with their possessions. Even the Mayor himself cleared out his own stock of goods and left town. Other merchants fled with their inventory. Banks hid some of their cash, delivered half of the money, and made residents sign promissory notes for the balance. Some Confederate sympathizers refused to sign the notes, indignant that they should have to bargain with a government they supported.

It soon became clear that no matter what the people of Hagerstown did, meeting the demand for clothing would be impossible. McCausland seemed to accept this, and agreed to settle for the portion of money already collected. But he still expected them to try harder, and extended the deadline another three hours to collect what more they could. Depending on the result, he said he would grant a short reprieve to remove women, children, and elderly before the burning of the town would commence.

The poorer residents, like Brideen's family, had little to contribute in the way of clothing. They owned little more than the clothes on their backs and a few garments set aside for Sunday best. John decided to put out some of their best hardware items and bags of nails, in hopes that the rebel soldiers collecting goods would just take what was on offer outside. To their relief, the goods were left just as they were. The Confederates were clearly not interested in awls and nails.

The crisis ended at the Court House when Gen. McCausland was given twenty thousand dollars in cash and all the suits, hats, shoes, boots, shirts, and socks that could be found. Within hours, McCausland's troops had left town. But word got around to other Confederate troops who showed up and began to loot what was left in the stores. It was then that Mayor Cook returned to town, inquiring what had happened.

"As if he didn't know!" John said. He and Brideen were among the many townspeople who were furious that the mayor had abandoned the town during the crisis. Other residents complained that the town fathers had overreacted, and questioned whether the ransom really needed to be paid at all. But for most, the terrifying prospect of witnessing their own homes and buildings torched reigned over the entire incident. And though it appeared as though the town had avoided a terrible fate, the ransom had an outcome that was almost as destructive. It divided a community that had, until recently, managed to overcome their differences and stand together against the trials of war.

* * *

Throughout this entire difficulty our borough council have done their duty fully and faithfully, and are entitled to the thanks of the entire people. Had they not paid the money and, to the utmost of their ability, furnished the clothing, the consequences to the people would have been serious in the extreme... The council knew that in the case of non-compliance with the demand, a system of pillage and outrage would be inaugurated, such as is only known in times of civil war... Those who had any intercourse with General McCausland must know that he is not the kind of man who would have been likely to throw constraints upon his men, but on the contrary would be disposed to give them unbridled license to do whatever they might desire. What would have been the condition of unprotected females, had the followers of such a man been permitted to roam at will throughout the place?

    -- Hagerstown *Herald and Torch,* July 20, 1864

Brideen was furious when the editorial was read aloud in the Lyceum. It was one thing for the city fathers to defend paying the ransom to keep Hagerstown from being burned to the ground. But for them to claim it was necessary to shield "unprotected females" from the "unbridled license" of Confederate soldiers? As if the women of Hagerstown were helpless damsels unable to take care of themselves, despite the tough resourcefulness they had shown in the operation of the infirmary at Rochester House. Worse, the editorial made no mention of the cowardly behavior of the town's own civic leaders, who, like Mayor Cook himself, had scuppered off with their own goods during the height of the crisis.

To Brideen, the way in which the ransom affair had torn the town apart was, in some ways, the worst thing about it. During the earlier days of the war, the townspeople— Rebel and Union—had pulled together when necessary. Even when Frances Kennedy had opened the infirmary at Rochester House to some wounded Confederate soldiers, the townspeople who objected to showing mercy to the enemy were eventually silenced. It was the selfish reaction to the ransom that ate away at that sense of unity, that strong sense of community exhibited in the early days of the war.

Now it was neighbor against neighbor and Brideen was growing disillusioned.

In the midst of war and the constant disruptions it brought to their lives, she and John had had no time to think about the future. She'd forgiven him for uprooting the family from Baltimore, but she'd never felt a true sense of belonging in Hagerstown. Would she ever find that feeling again? Were these the people among whom she wanted to live and raise her children? Where *did* she belong? Just who were her people?

From what she'd been hearing about many of the Irish who'd come to live in America, she was no longer sure.

** * **

THE MOB IN NEW-YORK.; Resistance to the Draft--Rioting and Bloodshed. Conscription Offices Sacked and Burned. Private Dwellings Pillaged and Fired. An ARMORY AND A HOTEL DESTROYED. Colored people Assaulted--An Unoffending Black Man Hung. The Tribune office Attacked--The Colored Orphan Asylum Ransacked and Burned--Other Outrages and Incidents. A DAY OF INFAMY AND DISGRACE.

-- New York Times, July 14, 1863

Instead of the bright, blue sky of America, I am covered with the soft, grey fog of the Emerald Isle [Ireland]. I breathe, and lo! the chattel [slave] becomes a man. I gaze around in vain for one who will question my equal humanity, claim me as his slave, or offer me an insult. I employ a cab—I am seated beside white people—I reach the hotel—I enter the same door—I am shown into the same parlour—I dine at the same table—and no one is offended ... I find myself regarded and treated at every turn with the kindness and deference paid to white people.

-- from *My Bondage and My Freedom* by
Frederick Douglass, 1855.

From the moment Brideen learned he would be coming to Baltimore to speak at the Bethel Church, she knew she had to go to Frederick Douglass' lecture. John and the children thought the trip would be too dangerous. But with the fighting having moved farther south, and the war appearing to be winding down, she convinced them she'd be perfectly safe on the two-hour train ride.

Ever since she was a child her father had spoken reverently of his two heroes: Daniel O'Connell, the Liberator, and Frederick Douglass, whom many had taken to calling the Black Liberator. Accounts of their meeting in 1845 had taken on a near-mythic quality, each leaving a powerful mark on the other's thinking, with their common goal of justice and equality for all people. Douglass said that his four-month stay in Ireland was the first time in his life that he experienced being "treated as a man, not a colour".

Now here he was, standing a few pews away, his very presence spellbinding to Brideen and everyone seated around her. She wanted to write Da and tell him she had seen the great man in the flesh, had been in the same room with him, listening to his deep, sonorous voice.

"Had any man told me four years ago," Douglass began, "That I should be here tonight, speaking to a Baltimore audience, I should have thought him about as insane as if he had predicted that I should some day go on a mission to the inhabitants of the moon! But this is a day of wonders. I left here a slave. I return to you a free man."

And if someone had told me, Brideen thought, *that a person like myself, who had never been to school, could command an audience's attention and speak with such clarity and eloquence, I would think that they were from the moon, too.*

She'd also assumed—naively—that the Irish who came to America would be supportive of the Union cause and fiercely opposed to slavery. But months earlier, the passing of the National Conscription Act had triggered four days of the worst rioting Americans had ever seen. In New York City, the free Black population became the rioters' main target. Irish immigrants, determined not to be drafted to fight for the freedom of a people they resented, turned on Black New Yorkers in a rage. Rioters lynched at least a dozen African-Americans and set the city's Colored Orphan Asylum on fire. Mobs assaulted any Black person they saw on the street, ransacked and burned homes in Black neighborhoods, and looted stores owned by Black people and those sympathetic to them. At least one hundred and twenty people, most of them Negroes, died in the violence.

As the lecture came to an end, Brideen summoned up her courage and joined the cluster of people gathering up front, hoping to speak to Douglass. She wanted to tell him how upset she was about the riots in New York, and let him know that they weren't a true expression of Irish sentiments toward Black people. As she waited her turn, her anxiety grew. She was afraid she'd babble incoherently when she did come face-to-face with Douglass (not literally, of course, because he was so tall). But just as he finished speaking with a woman standing in front of her, an aide came and whispered in his ear. Douglass nodded and turned to the waiting group, saying he had another engagement and must leave.

"I apologize that I am not able to speak with each and every one of you. I am grateful to you all for coming to hear my words tonight, for your generous donations, and for your commitment to the cause of justice and quality for the Negro and for all people. But know that we have a long struggle ahead of us. So please don't stop here. There is always more you can do. And you must. Always. Do more."

With that, the aide whisked him away.

Brideen was disappointed but also a bit relieved. She was grateful to have been in the living, breathing presence of one of her father's heroes.

She couldn't wait to get home and write to Da.

* * *

We, the undersigned Prisoners of War, belonging to the Army of Northern Virginia, having been this day surrendered by General Robert E. Lee, CSA, Commanding said Army, to Lieut. Genl. U. S. Grant, Commanding Armies of United States, do hereby give our solemn parole of honor that we will not hereafter serve in the armies of the Confederate States, or in any military capacity whatever, against the United States of America, or render said to the enemies of the latter, until property exchanged, in such manner as shall be mutually approved by the respective authorities. Done at Appomattox Court House, Va., this 9th day of April, 1865.

-- Official surrender document of Lee's troops to the Union Army, signed at Appomattox Court House on April 9, 1865

The War was over. Peace was declared, on the ninth of April, almost one month to the day after she gave birth to her fifth child, James. Yes, there were dozens of amendments to the American constitution she barely understood. But she read them because she wanted to understand that the war had truly come to an end and how it had come about. Living in a place like Hagerstown, divided between supporters of both North and South, Brideen had found much about the war confusing and difficult to understand. But neither she nor John had ever doubted their own loyalty to the North, because they never wavered in their belief that slavery was evil and must end. The important thing now was that the Union was restored and the slaves had been freed.

And the family was growing. Brideen had just given birth to another baby, a healthy son. She realized that she had been fearful about this birth, after the trauma of the stillbirth. Now she could breathe easier, knowing he was a child of peace who would not experience the agonies that her older children had endured the past few years, especially the turmoil of the battle of Hagerstown.

On the day of Lee's surrender at Appomattox, John and Brideen spent a quiet evening after the children had gone to bed.

When they had first moved to Hagerstown, they had no idea how long they would live there. They certainly hadn't been prepared for the intensity of life in a war zone. As hard as it had been for Brideen to leave Baltimore and the bosom of the Irish community, the desire to return there had largely faded. John had not given up his dream of living on the land, of owning a plot to farm. But how to find a way to do that? With the war finally over, it was time to think about the future.

"I wonder how true it is that the war is over?" John mused. "There may not be any more battles, but Hagerstown is still split between the Union and the Confederates. So is the rest of America."

"You're probably right," Brideen said. "But it's all too much to think about right now."

As they went to sleep that night, they had no idea about the new calamity that was coming within days.

Chapter 11: CHANGES

President Lincoln Shot by an Assassin.; The Deed Done at Ford's Theatre Last Night. THE ACT OF A DESPERATE REBEL
-- New York Times, April 14, 1865

It was like the end of the world. People walked around town doing normal, everyday things, saying, 'Yes, it's terrible what happened to the President', some sad, some even weeping. But almost as many weren't sad at all. They hated Lincoln and rejoiced at his death.

Something broke in Brideen when she saw the newspaper headlines. She thought of her Da, collapsing in grief at news of the death of O'Connell the Liberator. She didn't understand at the time, but now she burst into tears. How could such a thing happen? She'd never felt the deep devotion to President Lincoln that Da had felt for the Liberator. But now she was astounded at the depth of her feelings about his death. It seemed to open up a flood of reminders of all the suffering that she and her family had been through. Hunger. Near-starvation. The dead man standing in the doorway. The night of the Crowbars. The dying woman in the cabin on the way to Sligo, begging for help. All that they had endured, only to lose their beloved Mam to the fever. Waving farewell on the quay from Liverpool to Da, her sister, her brothers. Believing the pain of the good-byes would be relieved in America. The Land of Hope. Then the war, the dead, the wounded. Then finally, peace, and the prospect of life returning to what it had been.

But now a good man had been murdered. America's Liberator. God had taken O'Connell in old age, but Lincoln was taken before his time, just when his true work of bringing about equality was about to begin. They'd come to America believing it truly was the promised land, a country that welcomed even the poorest of the poor, like Brideen and her family. She had finally begun to feel at home in America, but the death of Lincoln changed all that. Is this what they left their people, their home country for? To go from hope to despair?

She felt a darkness inside her unlike anything she'd ever felt. She went to Mass with John and the children and prayed for the soul of President Lincoln. But the prayers felt meaningless. It all felt meaningless. Nothing would ever be right again.

Within days news came of the assassin's capture, and of the man who organised the huge countrywide manhunt for John Wilkes Booth: James O'Beirne, a Captain in the Thirty-Seventh New York Infantry, who had been born in Country Roscommon. The newspapers spoke of the pride that her fellow countrymen felt that an Irishman bore the responsibility for bringing the murderer to justice. But Brideen felt no such comfort. She and John were appalled at the people who rejoiced in Lincoln's death. Some of them were right here in Hagerstown. Her faith in the ideals of her adopted country had turned to dust.

Where should they go? Where *could* they go? The cities were where the Irish were. There were large Irish communities in the bigger cities, like Baltimore, where they had lived when they first came to America. But now there was a growing ugliness where the Irish were fighting with Black people over jobs. Originally there had been good relations between them: Black workers lived in close proximity to white workers in racially-mixed communities. Working-class African-Americans competed directly with the newly-arrived Irish for unskilled jobs. Even with the end of the war, racial tensions continued in workplaces and in working-class neighborhoods throughout the cities. When they heard these stories, Brideen and John were ashamed to learn that many of their own countrymen bore the same kind of prejudice that reigned in the American South. She was even beginning to doubt the Black Liberator, to wonder if his belief that the breach would be healed was wrong, that the Irish would come to a renewed understanding of their common bond with Black people.

No, the cities were not where they wanted to settle.

*** * ***

INDIAN LAND FOR SALE. Get a home of your own. Easy payments. Fine Lands in the West. Grazing. Agricultural.

-- from an1861 newspaper ad

Millions of Acres in Iowa!! The Iowa Rail Road Land Company, The Iowa Falls and Sioux City R.R. Land Co., The Sioux City & Pacific Land & Town Lot Co., AND The Elkhorn Land and Town Lot Co. HAVE NOW FOR SALE AT THEIR PRINCIPAL OFFICE AT CEDAR RAPIDS, IOWA, 1,880,000 Acres of Land, As fertile and desirable as any in America, at $8 to $10 per Acre on time or for Cash. For full information apply to W. W. WALKER, Vice President, CEDAR RAPIDS, IOWA.

-- from an 1871 newspaper ad

John continued to read and study the ads about land for sale in Iowa, preparing for the day when they'd have enough to even contemplate making an offer. But as time went on he began to despair that they'd ever be in a position to consider buying. In the early days the government was selling plots very cheap, but those were quickly snapped up by speculators and railroad companies, which jacked the prices up. There had even been a time in the 1840s when plots formerly inhabited by Indigenous tribes could be claimed for free, causing settlers to gather on the border and await the authorities' starting gun signal. But the days of those frantic land rushes were over. By now, John thought, most of the good land was already gone.

Barely a year after James was born, Brideen gave birth again, and at long last she had her girl-child, who was named Anna. She was overjoyed, not just because it was a healthy girl, but also because now she could relax and enjoy the baby. With the war well and truly over, the infirmary at Rochester House had shut down, and she didn't have to face the other ladies' unspoken judgement of her having yet another child. She spent all her time at home or at the hardware shop with John and the little ones while the older children were at school.

After each birth, Brideen went through a period of missing her Mam so keenly, but this one felt different, as if she could almost feel Mam watching over her from above. Maybe it was because she finally had a daughter. She found herself thinking about Mam as a tower of strength that she could draw on when she needed to. She recalled the time back in Castlebar, when she asked for a second piece of bread and Mam said no, they had to save it for the walk to Sligo, and Brideen was angry at her mean, heartless mother. But it was Mam's very ruthlessness that kept them going, kept them from starving, kept them alive long enough to get to England. It was a woman's strength, and Brideen hoped she had at least a portion of that strength to carry the family through whatever trials awaited them.

The next one wasn't long in coming, and it was completely unexpected.

Brideen and John had basically been running the store through the war years. George O'Faolin, the owner, had been an absentee proprietor, preferring the relative peace of Baltimore to the turmoil and street combat of Hagerstown. But one day he paid them a surprise visit.

"Mr. O'F, how good to see you," Brideen said.

"Business has really picked up since the armistice," John added.

"You've handled everything so well in my absence," O'Faolin said. "But some changes are coming that I want to tell you about myself."

"Changes? What kind of changes?"

O'Faolin took a deep breath.

"I'm selling the store, John."

He explained that with the peace, businesses were interested in Hagerstown, especially with the increase in railroad service. A gentleman named Foltz had made an offer, with the aim of expanding the business to farm equipment and railway hardware.

"Now, you've been a loyal employee and there's every reason to think that there will be an opportunity for you in the new operation, John. I'll personally commend you highly."

"But from what you say, it won't be a store anymore. It'll be more like a... a factory."

"To some extent, yes, but expansion is the way of the future," said O'Faolin. "Right now Mr. Foltz has got a crew working on a new kind of trough, rounded and made of steel."

"What pig is going to want to drink from a thing like that?"

"That's what Foltz' crew will find out. There's good money in it, John. More than I've ever been able to pay you."

"I worked in a factory in Birmingham. I don't want to do it again."

Brideen added, "We don't want to raise our children here in Hagerstown. We want a place more suitable to practice our faith."

"Maybe you ought to consider going back to Baltimore, then. There's lots of good jobs there. And believe me, they'd rather hire the Irish than the Nigras. Just because they're free men now doesn't mean they'll actually work for a living."

Brideen was appalled at his remark and was about to say so. But John cut her off, knowing that she'd likely raise the temperature of the discussion in a way that wouldn't help.

"Yes, so we've heard. But we really don't want to go back to Baltimore. Like my wife says, the main thing we think about is where we want to raise our family, and it's not in a city."

"You're just like my cousin Seamus Burns in Iowa. He's actually James but he still insists the family call him Seamus like back home. In his heart, he's never really left Ireland. He still prefers the country life, even here, in the Land of Opportunity. Myself, I couldn't stand it, living on a big, smelly farm."

"Smelly?"

"Back in Ireland you had those little potato beds and a cow and a pig or two. Out in Iowa they've got so much land they raise whole herds of cows and pigs."

"That sounds like just the kind of thing we're looking for."

"I have a thought," said O'Faolin. "James' son John, who's been working with him, wants to start his own farm, looking to buy a plot upstate. Maybe you should write to him and see if he needs any help, or if he knows anybody that does. They're surrounded by Germans in Quasqueton, and they want more Irish in the state. Complain that they don't have anybody to play at dances. Germans don't play anything but polkas."

"We got players right in our own family," Brideen said.

"You do?"

"Our oldest, Edward, plays banjo, and the next youngest, Thomas, is learning the fiddle"

"And my wife here has been playing the tin whistle since she was a girl. She knows all kinds of jigs and reels."

"You've practically got a whole *céilí* band right there. Play that up if you write to Seamus, John. Like I said, in his head, he's still living in Ireland

Later that night they sat down to write the letter. Brideen, whose printing was better, wrote as they jointly composed the text out loud.

"Mister Seamus James Burns, esq."

Brideen looked at John quizzically.

"O'Faolin said to use both names so we don't sound too familiar."

She shrugged and continued writing.

"I am writing to you at the suggestion of your cousin, George O'Faolin. I have been managing Mr. O'Faolin's Hardware business in Hagerstown, Maryland for the past several years. He

has recently sold the store and the business is undergoing a change, I would like to inquire about the possibility of taking up farm work. My wife Bridget and I have long sought to acquire a farm of our own, but did not have the finances to consider such a prospect until recently. We desire to live among other Irish people and raise our children to be good Catholics. From what we have learned about Iowa, we believe it offers a fine situation to do so. We are seeking a suitable parcel of land for a price that falls within the limits of our present resources, and would be grateful for any suggestions you might have that would help us attain that goal. Yours very truly."

"Wait," Brideen interrupted him. "Aren't you going to say anything about our music?"

"I feel a bit foolish going on about it. I think O'Faolin was just being polite."

"Maybe so, but we should play up the skills we have. Farmers are a dime a dozen, but from what he said, it sounds like musicians are hard to find. Now go on, tell him we have a full band with whistle, banjo, and fiddle"

"Little Thomas can hardly hold the bow straight yet."

"He'll work on it. He just needs to practice. By the time we actually get to Iowa he'll be fine."

* * *

For the men of our race whose highest aspiration is to see liberty triumphant, who are looking for the rise of that Irish Republic which is established in their souls, and which will yet bless the unborn generations – for these men there is but one side: "Liberty – her friends are our friends, her enemies, our enemies." That the Congress of the United States and the loyal people it represents are the guardians and friends of liberty – liberty not narrowed down by geographical lines nor races, but unversal as the love of God – that these are the friends of liberty they have given undoubted proof. To such men of our race we say: Get out from among the drove whose drivers are the herds of bigotry and slavery, and stand with the men upon whose banner is trace "Universal Liberty."

             -- from *The Irish Republic* Chicago, May 1867

They waited months. No response from O'Faolin's cousin Burns. John kept reading the land ads but was despairing of finding anything. He announced that he was taking the position at the new Foltz factory after all. "It'll be like being back in the Black Country, walking into this huge building. The machines they're making aren't like anything I've ever seen on a farm before. But what choice do I have?"

"Come to Chicago with me."

Since recovering from his war wounds, Liam had been living with Brideen and her family, drawing an army pension which was due to run out in the next year.

"Chicago? What's in Chicago?"

"There's a new group taking up the cause of Irish freedom, called the Fenian Brotherhood. They've got a headquarters in Chicago and started their own newspaper, *The Irish Republic.* They're also taking on the racial bigotry among the Irish workers. They believe in freedom and equality for all. There's a piece in the latest issue of *The Republic* about it, saying the Fenians are the revived spirit of O'Connell and Young Ireland."

"That sounds fine, but just how are they going to fight for Ireland from the other side of the ocean?"

"They have a secret plan."

"What secret plan?"

"You can't breathe a word of it outside this house. They're going to launch a raid into Canada."

"Canada? What good's that going to do."

"It will establish a foothold on British soil, to support the rebels in Ireland."

"Which will end the same as in 1848."

"There's lots of Irish here in America who are still committed to the cause, Brid. Just like you and John. So if you're going to work in a factory, why not go to Chicago with me, where you can get better pay and fight for Ireland too?"

"We don't want to live in a big city, you know that."

"You know this farm idea is a pipe dream. You'll never be able to afford one, with land prices going sky-high."

Brideen knew there was no persuading Liam from moving to Chicago and joining the Fenians. He had an inner drive to always be fighting for a cause, and this was another iteration of the eternal Ireland struggle. He and John were close as brothers when they first emigrated, and there was a time when John would have joined him in the struggle. But now he was father to six children, and nothing would dissuade him from his dream of living on the land once again.

A week later, Liam was already gone and John had left for the factory. Brideen was making soda bread with one hand and holding Anna with the other arm when Johnny called out.

"Mam? Is Iowa very far away?"

"Plenty far away. Why?"

"'Cause Da's got a letter from someone in Iowa."

"Bring it to me!"

It was scrawled handwriting, clearly written by someone who wasn't proficient at writing. But she could make out the name on the return address: Burns!

To Mr. John McDonnell, correspondent

I hope this reaches you. You wrote my father Mr. James Burns some time ago about land in Iowa. I have acquired a parcel of land six miles northwest of the town of Independence and there is an adjoining plot of land for sale that I would like to acquire, but both plots are uncleared and I cannot handle the work of clearing both myself. I am given to understand you have several sons and could provide the help needed and work toward ownership of the smaller plot yourself. I want Irish neighbors and my father says this exchange of work is the way they do it back in the home country. If this interests you we can discuss terms.

Yours truly, John Burns esq.

"Go to the factory, tell your father he's needed at home right away. Don't say why, or anything about a letter. Just make sure they let him off work."

She was excited, but also anxious. Was this offer too good to be true? They only knew this man Burns through O'Faolin's recommendation. What if it all fell apart? John would be devastated. She'd gotten over her anger at him for uprooting them from Baltimore, but this was different. They had six children now.

What were they getting themselves into?

PART IV: Buchanan County, Iowa, 1871-95

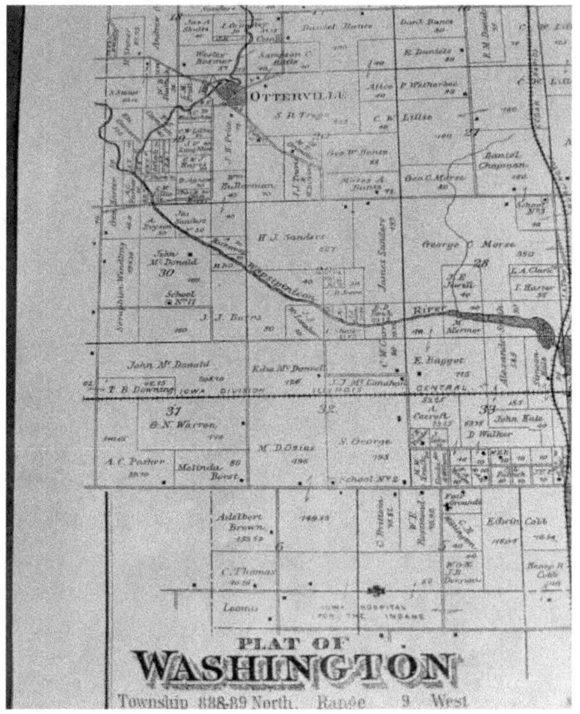

-- From 1886 plot map of Washington township, Buchanan County, Iowa, showing the McDonnell (McDonald) and Burns farms (courtesy of Buchanan County Genealogical Society)

Chapter 12: THE JOURNEY

Just imagine this county in 1842—a vast expanse of rolling prairie like a mighty sea of green, whose wild untrammeled grasses billowed like ocean waves with every breeze, streams whose clear, rippling waters teeming with fish life, flowed peacefully and tranquilly on, undisturbed except for the occasional rhythmic dip of a paddle and the splash of a canoe, or when some dexterous, agile Indian landed a fine specimen of the finny tribe; natural wood lands, whose rank and luxuriant undergrowth was never trod except by some fleet-footed animal or some stealthy moccasined red man on the chase, whose only echoes were those of wild animals or the guttural speech or war-whoop of the Indian, a country whose only use was a habitat for wild animals and still wilder savages, who challenged the advance of civilization and fought the usurpers of what they deemed were their inalienable rights... Thus did the pioneers of 1842 select this garden spot as an ideal on which to expend their efforts to assist Dame Nature in her well laid plan... The vast, waving prairies have given place to fenced and cultivated fields; roadways, bridges, houses, churches, schools, and towns dot the landscape. We have inherited all these material comforts from our forebears and those heroic pioneers who wisely selected this spot, Buchanan County, as their home-land.

-- from *History of Buchanan County, Iowa and Its People* by Harry Church Chappell and Katharyn Joella Allen, Chicago, S. J. Clarke publishing, 1914

It had been nearly two years since they received the letter from James Burns' son. First John and the two older boys, Edward and John Jr., had trekked out to Iowa on foot and by rail, to meet their new neighbor and see the land. They built a rough shelter for the three of them and set to work clearing the fifty-seven-acre plot. John admitted it was going to be difficult to render it fit for cultivation, but the presence of the river was crucial.

"Why has it taken so long for this land to be claimed, with such an abundance of fresh water?" he wondered aloud.

John Burns explained that most of the treaties with tribes in the southern half of the state had been settled over twenty years ago, and the land had been snapped up quickly in federal sales. But Buchanan County had been part of the territory of the Sauk tribe whose Chief, Black Hawk, mounted a fierce war to retain possession of their lands. After the uprising's defeat, much of the state northeast of the Mississippi became part of what was known as the Black Hawk Purchase.

"Just took a while to sort it all out, and by then people thought all the good land was gone. They saw all those nice cleared farms down in Jefferson County, but up here it was all scrub and trees and rock. How do they think you get good farmland? You have to put in the work to clear it."

They returned to Hagerstown to winter with Brideen, who had stayed behind with the younger children. She was reassured by what she heard about the land, the work they'd already done on it, and especially John's impression of John Burns, whom he judged honest and trustworthy. The following spring John and the boys planned to go back to Buchanan Country and build a proper house on the section they'd cleared. "You better build me a nice big one," Brideen told him. "Because we're going to need it."

"Are you telling me what I think you're telling me?" John asked.

"Yes, and I sure hope it's another girl. Don't we, Annie?"

"A sister! Yes!"

That year the family celebrated a joyous Christmas together, marked by constant talk about living and working on their own farm in faraway Iowa. On New Year's Day the traditional rituals took on deeper meaning, especially the chant: "Blow out the old, blow in the new, blow out the false, blow in the true." On each line the family members were meant to run between the front and back doors of the house, blowing in and out the named spirits. Which always sent them into fits of giggles as the little ones protested, "We don't *have* a back door!" This year the New Year brought back Brideen's sorrow at missing her family back in Ireland, and the thought that her children didn't even know their aunts and uncles there. But she reminded herself that the chant's message was the coming of new possibilities, which turned her mind to the challenge of getting the whole family to Iowa.

Spring came and as planned, John and the two eldest set out again for Iowa. They got back to Hagerstown in late fall, just in time for the birth of a seventh child.

When the midwife came out of the birthing room she had a sly smile on her face.

"Well?" demanded John.

"Annie, you got the little sister you ordered. And she's a beauty."

They celebrated their last Christmas in Hagerstown. Then, early in the New Year, they began loading up a wagon for the final move to Iowa.

"It's at least two weeks by wagon and on foot," John said, suggesting that Brideen go by train with the baby, Annie, and James.

Brideen was adamant that the train was too much money.

"Why not give our young ones a taste of what it was like when we were growing up in Mayo? We can all take turns riding and walking."

Next came the discussion of whether to have oxen or horses pull the cart.

"Horses are more expensive," Brideen said. "And they don't have the endurance of oxen."

John shook his head.

"I'll not drag my family a thousand miles behind a couple of slowpoke ox."

"A thousand miles," exclaimed young William. "Are we really going that far?"

"Yes, we are, boy. *Really,*" John assured him, gently mocking his son's drawing-out of the word. He launched into an explanation of the vastly longer distances in America, and Brideen let the matter drop. There'd be no point arguing with him.

It was going to be a difficult journey to their new home, and they were eager to get started. Initially, the most daunting task was loading the wagon—deciding what they wanted to take with them against what they had room for. They'd be camping and cooking along the way, so buckets, cooking pots, and dishes were essential. But aside from a few chairs, they had to leave all the furniture behind.

"What'll we sleep on?" Annie asked

"The ground," said John.

"But what if it's raining?"

"We huddle under the wagon," said Brideen.

They set off on a cool, dry morning in March. They had two horses to pull the wagon, and a smaller cart pulled by the older boys, while the younger ones took turns riding on the big wagon. They periodically surrendered their seats so their mother could get some rest from walking, while Annie rode the wagon holding her baby sister, Margaret. They soon arrived outside the town of Cumberland, where there was a large, official-looking sign that read: "National Road. United States of America, Built 1811" The road extending beyond it consisted of small pebbles that appeared almost locked together.

"Here's our gift named after the Scotsman McAdam," said John. "And it goes on for miles and miles!"

No one other than John seemed to know who this McAdam was, but they appreciated the way the wagon moved so much more smoothly over the small stones.

Within a day's walk they had crossed into Pennsylvania. Following the macadam road it took nearly three more days to get across the state. They knew they were coming to the state border when John pointed to a cluster of smoking towers in the distance.

"Must be the steel mills of Pittsburgh," said Brideen. The closer they got, the more the terrain reminded her of the Black Country where she and John had lived and labored when they were young. To Brideen it seemed like a lifetime ago, but the smoke-ridden, darkened countryside brought the memories back. She was anxious to move on and put thoughts of that hard time out of her mind.

They spent the night a few miles from the Ohio border. The weather had turned cold, so all nine of them huddled together under the cover atop the big wagon. They had to unload a couple of large trunks to make room. John hated having to do it, because it meant taking time in the morning to re-load. But woolen blankets and the warmth of their bodies were all they had to get them through the freezing night.

The morning was still cold, but the bright sun warmed them as they re-packed and set off into Ohio. Already the young ones were talking about Chicago, where they planned to stop a few days and visit with their uncle Liam. John knew they had only covered a small part of the journey. The hundreds of miles that lay ahead of them across Ohio, Michigan, and Indiana meant that Chicago was yet many days away. But not wanting to dampen their enthusiasm, he said nothing.

What followed were what seemed like an endless stream of identical days: Waking before dawn, feeding the horses, making breakfast, setting off on the road, stopping briefly for lunch and carrying on until dusk, when they had to find a sheltered spot to build a fire, cook dinner, and spend the night. Ohio was dotted with farmhouses and they sometimes encountered a generous family who would offer them some milk and warm biscuits, for which they were grateful. They were also grateful for a late-March gift, a run of several dry, sunny days. Which of course was bound to come to an end—and did, just as they were approaching the

Indiana state line. A ferocious storm came up, with wind and hail threatening to rip the cover off the wagon.

"Hold it down!"

John stopped the horses while they worked in pairs to hold down the corners and sides. Even the little ones, James and Annie, managed to hang on to the front right corner. When the storm finally began to let up, they found the road so saturated with rain the pebbles were becoming loose and the wheels got stuck in the mud and slurry. There was nothing to do but wait until it started to dry out. They spend a damp night under the canvas over the wagon, cold and hungry.

It took until the middle of the next day before the mud had hardened enough to move the wagon again. But their progress was much slower, and the struggle with the storm had worn them out. When it was time for Thomas to ride, he climbed into the back of the wagon and began rifling through the items.

"What are you doing?" his father said, clearly annoyed.

"Trying to find my fiddle."

Brideen spoke up before John could upbraid the boy for wasting time.

"That's a fine idea, Thomas. You can catch up on your practice time and it might raise our spirits to hear a tune or two."

He managed to find the instrument case and pulled it out of the stack. When he applied the bow, a couple of strings had gone badly out of tune from the dampness.

"Here, let me take a try at it," said Brideen.

She adjusted the pegs until the strings sounded close to what she expected to hear when plucked. She handed it back to Thomas, who ran the bow across them again. He nodded.

"Sounds pretty close. Good job, Mama."

It had been many days since he'd played, but he managed to get a pleasing tone in the bowing, then without stopping he slipped into a recognizable tune, a waltz Brideen recognized but couldn't remember the name of.

For the next hour Thomas played through the tunes he'd learned from Paddy O'Flaherty. Brideen was right. It did lighten their spirits. And the orange-and-pink sunset settling over the horizon seemed to dry out the air even more as they stopped to set up for the night.

As night fell, John announced they'd crossed the Indiana border.

"No more Scotsman's road," he said, as the wagon turned rightward.

They could tell the road surface had changed.

"Can't we stay on the nice road?" James asked.

"Sorry, *buachaill daor*. We head up near Fort Wayne now."

It was the first time in ages that Brideen had heard her husband speak Irish.

They continued a bit farther into Indiana 'till nightfall. In the morning they skirted the town of Fort Wayne, then John turned the wagon sharply west again. There were fewer farms, and they were farther apart. No one offered them biscuits.

They walked for hours, then finally stopped to make camp. By now even the older boys were getting snappish.

"How much farther to Chicago?"

"Oh, we're getting there."

"When? Tomorrow?"

"Let's hope so," John said.

They were well into the next day when a series of hills appeared in the distance.

"What are those hills?" William asked.

"Not sure," said John. He looked at Brideen and smiled. They'd looked at the map the night before.

"Why don't you run on ahead and find out for yourself?"

The terrain before them was quite flat. Edward and Thomas took off, with little William trailing behind. Their parents watched from a distance as the two older boys arrived at one of the hills and started to run up. It was all sand, and they had to fight to keep from sliding back down. Finally they scrambled over the top and disappeared from sight. Then back at the wagon the family heard a string of loud shrieks.

"WATER!"

The two boys reappeared and scrambled down the hill again, joined by William as they raced back to the wagon.

"There's water up ahead."

"A big body of water!"

"As big as an ocean. And there's dunes!"

John smiled.

"That's Lake Michigan. It's one of what they call the Great Lakes. They're like inland seas."

"Where do you think we'll get to if we keep going beside it to the other shore?" said Brideen.

The boys looked at one another.

"Where?"

"Try and guess."

Edward thought for a moment.

"I know! Chicago!"

"Right!"

"So we're almost there?"

"Oh, you've got a ways to go yet," they heard a voice call out.

They were passing a farmhouse a short distance from the road. There was a man standing in the doorway, looking their way.

"How much farther, you think?" John called out. They'd found that people in the farmhouses they passed often called out greetings and offers of help.

"Illinois state line's still another ten miles or so," replied the man. "You won't get to the big city 'till sometime tomorrow."

Brideen, at the front of the cart, had to lean sharply to her right to see who John was talking to. She caught a glimpse of the man standing in the doorway, his head and one shoulder leaning on the right jamb. She took a sharp breath inward, as her mind was seized by a long-forgotten memory.

The farmer's stance at the farmhouse door was exactly the same as the skeletal figure that had terrified her all those years ago, that had invaded her dreams that night in Castlebar. It was like it was happening again, now, at this moment, and she felt the same terror rising up in her chest. Her heart raced. Her breathing became shallow. It was all she could do to keep from screaming.

Annie, who was sitting next to her on the front bench of the cart, could see that something strange was happening to her mother.

"Mama! What's wrong?"

After a moment Brideen managed to catch her breath, and began to shake her head vigorously, as if to drive the image out of her mind.

"It's nothing, Annie. Nothing at all. Just a bit short of breath."

John and the boys were carrying on a friendly conversation with the farmer, who was still standing in the doorway. None of them noticed Brideen's strange reaction, which was a relief to her. Annie was soon distracted by Margaret's squirms and wiggles as she lay between them on the bench, and Brideen picked the baby up as if to soothe her. But it was Brideen herself who needed soothing.

It had been many years since she thought about that terrible time. For the memory to come flooding back so vividly and unexpectedly... Why? What if it happened again?

They bid the farmer farewell and started up the wagon again. Crossing into Illinois would take them into the last leg of their journey, and they were in good spirits. Except for Brideen, who was still shaken. Even as she did her best to hide her inner turmoil, her mind was being roiled by a wave of other memories of that long-ago trek to Sligo—the corpses lying by the side of the road, Mikeen warning her not to look at them. The desperate whispers of the dying woman in the cottage they thought was empty. Da, Mam, all of them weakened, rail-thin, yet forging on with tremendous effort. Things that she hadn't thought about in more than twenty years, coming back now in all their vividness and clarity, almost as if this journey to Iowa was a re-living of the earlier one.

That journey is over, she told herself. *It's long over, it's in the past, we're on our way to our new life.* But the memories kept coming as they pushed on toward the Illinois border. It was only when the trail took them close to the Lake Michigan shoreline that Brideen began to regain control over her thoughts. She told John to stop and let her off the wagon. He thought she needed to relieve herself but instead she ran toward the water.

Reaching the shore she whispered a fervent prayer.

"Relieve me of these dreadful memories, Lord. Please, let them pass from me and wash away into these waters."

As gentle waves lapped the shore, she felt a peace enter her soul. A kind of grace, a knowing that there was nothing more to fear.

We survived that journey. We survived. We survived.

She made her way back to the cart. John looked at her quizzically.

"I needed a moment to pray," Brideen told him.

Nothing more was said between them.

* * *

FENIAN WAR COMMENCED. Canada Invaded! Fenians in Possession of Fort Erie and Waterloo! Telegraph Wires Cut! Railroad Tracks Said to be Destroyed! Families Leaving Canada for this Side etc. etc. etc. The long anticipated movement of the Fenians would seem to have taken place at last. What the result will be cannot now be foreseen.

-- The Buffalo Commercial, June 1, 1866

The clip-clop of the horse's hooves was loud and sharp on the pavement as the cart made its way up Michigan Avenue, a wide street lined on both sides with buildings several stories high.

170

They craned their necks to look up at these structures, a few as tall as any they'd ever seen. They were awestruck by the sheer number of people around them, some walking, some riding in carriages, some on velocipedes, going this way and that, all seemingly in a mad scramble to get to a destination. Most intimidating were the horse-drawn trams that whizzed by them, carrying dozens of passengers.

"Do we even know where to find Liam?" Brideen asked John, who was holding the reins.

"He wrote something about an office just off Michigan Avenue. This street is so long, how are we supposed to find it?"

"Maybe ask someone? There are an awful lot of Irish people here."

"We have to be careful. The Fenians are considered an outlaw group by the authorities here. Some of them are in jail for those raids into Canada."

"We're not looking to join them or cause trouble," Brideen pointed out. "We're just trying to find our brother."

She spied a man wearing a green jacket.

"That could be a Fenian, couldn't it? Stop," she told John. "I'll go ask that man over there."

He stopped the cart and Brideen stepped down to the street and approached the man. As she came closer she could tell right away from his coloring that he wasn't Irish. But he'd already become aware of her approach, and stopped.

"Pardon, sir? May I ask you a question?"

The man looked at her curiously, then came out with a torrent of words in a language she didn't recognize. *A city full of Irish*, she thought, *and I pick one who isn't.* She nodded a thank-you to the man, who was still babbling on about something, and started back toward the cart when she heard some voices, distinctly Irish ones, coming from farther up the street. A cluster of men were having a spirited debate, and Brideen caught enough words and phrases to conclude that they were either Fenians or sympathizers. She approached them, but before she could say anything, one of the men turned to look at her and said something that brought her up short.

"Well, look who's finally arrived in our windy city."

"I'm sorry to interrupt you, but..."

"The sister of a Fenian man can interrupt any time at all."

"Excuse me?"

"You're the one Liam Sweeney has been waiting for, aren't you?"

"How did you know?"

"You two are the spittin' image of one another! He told us you'd be stopping by on your way to Iowa. I'm Michael O'Brien, pleased to make your acquaintance. Come on, I'll show you where you'll find your brother."

She gestured to John to start up the cart, but the man said, "Oh, you won't be needing to ride. We're not going far."

Brideen gestured John to follow as Michael O'Brien turned up a side street and stopped a few doors up in front of a tavern called Mulcahy's.

"Comrade Sweeney!" he bellowed. "I've brought you a lovely gift."

Brideen followed O'Brien inside and saw her brother standing at the bar.

"Liam!"

"Sweet Jesus, it's you, Brid!"

He ran to her and they embraced while all the tavern patrons shouted and applauded.

"I was worried you wouldn't make it."

"You can thank your friend O'Brien there that we found you at all!"

John was in the tavern doorway, followed by the children.

"Ye didn't exactly make yourself easy to find!"

He embraced John warmly while the young ones clustered around him.

"Uncle Liam!"

"We looked all over Chicago for you, Uncle Liam!"

He greeted each one with a hug and kiss, then got to Annie, who was holding the baby.

"And who's this?"

"Her name's Margaret," Annie replied.

"She came along after you left," John added.

"Well, then, pleased to meet you, new niece named Margaret. This family needed more females."

Liam looked around. "This is no place for little ones. Let's go up the street. There's a place where we can get a nice big batch of lamb stew."

Brideen said they couldn't afford to pay for such a meal but Liam insisted it was on him. They arrived at another tavern, where Liam chose a table. Soon a woman came out of a back room carrying a large pot. They all sat down as she ladled steaming hot stew into bowls.

"Ah, that's the way, Miss Maggie," said Liam.

They emptied the bowls quickly.

"A fine stew, isn't it?"

"'Tis," nodded John between spoonfuls.

"It's so fine to see you, brother, even if it's a short visit," said Brideen.

Liam looked at her with a squint.

"Well, sister. It may not be all that short."

"Oh?"

"I'm not sure how much longer I'll be here meself."

"How do ye mean?"

By way of answering Brideen's question, her brother launched into a capsule account of recent Fenian history. Before he'd joined the movement, they'd embarked on several raids into Canada, all failures. Demoralized, the members had argued over the causes of these failures and where they should direct their future energies, which led to an overt split in the organization.

One faction planned to return to Ireland and continue the struggle on Irish soil. The other faction was staying behind in America and was considering yet another raid into Canada, through the Dakota territory.

"They want to join forces out west with an Indian group called the Metis Nation, who're fighting to hold on to their homeland, which the government is trying to claim for English settlers. Their struggle is a lot like Ireland's, and they've got the numbers to do it."

"Are you're going to go along with them?"

He paused, then let out a sigh.

"I wish I believed this Dakota thing had a chance. But it's going to be another lost cause. And once the rest of them go back to Ireland, there'll be hardly any of us left. You were right, Brid. We can't free Ireland from an ocean away."

"So what are you going to do? Go back to Ireland with the others?"

"I'd rather stay here. But not in Chicago. I need more than political comrades. I need family. I was thinking I might... go to Iowa with you."

"Really? You mean it?"

Her loud reaction drew the attention of John and the children.

"What's going on?"

Brideen gestured to Liam, who directed his words to John.

"Well, brother-in-law, I'm hoping you can use another set of hands on that farm of yours."

"You mean you'll come with us to Iowa? Jesus, Mary, and Joseph, of course we can!"

As the children gathered around the two men, shouting, "Uncle Liam! Uncle Liam!" Brideen held back. She was aware of an odd sensation inside her, and realized it was the same feeling of grace, of peace that she'd experienced standing on the shore of Lake Michigan, following that frightening flood of memories of the famine. Being reunited with the brother who'd endured the same trials and agonies felt like an answer to her prayer.

We survived that journey. We survived. We survived.

Chapter 13: THE CROSSING

The Great Calamity of the Age! Chicago in Ashes!!!
-- headline in Chicago Evening Journal-Extra,
October 9, 1871

As the wagon made its way across the state of Illinois, one topic of conversation preoccupied them: The wide barrier of rushing water that awaited them at the western border of Illinois, and how they would get across it into Iowa. Ferries run by steam power had become the main method of crossing the Mississippi, but only the largest ones could handle big wagons like the Sweeneys', and the fare was expensive. Another option, they learned, was to unload the wagon, carry all their goods separately onto the ferry, and ride to the other side. But that would mean leaving the wagon behind.

"Then how are we supposed to get that load of stuff from Dubuque to the new place?" Brideen asked. "Buy another wagon, just to go another sixty miles?"

"Is there a railroad?"

"I don't know, but if there is, it would only get us as far as Independence. That's still another five miles or so to the farm."

When they got to the town of Galena they stopped in at the local general store. The proprietor could see they'd travelled some distance.

"Where are you coming from?" he asked.

When they answered "Chicago" he looked startled.

"How long ago did you leave there?"

"Five days ago," Liam answered.

"Count your blessings, friend," said the storekeeper.

"Why do you say that?"

"There's a huge fire there, started a couple of days ago. Half the city's burnt to the ground."

"Half the city?" Liam said. "That's not possible."

"That's what the papers are saying."

"What about your friends, Uncle Liam?" said Annie.

"Do you think they're okay?"

Stunned, all Liam could do was mumble, "I hope so." Half the city in flames? What about the people? At this distance there was simply no way to find out. They all fell silent, unsure about what to do next.

"We have to keep moving," John finally said. He turned to the proprietor. "Is there a cheaper way to get across the river to Iowa than the steam ferries?"

"There's flatboats," he replied

"What's that?"

"Big wooden platform. You just row it across."

"*Row?* With what?"

"They got extra-long oars called sweeps. It's how everything got to the other side before the steam engines. Hardly anybody uses them now, but there's a fellow down near Davenport who'll still take carts across. It's all done by human power. That's why it's so cheap. With your bunch he'll hardly have to hire anybody."

"But we want to cross up here, not go all the way down to Davenport."

The store owner shrugged.

"Your choice, my friend."

They debated what to do. Liam argued that it was only a couple of hours down to Davenport, and the ease of just rolling the cart onto the flatboat was appealing. And with so many arms to work the sweeps, how hard could it be to cross the less-than-a-mile distance?

They turned the wagon around and headed south in a track near the river. There was quite a bit of traffic on the wide stretch of water—canoes, small craft, even a ferry powered by horses turning a treadmill. But most imposing was the huge steamboat heading to the opposite shore. They watched with envy as it moved at a speed they'd never seen for a watercraft. But such luxury wasn't for them, and they continued on for a couple of hours down to Davenport.

There was no difficulty finding the flatboat—the large wood platform was tied up at a dock just as they reached the outskirts of the city. There was no sign of the operator around, but there were a number of sweeps bundled on the shore.

"Should we wait for him?"

"We have to."

"Why? Everything we need is right here. It's late in the day, we should head out and pay the owner when we bring it back. It's nice and calm on the river. We should be able to get across in no time," said Liam.

To be so close, after all they'd come through, it was just too tempting not to push on.

There was a wooden ramp to drive over onto the flatboat, and John guided the horse onto it with little trouble. Brideen, Liam, and the older boys each picked up one of the sweeps, and John untied the rope anchoring the platform.

"Iowa, here we come!" shouted Edward as they pushed off from the shore.

"Let's angle toward the north, so we can get as close as possible to Dubuque."

At first the sweeps got a nice, smooth glide going, but it took tremendous effort to keep the platform moving, and soon they were making no headway at all.

"We're just floating in place," Brideen said. "The current is too strong."

Liam agreed.

"We can't keep trying to go upriver, John. Straight across is the best we can do."

"Fine, but what do we do on the other side? Do you see a ramp anywhere?"

"We should have thought it through before we started out," Liam retorted.

They realized that while they were debating, the raft was getting pushed farther downstream. They had to work even harder to make up the distance they'd lost. Then they heard a noise coming from up ahead. It was the puffing of a steamboat—not too large, but coming fast upon them, enough to create a wake rippling through the water.

"Uh-oh."

As the steamer began to pass them, the flatboat started to bobble in its wake. John ordered all of them to hold on to the wagon to keep it from sliding off the platform, while he jumped into the water to hold up the other side and keep it from tipping further.

"Hold on! Hold on!"

The wake was growing stronger as the steamer moved on, leaving them behind. As the wagon began to skid toward the edge of the platform, Brideen jumped into the river and worked beside John to keep it upright. The rest of them were hanging on to the other side of the cart.

"Hang on tight!"

It was very difficult to hang on to the raft while pushing it up at the same time, and it took all the effort Brideen could muster to keep her head above water. Just when she felt she couldn't hold on any longer, the wake finally began to recede, and the flat boat stabilized itself. John was able to vault himself back onto the platform, then he and Liam pulled Brideen up. Both of them were drenched and chilled to the bone. Once on the platform, they locked in a three-way embrace and cried with relief.

"How brave is my wife and your sister?"

They realized they'd have to find a spot to pull up on shore soon, so that John and Brideen could get into dry clothes. It was getting dark as Liam, Edward, and Johnny worked the sweeps to get the flatboat close to shore, where the current wasn't as strong. Up ahead they could make out a small settlement with a dock.

"We can stop over here."

"But there's no ramp for the cart."

"Too bad. We'll have to do it the hard way after all."

They pulled over and started unloading everything from the cart onto the dock—the very thing they'd hoped to avoid if they'd opted for the steam ferry. They hoped the lighter weight might enable the horses to leap onto the dock and pull up the cart. They managed with an assist from the older boys, who grabbed onto the back wheels and tugged at them.

As Brideen searched through the cargo for dry clothes, Liam made a joking comment about the ordeal.

"I guess the lesson is, figure out how you're going to get out of the water *before* you get in the water."

"That's what I tried to tell you. But no, you were in such a hurry to get across."

"What? We got over fine."

"We could've lost our entire load."

"Well, we didn't. Why are you harping on it?"

The two men argued back and forth, while an exasperated Brideen shouted them down.

"Stop it, you two. Look down! What are you standing on?"

They both looked down, mystified.

"Some dirt! What about it?"

"The soil of what state?"

The kids all laughed and shouted.

"IOWA!"

"That's right, you idiots. We've made it to Iowa, so stop fighting and start re-loading the wagon so we can get going in the morning."

* * *

Wapsi, a young warrior, and Pinicon, the daughter of the chief of a rival tribe, eloped, but were found by Pinicon's father and the other chiefs. The couple decided they would rather die than be taken back and separated. They raced to the river, clasped each other, leaped into the stream, and drowned in the swirling waters. The sorrowful Indian chief later named the stream Wapsipinicon.
  -- from *History of Buchanan County, Iowa.* by A.G. Riddle, Williams Brothers, Cleveland, 1881

West Bromwich, England, May, 1872
My dear sister Bridget,

I write with sorrowful but perhaps not surprising news. Our darling Da has at long last gone to his eternal rest in heaven. This event occurred on March fourth, and I am sorry it has taken me so long to write to you. He had suffered for a long time with chest pain and shortness of breath. The physician in Walsall, Dr. Doyle, said it was a miracle he lived as long as he had, with the lung condition he acquired during our time in the Black Country. Dr. Doyle said it was probably because Da had got out of working in the mines after only a couple of years, that if he stayed longer he would likely not have lived past the age of forty. For all that he suffered in his last years, his death was a peaceful one and we are fortunate to have had so many years with him. He is buried next to Sean Brian and in the same cemetery as our Mam. Every time I think of the three of them being together once again my tears of joy flow.

The other joy was having so many of our siblings together again. Ciaran is a young man now, working at the steel foundry and courting a lovely Welsh girl named Bryn. Mikeen and Margaret and their family came from Walsall, and our own Father Manus came from St. Peter's in Birmingham to perform the last rites, at Da's request. Luckily with the frequent horse carriage runs he was able to arrive in time. We hoped that Manus would be able to convey some news of the final resting place of our brother

Seamus back in Mayo. But in recent years, and especially since his ordination, Manus has lost contact with his fellow Ribboners in Mayo, and with so much time having passed, I doubt we will ever know. But we know our dear brother Seamus is with God, and that is all that matters.

Da never lost interest in the great events of the time, in America, or in Ireland. He was proud of the fact that Liam fought in the war that ended the great evil of slavery, and that you and John and the children did your part to prevent the enemy army from destroying your city. Among his last wishes was to send his blessings on you from heaven, and his prayer that Mother Ireland will achieve freedom within your lifetime, since she did not do so within his.

I know it must seem that I have become almost as fluent a writer as you, but it is still very difficult for me to put thoughts into words, especially in English. Fortunately our daughter Roisin is very quick and intelligent, and much of this letter is my words as dictated to her. She rarely speaks Irish anymore, which makes me sad.

I took the most remarkable trip back to Ireland some months ago. We took the steamer from Liverpool, where we landed in England all those years ago. But instead of walking or even taking a coach, we were able to take the railway to Castlebar, where we spent several days with Mikeen and Margaret. You may not know that they moved back to Ireland a year ago and live there now. You will be pleased to learn that Mikeen has acquired a concertina and is learning to play tunes on it. It is quite an undertaking to learn an instrument at his age, but he seems to have some natural ability to figure out how to pump it in and out to get the proper notes. His inspiration seems to come from an attempt to keep up with his daughter Sinead, who is learning to play the tin whistle. Inspired by her aunt an ocean away! She is getting to be a fine player, and hers is a black whistle with the maker's name "Clarke" on it, just like yours.

After our visit in Castlebar we then took another train to Westport and the coach from there to Achill Island, where I was able to visit our sister Máirín! We had not seen each other in twenty-five years, and yet she seems hardly much older and is still beautiful, as we always thought of our big sister. And just imagine! There are plans to extend the railway line all the way to Achill Sound in the coming years. So it will become even easier for us to visit. Missed, of course, will be you, darling Bridget, the third Sweeney sister who lives an ocean away.

Roisin's hand is getting tired and I think I have shared all the family news at present. I promise I will not wait so long before my next letter. God bless and watch over you and yours in America.

Your beloved sister,
Siobhan

Da! She suddenly remembered a dream about him she'd had some weeks back. He was walking down Barr Beacon, the hill outside Wednesbury where she'd met up with Manus all those years back. She was standing at the top and Da was making his way down, not climbing upward as Manus had been. Partway down the hill he'd turned and waved at her, then continued on. She'd forgotten all about it, until Siobhan's letter arrived. He was saying good-bye in the dream and she'd completely missed the significance.

She was angry with herself. She should've known. She felt terrible that she hadn't understood his parting gesture. But he'd been gone from her life for so long. What an awful thing it was, to live far away from your family, so far that you would never see them again in this lifetime. It was against nature to do such a thing, and yet so many of her countrymen and women had done so. You tell those you love that you will never forget them, but you remember them as they were when you were together. The bond grows weaker over the years, and letters can only do so much.

Da, dear Da, forgive me. Now there would be no chance to write and tell him about the paradise that was Iowa, the land of plenty, its huge farms so different from tiny plots they tilled in Ireland, a land where the gnaw of constant hunger would remain a distant childhood memory.

She was grateful for the news that he'd had a peaceful passing. But if he hadn't, if he'd suffered greatly, would Siobhan even tell her?

She would ask Father Gosker to say a special Mass for Da. That way the family could honor his passing, along with the parishioners at St. John the Evangelist, even though they never knew him in life. She was grateful that the family had been so warmly and fully embraced by the parish in the short time they'd been here. She was also grateful to be once again part of an Irish community.

She felt a sudden urge to play her tin whistle, his long-ago gift to her. Where was it? Brideen was certain she had packed it in the wagon load from Hagerstown. But they had arrived here in Buchanan County and took possession of the farmhouse on the Wapsipinicon River months ago, and she hadn't seen it since. What had she done with it? Where was it in this big, new, unfinished house? There was still so much to unpack. She had to trust it would turn up sooner or later.

She looked out the upstairs window and noticed a woman and a child, a girl about seven years old. They were near the shore of the river, digging what looked like knobbly tubers out of the ground. What could those be? They were putting the tubers in a sack, clearly planning to take them away for some use or other.

Brideen wondered if she should go out and let them know that they were on private land. From the way they were dressed she thought they might be from one of the Amish settlements a few miles north. But the Amish kept to themselves and likely wouldn't go on someone's land without permission. Before she could decide what to do, they were on their way, walking along the river, the woman carrying the sack in one hand and holding the child's hand with the other. It was just as well. They were doing no harm and Brideen knew she would feel uncomfortable suggesting that they shouldn't be on "her" land. No one would ever have done such a thing back in Mayo, where they all worked plots that belonged to a distant landlord. Still, she was curious. Who were these people, and what were those tubers they were digging up? Surely they weren't for eating.

As the family settled into farm life over the coming weeks, Brideen had to laugh at her own idyllic first impression of Iowa. This so-called "paradise" demanded backbreaking, unceasing work. The men had to be out every morning before daybreak, working the vast fields of tall corn and wheat. The potato plots required more labour than the lazy beds they tended back in Ireland. John and the elder sons worked their own fields as well as the adjoining ones of the Burns', as part of their agreement to pay for their share of the land.

Everyone had a huge meal at midday, cooked by Brideen on an open fire. She looked forward to the day when they could afford to buy one of those modern wood-burning cookstoves. But for now, she was doing her best to catch up on the farm-wife skills she'd never had a chance to develop in her youth. As a girl, she'd worked in a nail shed; as a young woman, she'd assembled pens in a factory and managed the stock in a hardware store. The one vital skill she lacked was making bread. In Hagerstown they'd bought loaves from the local bakery, but here on the farm they had to make their own. Early on she produced quite a few loaves that failed to rise, which the family dutifully but grudgingly consumed.

After the big midday meal, the men went back out to the fields. In the early weeks, Brideen sometimes went with them, eager to see and experience the land for herself. She found the cornfields had an unsettling effect on her, which she at first supposed was due to their size. They were only a few inches high now, but she'd heard that the stalks would eventually grow tall enough to get lost in. Then it occurred to her that her uneasiness came from something else: memories of the dreaded stirabout – the watery gruel of milled corn that kept them from starving back in Mayo. The thought of those terrible times sent a shudder through her, triggering a renewed rush of memories. She couldn't afford to let herself slip back into that earlier, disturbing state of mind, triggered by the image of the corpse in the doorway. She had to make it stop.

She hurried to the henhouse, greeted by the squawking of the chickens. In Ireland, they'd never raised chickens and only occasionally had eggs from trading with neighbors. Now they had a seemingly endless supply of eggs. *The hunger times are over,* she told herself. *They are in the past. Look at this magnificent land. We will never be hungry again.*

Back at the house, which was still in an unfinished state, she set herself to work, using some carpentry skills she hadn't known she had. She joked to the children that she looked forward to the day when her life no longer had anything to do with nails.

After the early weeks, life on the farm settled into a predictable rhythm, set by the days' chores. In the evenings after supper they sat around the fireplace, not minding that there still weren't enough chairs for them all. It reminded Brideen of her childhood home in Ballyhean, when they had to share stools sitting around the table. This house was so much bigger. How had they all managed to live in that tiny cottage?

She looked around the room at her children. Edward and John were nearly grown men now, and bore a more serious mien than their younger siblings—the burden, Brideen believed, of the horrors they'd experienced on the sea passage to America. She felt a wave of gratitude to God for bringing them safely to this place, their true and permanent home, and leaned over to squeeze her husband's hand. He returned the gesture, and she guessed he was feeling the same.

Not that family life was an oasis of calm. The middle boys, Thomas, William, and James, carried on a constant round of activity, sometimes teasing, sometimes arguing, sometimes wrestling one another. She'd taken to calling them her *gasradh,* as her Mam had called Brideen's quartet of raucous older brothers. They all knew that she shared a special bond with Annie, the daughter she'd waited so long for. As for Annie, she was eager for baby Margaret to grow up to be her playmate in the sea of males that made up the rest of the siblings.

The main task of the younger children was tending to the cows. They had to be milked in the early morning, and they took turns getting up at first light to carry out the chores. Brideen mostly did the afternoon milking on her own, giving the children some free time. Back in Mayo she'd been too small to do any milking herself, instead helping Mam with the buckets. She found she enjoyed the quiet, alone time, just her and the cows. One afternoon a song in Irish popped into her head, one they sang as children. It was a farmer's lament for the death of his cow, which was no small matter back in those days of hunger.

Agus oro Drumion Dubh oro ah!
Oro Drumion Dubh mhiel agrah!
Agus oro Drumion Dubh O, ochone!
Drumion Dubh dheelis go dea tu slan.

It gave her pleasure to sing in Irish, given that she rarely spoke it now, and in fact was slowly losing her memory of it—not just the words but the rhythm, the musicality of it. Edward and Johnny had spoken it as children, but the others, all born in America, never learned more than a few words. She and John used to speak Irish between themselves but gradually fell out of the habit. Now she was fully fluent in speaking, reading, and writing English, but was losing her native tongue.

As the verses inched back into her memory, Brideen kept singing and milking. At one point she looked up and noticed two people standing on the riverbank, listening to her sing. It was the same woman she'd seen weeks earlier, digging for tubers, but with her this time was an older girl, perhaps twelve or thirteen years old. They both smiled and nodded in Brideen's direction, indicating that they enjoyed her singing, and she smiled back, making a slight wave of her hand.

This time she realized the women couldn't be Amish—their heads were uncovered. From their complexions she guessed they might be from the Indian settlement a few miles past Cedar Rapids. She wondered if she should say something to them this time, when she heard angry shouts coming from behind her. It was Johnny, rushing toward the riverbank.

"What are you doing here? Get out, this is our property."

The women, startled and frightened, began to run away. Brideen ran after them, meanwhile upbraiding her son.

"What's the matter with you? Don't yell at them, that's rude."

"They're on our property."

"There's no need to treat them like that. They're doing no harm."

She caught up to the woman and tried to apologize and explain what had happened. She quickly realized the woman didn't understand what she was saying. But the girl with her clearly did.

"She doesn't speak your language," her companion said. The woman continued speaking and now the girl interpreted for her.

"My grandmother begs your forgiveness. These swan potatoes don't grow on Tama land. This is where our people used to gather them, right here on the river."

Tama? Brideen thought. Yes, that's where the Indian settlement was.

"Oh, but you're welcome to keep coming here to gather your.... Swan potatoes, you call them?"

The older woman spoke up, pointing to the tubers and saying an unfamiliar word.

"She's telling you the name for them in our language, *wapsi pinion*."

"Oh, that's the name of the river, too. We were told that there was a legend about two lovers named Wapsi and Pinicon who drowned in the river."

The girl told her grandmother what Brideen had said. They both started to giggle.

"My grandmother says that story is not from our people."

"Oh? Where does it come from?"

The girl started to giggle again, then collected herself.

"From white people."

"Oh, I see," Brideen said. But she didn't see. The story came from a book about Buchanan County. Didn't that mean it was true? Confused and embarrassed, she apologized for her son's behavior.

"You're welcome to come back. Anytime. Really."

The pair started to make their way along the riverbank and out to the road.

"Thank you," the girl called back. "We enjoyed your singing."

* * *

THE NEW PURCHASE: The Whites are now in full possession of the land recently ceded to the U.S. by the Indians in Iowa territory. Nearly all the tracts are under claim and to some of the more valuable, there are conflicting claims. The rush of population has been immense. It is estimated that the number of people who have already located themselves on the new lands is near eighty thousand.

-- from an 1843 newspaper article about the land rush for the Black Hawk Tract, quoted in the Iowa Historic Indian Location Database (HILD) of the Office of the State Archaeologist, University of Iowa.

"We're going to a *ceili*!"

Annie and Johnny jumped up and down with excitement when they heard the news. The whole family would be going to the *ceili* down in Washington County. It would be their first real Irish gathering since they'd left Baltimore.

"Washington's quite a ways downstate," their father pointed out. "It'll take a couple of hours to get there in the wagon."

"It'll be worth it!" Brideen insisted. "They'll play jigs and reels and there'll be some set dancing. We haven't had a chance to do that in years."

John Burns said his elderly father Seamus was eager to go and asked if the Sweeneys would take him in their wagon. They stopped at his farm near the town of Quasqueton or Quasky, as the locals called it. Brideen hoped to find out more about the nearby Indian community, so she made sure to sit next to him. Seamus Burns had lived in Quasky for many years and knew a great deal about this part of Iowa.

"They're the Fox tribe but they call themselves the Red Earth People, or Meskwaki in their language. There's a few hundred of them living by Tama. They're the only Indians left in Iowa."

When Brideen asked why that was, Seamus explained that more than twenty years earlier, all the tribes, including the Sauk and the Pottawatomi, were ordered to leave Iowa territory and move to reserves set aside for them in Kansas. The government took possession of the land, put it under the jurisdiction of the state of Iowa, and started selling off plots for farming.

"That's when whites started to move in. There was even a land rush in this part of the state. Folks crossed the river and lay claim to some of the best farmland."

"So the government just took their land and gave it away for free?"

"That's about right. But those Fox people, they're a wily bunch," Seamus continued. "They only pretended to leave. Or they'd leave for a while and keep coming back. They figured out that they'd be in a stronger position if they got some land of their own. They got a farmer named Isaac Butler to sell them eighty acres over near Tama, and they're still there."

"Why didn't the other tribes do that too?"

Seamus explained that Indian tribes were forbidden to own land in the United States. But the governor at the time was sympathetic to the Meskwaki and found a way around the ban. He had to face the wrath of some large farm owners, who were doing their best to prevent the sale.

"Those folks just didn't want Indians living next to their farms. But they lost that battle. It's been over ten years now, and most people who live nearby consider them good neighbors. Not that there's much contact. They keep pretty much to themselves."

"There's a woman who's come to our place a few times with her daughters. They go to the riverbank and dig for some kind of tuber. They call them swan potatoes."

"Yep, that stretch of the Wapsi is prime territory for the Meskwaki. They used to come year after year, spend the whole summer hunting and fishing and gathering wild plants."

"You mean, they used to live right on our farm?"

"Well, for part of the year, yes. They build these grass huts they call wickiups. In the fall they'd move on to their winter grounds. I'm not sure where those were."

"It sounds like what the Irish used to do, like our family did when we went to the booley huts on Achill. We'd spend the summer there to let the cattle graze on fresh grass, and we girls would milk them and make cheese to send back to our families."

"Those old ways died out in Armagh before my time, but my late wife, who hailed from County Clare, she used to talk about the booleying times."

"Maybe we're not so different from them. Their land got taken away, just like what happened to us back in Mayo. The landlord sent men to throw us out in the middle of the night and tore our cabin apart with crowbars."

Seamus had come to America well before Brideen, and he began to pepper her with questions about how they managed during the hunger times. As always, she was reluctant to revisit that time and was relieved when they arrived at the *ceili*. As she approached the hall, all those painful thoughts were swept away by the spirited rhythms of the music. The high-ceilinged barn was full of people, and a huge circle dance was just finishing up. As the band's last notes sounded, the dancers all ran into the center of the circle to clap and cheer. Then lines began to form for a set dance, and as the band started up, Brideen recognized *The Siege of Ennis*, one of the most popular dance tunes.

Set dance tunes were long, with multiple sections, and she'd never learned to play any of them. Nor had she and John had the chance to learn the dance figures, so they could only watch as Seamus scurried off with a partner. Still, it was a joy just watching the dancers as they did pass-throughs and formed right- and left-hand stars. After the set dance, the band let loose on a fast free-dance reel. It was Brideen's beloved *An Giolla Ruadh,* "The Red-Haired Boy"! She was overjoyed to hear it, but it also made her ache to play along with the musicians.

On the ride home, they were still exhilarated from the *ceili*. They'd been far from the bosom of the Irish community during their time in Hagerstown, and now they'd recaptured it right here in Iowa. Seamus promised to teach the children some of the dance steps, but it was the prospect of playing the music that Brideen was focussed on. She was determined that, sometime in the near future, there would be a *ceili* in Buchanan County, for which Brideen and her musical offspring would provide the music. She'd get the boys practicing jigs and reels on their instruments, and learning a couple of longer tunes to play for the set dances.

She still hadn't managed to locate her tin whistle, and was about to give up, figuring it must have fallen out when they unpacked the wagon one of those times on the journey. Here in

America, she'd learned, there were things called mail-order catalogues, where you could buy something and have it delivered to the local post office. She'd seen a whistle in a catalogue at the general store in Independence, with the same name, Clarke, as her lost one, and decided that next trip to town she'd order one. But once James was unrolling a pair of pants and something fell out, making a clanging noise.

It was her whistle! Just when she'd given up ever finding it!

* * *

"The undersigned citizens of Tama County State of Iowa respectfully ask that the Sacs and Foxes Musquakie Indians living in this County may be removed from said county to some other locality for the reason that they are a great annoyance to the white population in their vicinity and that their ponies are constantly breaking into the fields of the surrounding farmers, and that in the opinion of your petitioners it would be vastly for the benefit of the Indians to remove them to their reservation. That in the case their true interests could be much better served. The presence of these Indians here has become almost intolerable to the white citizens."
-- Petition to the U.S. Secretary of War. May 14, 1878

It wasn't easy getting the boys to practice the tunes. And finding time in between their farm chores was a challenge. But Brideen was determined that a *ceili* would be held in Buchanan County and that her family would provide the music: Thomas on fiddle, Edward on banjo, and herself on tin whistle. William and James were competing with one another to learn the concertina, but neither would be ready to play for an audience. As for Annie, she wanted to learn to play *something* but was still too young to make a decision, much less to start learning.

They had the perfect space for the *ceili*—the big barn on John Burns' farm. The only detail left for Brideen was to find someone to call the dances. She tried to locate the person who'd filled that role at the *ceili* in Washington County, but had no luck.

Finally things fell into place. A young Irish immigrant named Norah, who worked as a domestic for a well-off family in Dubuque, came forward just before the date set for the *ceili* and said she knew how to teach hornpipe and jig steps, and call *The Walls of Limerick* and *The Siege of Ennis.* Teaching two set dances would take up more than half the evening, and jigs and free dances would fill the rest. Brideen was relieved and excited. Now she just had to make sure her musicians were up to the task.

"The main thing," she told her sons, "is don't stop playing, no matter what. If you mess up a few notes, just keep strumming or bowing until you catch up to the other players. The tunes come around again, so you can always get back on the melody."

On the night of the *ceili,* Burns' barn filled up quickly. There were local people as well as many from the nearby counties. Brideen got the boys playing some easy hornpipes right away so they'd get over their nervousness. They got through the dance without too many stumbles, then Norah taught steps to *Red-Haired Boy.* After that they played a waltz, *Southwind,* and then Thomas launched into the opening notes of *Waiting for the Federals,* one of the first tunes he'd learned from Paddy O'Flaherty back in Hagerstown. Brideen was pleased that her son had kept playing the tune over the years. It was well-known in America as a commemoration of the Union victory in the Civil War, though in her mind it still bore the name of an Irishman named Hoban.

Lively conversation filled the hall during the break, and Brideen noticed a cluster of people gathered around a fellow holding some sheets of paper. She drew closer to listen to what he was saying—something about a petition he was seeking people to sign. Her ears perked up when she heard the word "Meskwaki". She had trouble hearing through the din in the hall, but she picked up other phrases as he read from the petition, "They are peaceable, quiet, honest and law-abiding people... It would be a great injustice to remove the Meskwaki from their lands..."

Remove? It suddenly occurred to Brideen that she hadn't seen the Meskwaki woman gathering swan potatoes by the river for some time. Why? Had the rich landowners finally won their fight to force the Meskwaki off their land? The land they bought and paid for?

The man finished reading and put the papers and a pen on a table for those who wanted to sign. For those who couldn't write, he assured them it would be fine if he wrote their names and they added an "X" next to it, and several did.

Brideen introduced herself to the man.

"Good to meet you," he replied, shaking her hand. "Karl Harbach. I have a farm over in Black Hawk County. I hope you don't mind me being here talking about the petition. Dances are where you always find a lot of people."

"I don't mind a bit," she replied. "What's this about? Have the Meskwaki tribe been forced to leave their land?"

"Not yet," he replied. "But some of the big landowners want the government to send them to the reservation in Kansas."

"How can they do that? I thought they owned that land."

"They do, but it may not matter. Some of those landowners tried this before, and this time they might succeed. They're trying to get a law passed in Washington, ordering the state of Iowa to remove them."

"That's not fair!"

"You're right, Ma'am. That's why we started this petition."

"They should leave those poor people in peace," she said as she added her name.

Karl Harbach thanked her and turned to a couple waiting to sign.

"Excuse me, Mr. Harbach. There's something I want to ask: Do you know any of the people in the settlement there? There's a woman I've met. She's come to our farm to gather wild plants, but

I haven't seen her for quite a while. I don't know her name, but she's older than I am, has granddaughters who come with her."

He pondered a moment, then shook his head.

"Wish I could help you out. I've only dealt with the menfolk."

Brideen thanked him and wished him good luck with the petition.

"Let us know how it turns out."

"I'm sure something will show up in the Waterloo paper."

She gathered up her musician sons to resume playing for the dancers. The rest of the evening was a great success, and there were many expressions of gratitude and hope that there would be more *ceili* dances in Burns' barn. As Brideen and the rest of the family prepared to walk across the field to their house, she heard Liam calling out to her.

"Go on without me, Brid. I'll be along later."

He was lifting someone up onto the seat of the wagon. It was Norah, the dance caller. Clearly, Liam intended to drive her back to the house in Dubuque, a distance of over sixty miles. He wouldn't make it back till the middle of the night.

She heard her husband's voice behind her.

"I know what you're thinking, Brid."

"Oh, you do, do ye?"

"You're thinking it's time that restless brother of yours settled down and got himself a wife."

She pushed him playfully.

"Oh, shush now! Ye know it's bad luck to say a thing like that out loud! It could curse the whole idea."

* * *

"We, the undersigned citizens of Tama Co. Iowa: Would respectfully remonstrate against the removal of the Sac and Fox Indians now residing in Tama Co.: As we believe that it would be an act of great injustice to them and a breach of faith on our part,

to remove them without their consent, from their own lands which they have purchased from time to time, of citizens adjoining them paying the full value of the same, with their own money, paying as high as $31.25 per acre and having purchased in all six hundred and ninety two acres as shown by report from your office, and they are now paying taxes on the same and were permitted to locate here by an act of the Legislature of the State of Iowa in the of 1856. These Indians are a peaceful, quiet, honest and law abiding people and compare favorably in their obedience to the laws with the same location here which, we believe would be retarded by their removal to the Indian Territory... We would earnestly request that they be permitted as an act of justice and good faith to remain on their lands in Tama County which we believe they hold by every right."

-- Petition to Commissioner of Indian Affairs, 1878 in Letters Received by the Office of Indian Affairs, Sac and Fox Agency 1824-1880. National Archives

* * *

"Siobhan! It's coming right at me! Siobhan!

Brideen was still screaming when she woke up from the dream. She looked over at the other side of the bed, where John was sound asleep. Her husband's ability to sleep through the loudest noise never ceased to amaze her. But she was grateful he hadn't heard this time. What would he have made of her calling for her sister, thousands of miles and an ocean away? She lay back down and closed her eyes.

It was still there. She could see it: the long metal bar with the curved end. Coming straight for her head, her face, her eye... She'd heard about this. A waking dream, one that you can't get out of, that keeps going even after you open your eyes...

She shut her eyes and shook her head vigorously to make the dream vanish. It did, though the sounds were still deep in her head—the men shouting, Siobhan screaming, Mam's voice, "Please don't..."

Finally the voices receded, and she drifted back to sleep. A different dream commenced, a quieter one. The Meskwaki woman was there—not crouched over digging for swan potatoes, as Brideen had usually seen her, but standing still, almost motionless, on the riverbank. Then another figure appeared, a very tall Black man, wearing a formal jacket and waistcoat. It was Frederick Douglass. He nodded to the Meskwaki woman, but neither of them said anything.

When she awoke in the morning, Brideen was mystified by the incongruous figure of Douglass standing on the riverbank. Why was he there? Why was the great orator silent? Then she recalled the words from his speech in Baltimore: "You can always do more."

Do more. Do more.

Signing the petition wasn't enough. Not nearly enough. She had to do more. Write a letter. A letter in her own words.

But what to say? And to whom?

At the *ceili*, Karl Harbach had said the big landowners were trying to get "a law passed in Washington". She figured that must mean the Congress, the governing body. But a letter had to be addressed to an individual, not just to "Congress". There was a name she'd seen many times in the newspaper: "Allison". He was an important man, a Senator who represented the people of Iowa. Would he be dealing with this matter, in some one way or another? Should she address her letter to him? To "Senator Allison," without his given name?

She felt foolish. Why would a U.S. Senator listen to a farm woman? Several times she started to write, kept putting it aside, then coming back to it. She was feeling such inner turmoil that she decided the only way to calm herself was to write the thing, to obey the dream's command to "do more," even if she made a fool of herself.

"Dear Senator Allison," she wrote. "I write this letter to ask for your help to prevent a terrible injustice. I live with my husband and children on a farm in Buchanan County. Our farm is not far from the land where the Meskwaki people live. Some people in Iowa do not want the Meskwaki living near them, and have asked the government to force them to leave. I do not believe it would be right for the government to do this, and my family and many of my neighbors agree with me.

"Let me tell you my own story and why I believe this is unfair. I was born in Ireland, where my family grew potatoes on a small plot. Like most of our neighbors, we were tenant farmers, and paid rent to the owner of the land. We always paid our landlord on time, until the black blot ruined the potato crop and we had nothing to eat and neither did anyone else. One night men came without warning and turned us out of our home. They tore it down with crowbars. I was nine years old. It was the most terrible thing that ever happened to me. That night still haunts my dreams.

"My family did not own our land but what our landlord did to us was cruel. We were poor and had nowhere to go. We are grateful to this great country for taking us in, and allowing us to earn a living by the sweat of our brow.

"But turning out the Meskwaki would be even more unjust than what happened to us. They own their land, they paid for it many years ago. They should be left in peace. I do not want the Meskwaki children to go through what my family went through. I hear you are a good man and that you represent the people of Iowa honestly and fairly. Thank you for reading my letter.

Yours very truly,

Bridget McDonnell, farm wife"

Now she had to get it to Washington. And quickly. She got Johnny to drive her into Independence. He drove the wagon faster than she did. She had him stop at the Post Office and went inside. A woman was working behind the service window. Brideen bid her good-day and held up the letter.

"I want to send this to Senator Allison in Washington, D.C."

"Fine," said the woman. "You need an envelope."

"Oh. I forgot to bring one."

"Here." The woman slid a blank envelope under the glass.

Brideen thanked her, folded the letter neatly, and stuffed it in the envelope.

After a moment, the woman said, "Aren't you going to address it?"

She was a bit flustered. "I'm not sure how to do that...."

"Here, I'll do it for you."

The woman took the envelope and wrote on the front with an ink pen.

Brideen thanked her again. "You're very kind."

"Now the last thing you need to do..."

"Of course, it needs a stamp, doesn't it?" Brideen interrupted. She'd mailed things many times when she worked at the hardware in Hagerstown. But her nerves were still jangly.

She gave the woman three cents and watched as she applied the stamp and dropped the letter in a canvas bag under the counter.

"So, it'll get to Senator Allison's in Washington, then?"

"Yes, Ma'am. 'Nor rain, nor snow, nor sleet, nor hail, can e'er defeat the U.S. Mail.' That's what we say around here."

* * *

IN THE SENATE OF THE UNITED STATES, January 14, 1895 – Referred to the Committee on Indian Affairs. MR. ALLISON presented the following Memorial on behalf of the Sac and Fox Indians of the Mississippi: "Purchase of Land for Home in Iowa. On July 13, 1857 they purchased their first tract of 80 acres of land from a citizen of the United States, paying therefore

$1,000 and taking a deed therefore in trust to the then governor of the State of Iowa.",

-- U.S. National Archives

Weeks went by. There was no news, nothing in the Waterloo *Courier.* One day walking over the bridge in Independence, Brideen heard a voice behind her.

"Mrs. McDonnell. Is that you?"

She turned around. It was Karl Harbach, the man with the petition.

"Mr. Harbach!"

"It's good to see you again, Ma'am."

"And you as well. I've been wondering about the results of your petition. I've been watching the newspaper but I haven't seen a thing about it."

"Well, that's because there was nothing to report. Nothing happened."

"What do you mean?"

"The motion to remove was approved by the House..."

"House....?"

"...Of representatives, which wasn't surprising. Then it had to go to the Senate. And that's where nothing happened. It didn't come forward for a vote."

"Why?"

"We have no idea."

"So what happens then?"

"That's just it. Nothing."

"Is that good news?"

"It would've been better if the measure had been voted down completely. But 'twould be foolish to look a gift horse in the mouth. So yes, it means the Meskwaki can stay on their land in Tama, at least until the next time some rich landowner objects. After this, I don't think they'll have much luck."

"So you have no idea what happened?"

"Some people think Senator Allison might have had something to do with it. He's a big man in the government, been the head of a lot of committees, including Indian Affairs. Who knows? Maybe he just took it off the docket."

"Why would he do that?"

Harbach shrugged.

"It's politics, Ma'am. Politics."

Brideen wondered if her letter could have made the difference. But she was too shy to mention it.

"That is such good news, Mr. Harbach. You should be proud. Through your efforts an injustice has been prevented."

"It wasn't me, Mrs. McDonnell. It was all the good people who signed my petition. And you were one of the first. I should be thanking you."

Brideen smiled her appreciation as they said their good-byes and headed in opposite directions over the bridge.

"Wait, Mrs. McDonnell. There's something else."

"Oh?"

"You asked if I could find out who it was that came to your farm to pick those tubers. When I took the petition to the Settlement there was a young woman there—a very impressive person who spoke excellent English. She goes to the University in Iowa City. We got to talking and she remembered going to your farm with her grandmother. She said you were very welcoming and told them they could come back to get some more any time they wanted. The young woman said those swan potatoes weren't the tastiest, but picking them meant a great deal to her grandmother, her *nōhkometha,* she called her. Reminded her of her childhood."

"That's so good to know, Mr. Harbach. How is her... what is the word? *Nōhkometha?*"

"Oh, she passed away some months ago. As I understand it, she lived out the fullness of her days."

* * *

Mr. Speaker, and gentlemen of the House of Representatives, the remedy that we propose for the state of affairs in Ireland is an alteration of the land tenure prevailing there. We propose to imitate the example of Prussia and of other Continental countries where the feudal tenure has been tried, found wanting, and abandoned; and we also propose to make or give an opportunity to every tenant occupying a farm in Ireland to become the owner of his own farm... It has been abundantly proved, that terrible suffering and constant poverty are inflicted upon millions of the population of Ireland, then we may reasonably require from the Legislature that... they should terminate the system of ownership of the soil by the few in Ireland and replace it by one giving the ownership of the soil to the many.

    -- from Charles Stewart Parnell's Speech to the United States Congress, Feb. 2, 1880, U.S. National Archives.

Brideen accosted John as he was coming in from the fields.

"Parnell is coming to Iowa!"

"Charles Parnell? What are you on about, woman?"

"It says so right here in the *Daily Herald*. He's going to Washington to address the United States Congress in February, but first he'll be coming to Iowa and he'll be making stops at Dubuque and Davenport."

"Now why would the great Charles Parnell come all the way to Iowa?"

"'Cause there's so many Irish here, don't ye know? He's raising money for the Land League. We can go see him in the flesh, John!"

Brideen and Liam had continued to follow the news out of Ireland, while John hadn't shown much interest. He had grown cynical about the possibilities of meaningful change in Ireland, but that began to change when he heard about the Land League, an organization working for the reform of the country's landlord system. It was led by Michael Davitt, the son of an evicted tenant farmer and a member of the Fenian Brotherhood, and Charles Stewart Parnell, who'd been elected to the British Parliament as leader of the Irish Home Rule Party. Parnell's victory had revived the Irish independence struggle, and the newspapers started referring to him as the "uncrowned King of Ireland". Parnell's success also helped to revive John's fundamental belief in land reform that dated back his days in the Birmingham radical movements.

"He actually believes that land should be owned by the many, not the few," John would say of Parnell. "That's what will make Ireland her own country, at long last."

They made plans to go to Dubuque for the great man's arrival—Brideen, John, their children, along with Liam and Norah, who had recently announced their engagement. The *ceili* dances in Burns' barn had become wildly popular, and the family band had developed into excellent musicians. But city officials in Dubuque didn't want a *ceili* band, they wanted a big marching band for the occasion. Brideen suggested to the officials that Parnell also be greeted with a rendition of a true Irish song. Despite the large Irish population of Dubuque, none of the city leaders were Irish, but they gave her approval, with no idea what she actually had in mind.

On the big day, everything went off as planned. A marching band preceded Parnell's carriage through the city, followed by an enthusiastic crowd. When the parade arrived at the courthouse, the great man emerged from his carriage to cheers and a cannon shot. As he approached the courthouse steps Brideen raised her hand, calling for quiet. Amazingly, everyone obeyed as the small choir she'd assembled began to sing, in the old unaccompanied style, one of the oldest of Irish ballads:

Óró 'Sé do bheatha 'bhaile / Óró 'Sé do bheatha 'bhaile / Óró 'Sé do bheatha 'bhaile,
Anois ar theacht an tsamhraidh!

It was a song Brideen recalled her Aunt Mary singing during booley times, and she was glad she remembered the words. Some of the older people in the crowd knew it, too, and began to sing along. Brideen could see that Parnell himself was greatly moved to hear the old song of welcome, little known here in America, but still strong in Ireland.

As the final chorus ended, tears rolled down her cheeks, but when she looked over at John, she was surprised to seel that he too was weeping. He leaned over and whispered in her ear:

"He gives me hope that I will see a free Ireland in my lifetime."

Chapter 14: THE PASSING

Go into the length and breadth of the world, ransack the literature of all countries, find, if you can, a single voice, a single book, find, I would almost say, as much as a single newspaper article... in which the conduct of England towards Ireland is anywhere treated except with profound and bitter condemnation. Are these the traditions by which we are exhorted to stand? No; they are a sad exception to the glory of our country. They are a broad and black blot upon the pages of its history; and what we want to do is to stand by the traditions of which we are the heirs in all matters except our relations with Ireland, and to make our relations with Ireland to conform to the other traditions of our country... That will be a boon to us in respect of honour, no less than a boon to her in respect of happiness, prosperity, and peace.

-- from a speech by William Ewart Gladstone MP, British Prime Minister, to the House of Commons on Home Rule for Ireland, given on 7 June 1886

It was more than a decade since John, Brideen, and their family had arrived at the plot of land four miles west of the town of Independence, and it had taken most of that time to pay off their debt to John Burns and his father. But after clearing the land, constructing a farmhouse and outbuildings, season after season of planting, cultivating and harvesting, they became the rightful owners of a highly productive farm. There were times when John shook his head in disbelief.

"Here I am, once a poor, landless Irishman, now a landowner."

Brideen nodded but left her own thought unsaid: *We, who were starving, now have food in abundance.*

In recent years farming was becoming a more complex operation, and even John was coming around to what he called "newfangled" methods. His sons talked him into investing in a two-horse plow with a seat for the driver.

"Think of it," Edward told his father. "All those years of walking behind the plow, bending over to hoe the weeds, and now you can work sitting down!"

Changes were even more marked with their cattle and dairy cows. Butter was no longer made on site but at a large separator plant, to which the milk had to be hauled by cart. Brideen still preferred to churn butter for their own household by hand.

"What else can I do?" she'd say, laughing. "Don't I owe my very life to a butter churn?" She had no memory of the incident herself, but the story of how she was saved from being swept away by the great storm had become an unshakeable part of Sweeney family lore. Now she was passing it down to her own offspring.

By now all Brideen and John's sons had grown into adulthood and, after years of working the farm, were embarking on their own lives. John followed the traditional Irish practice of passing on a parcel of his land to his eldest son, Edward. But he was reluctant to further subdivide among his other sons, the practice that had caused so many problems through Irish history. John hoped that his second-born son would stay and eventually inherit the family farm. But Johnny wasn't happy about having to wait for his own farm. He decided he would head west to Arizona territory, where there was money to be made in silver and copper mining. He was the first one of the family to leave home, and his parents hoped it wouldn't be for good.

"Maybe you'll earn enough to come back and buy land in Iowa," Brideen told him. "They say there's still some good farmland in Fayette County."

Thomas had taken a job managing a store in Waterloo, and he seemed content. William and James were still at home and between them were running the farm, though Brideen could see that William was a restless soul, like his namesake uncle. Still at home too were the youngest, Annie and Margaret, but not for long. Annie was already engaged to be married to John Diggins, who had a farm near Winthrop, east of Independence, and Margaret was being courted by a young fellow named John Berne.

John spent less and less time in the fields. He had developed a persistent cough, and Brideen was worried. He'd smoked a pipe since early adulthood, and as he got older and more sedentary he smoked even more.

"That pipe's never far from your lips, and it's not helping that cough of yours," Brideen would tell him, and he'd agree, but without changing his habits in the least.

He was also becoming more and more focused on the political situation in Ireland. He followed the news from the homeland, and his newfound devotion to Parnell reminded her of Da's for the Liberator. He was excited when news came that Parnell's party won the balance of power in the British Parliament, and that he'd managed to convince Prime Minister William Gladstone to support Home Rule for Ireland.

"Gladstone himself is going to introduce the bill. It's going to happen. Ireland is going to be a free country. It's only a matter of time now."

His offspring listened politely to his enthusiastic outbursts, but having grown up in America, they weren't that interested in Irish politics and the struggle for home rule. The exception in the household was Liam, whose Fenian views had never diminished. He wanted to be part of the movement again, and he and Norah began to talk seriously about moving back to Ireland.

In the end, Gladstone's party was split on the issue, and the Bill was defeated by three hundred and forty-one to three hundred and eleven in June 1886. It was a bitter pill to swallow, but Parnell vowed they'd re-introduce the Home Rule bill and keep on until they won. John was optimistic, but with all the times he'd spoken of a free Ireland "in my lifetime", Brideen feared his time might be running out.

* * *

Although not unexpected the announcement of the death of John McDonnell on Thursday last was greeted with unaffected sorrow by all who knew him. He was born in the County Mayo Ireland in 1839. In 1860 he came to the United States and settled in Baltimore, Md. After a residence of eleven years in that city, he removed to Buchanan County in 1871 and purchased a farm four miles west of the city where he resided ever since. He was one of those quiet, unobtrusive citizens who move through life with but little if any friction. In every relation of life he aimed to do his duty, and success attended his efforts. The deceased had many reasons to be thankful. He had for a life partner a lady of strong character, a helpmate indeed, and his children, seven in number, emulating his example, proved to him a source of solace and comfort in his advancing years... To the bereaved widow and stricken children, the community extends its only solace, sympathy. The funeral occurred on Saturday, and was one of the largest ever seen in Buchanan County, over one hundred conveyances being in line. At St. John's Church, Father O'Dowd paid a touching tribute to the memory of the deceased.

-- Waterloo *Courier,* 18 April, 1894

There was a Wake at the farmhouse the night before the funeral. Only the Irish neighbors from Buchanan and the surrounding counties were invited, and all were sworn to secrecy, to keep Father O'Dowd from finding out about it. The Catholic hierarchy in America disapproved of the old-style Irish wakes, and not just because they were invariably occasions of heavy drinking. It was the rituals associated with the old pagan ways that concerned them. Back in Ireland the church tried to discourage the use of Holy Wells for worship, but even they knew the Wake was so embedded in the culture there was no point trying to ban it.

John's body was in a casket on the dining table, the only surface in the house big enough to accommodate it. Brideen and the neighboring women had washed the body and dressed it in

John's finest clothes. Annie and Margaret went through the house, making the various preparations as directed by their mother. They closed all the curtains, except for the window nearest the casket, to allow the deceased's soul clear passage to heaven. Margaret also covered the one mirror in the house, to keep out unwelcome spirits. A candle was placed at John's head, to light the way, and a pair of shoes at his feet, for the journey to the other world.

Next to the casket Brideen placed his clay pipe and a jug of whiskey, into which the male mourners would dip the pipe and take a puff. She found this ritual distressing because she firmly believed that John's heavy pipe-smoking had hastened his death. But she knew she had to bow to tradition. The mourners would expect it to be part of the Wake. In fact, when the tobacco in the pipe had nearly burned down, Brideen surprised everyone by picking it up, dipping it in the whiskey, and taking a draw of it herself. It was a gesture of defiance, aimed not at the men present, but at John himself.

"What did I tell ye, stubborn man?" she said through angry tears. "Ye wouldn't listen."

After that the women's keening started up, and then the drinking and eating and singing and storytelling went on far into the night. It was the way John would have wanted it

In the morning, they had to drag themselves off to St. John's for the Requiem mass, a solemn affair with Latin chants, then off to the cemetery at the north end of the city, where the Wapsipinicon River widens out. The children all watched to see how their mother would react as the casket was lowered into the freshly-dug grave.

For days, all her attention had gone to the arrangements, the preparations, the details, and now it was over. Everything was done. She was free to give vent to her feelings. But Brideen was stoic, showing nothing, even as the last shovelfuls of dirt were tossed onto the lid of the casket. It only began to hit her when the line of carriages started exiting the cemetery. All these weeks she knew John was dying but she never gave a thought to what life would be like with him gone.

For the next few days she threw herself into chores around the farm. Annie was concerned about her mother and tried to get her to take it easy and rest, but Brideen wouldn't hear of it. Not only that, she badgered her sons to get back out into the fields.

"Too much has gone undone these past days. Those turnips aren't going to plant themselves."

One day she was milking the cows, and noticed that one of them, Jenny, seemed skittish, much more so than usual. She was expecting her first calf, and Brideen wondered whether something was amiss with the pregnancy. She'd have to get John to examine Jenny, to see how far along she was. He was always much better with the young cows than... *Oh, wait, he's...* For a few moments, she'd completely forgotten. For a few moments, it was like none of it had happened. But it soon flooded back: *John died. Last week. He's gone. My husband is gone.* The lapse of memory had brought her a moment of relief, of happiness, even. But then it returned, and she found herself staring back into the abyss.

How would she bear it? Living the rest of her life? How could she bear to go on? She whispered a prayer. *Holy Mary, Mother of God, please send your bountiful grace and free me from this despair. I pray you. Please.*

She thought she heard a rustling in the barn. When she looked around there was no one there. A long-forgotten memory surfaced: That day on the barge from Birmingham, when she and John sang the chorus of *Peigin is Peadar.* And laughed about the bearded baby till their sides ached.

Ó a hó a, hó a óa.

Without conscious effort on her part, the notes and syllables began to emerge from her body...

Ó a hó, a stóirín mo chroí.

...drawn out by another voice. He was right there with her. Singing. She couldn't hear his voice, but she could feel his presence, their voices joining. It was the feeling of rightness, of something missing put back in its place, just like it was on that day so many years ago.

Then slowly, the feeling faded. She had a sense of him slipping away. She felt a burst of joy, a feeling of deep gratitude. She knew he was rising to join the blessed souls of the departed.

John was with the angels now.

Chapter 15: THE LAST MOVE

There is no instrument in the history of music which has attracted so much attention as the Pianola. It has revolutionized formerly accepted pianistic standards and has made possible *that what was considered* impossible, *namely artistic piano playing, irrespective of musical training... the Pianola performs that part of the playing that was formerly allotted to the human fingers!*

-- from a 1906 Aeolian Company advertisement, source: Wikipedia

Near the end of her first year of widowhood, Brideen's spirits were not much improved. Try as she might to put on a brave face, her children could tell she wasn't herself. They were concerned, though for the most part, her sons considered her melancholy normal, something that arose from the loss of her husband, nothing to be done about it. Annie and Margaret disagreed. They believed that something could be done, had to be done. They began to talk about persuading her to move to Waterloo to live with Margaret and her now-husband John Berne.

"She's lonely out there on the farm. She doesn't see anyone but James and William, and they're out in the fields from dawn to dusk."

Margaret agreed. "She's too isolated. She needs to see people."

As they expected, when they put the idea to Brideen, she brushed it away.

"Why would I want to move to the city?"

"Because there's people there," Margaret shot back. "Out here you don't talk to anyone from one week to the next, except when we come to visit."

"Well, keep on doing that, and I'll be just fine."

The sisters let the idea drop, knowing there was no point trying to persuade their mother to do anything she didn't want to do.

But when Margaret dropped by the farm a few days later, she was surprised to hear a comment from her mother.

"Maybe you're right."

"About what?"

"It's true, you only come by here once or twice a week. It's not enough."

Margaret was flustered, ready to head off her mother's anger and promise to come more often, but Brideen cut her off.

"Where would I live?"

"What do you mean?"

"In Waterloo. Where would I live?"

"Why, you'd live with John and me, of course. We have plenty of room."

"What about when you start having babies?"

"We'll still have plenty of room. We have a big house. Why? Are you going to do what Annie and I suggested?"

"I'm thinking about it. I don't know yet."

Margaret knew better than to push Brideen. But "thinking about it" was more than she expected from her mother. She had an idea.

"Actually, there's an event coming up I think you might enjoy. You could just come to town for the day and get a feel for what it might be like. John could come pick you up in the morning and bring you back here after supper."

"An event? What kind of event?"

"Oh, some neighbors have invited people to come see their new piano."

"Why would I go to someone's house to see their piano?"

"It's a different kind of piano, Mother. It'll be worth it, you'll see."

"Fine," Brideen agreed. "But this doesn't mean I've agreed to anything."

"Oh, I know, Mama," Margaret assured her.

On the appointed day John came to fetch her. When they got to Waterloo, Margaret came out and got in the wagon beside her mother. They drove a short distance outside the city, past a sign that read "Cedar Falls", and soon turned onto a street with a number of large, fine-looking houses. John parked the buggy in front of one that, to Brideen, looked the size of a mansion. At the door, they were greeted by a servant and ushered into a large, high-ceiled room where a number of people were already gathered. Against one wall was a piano, a handsome upright, clearly brand-new, but Brideen couldn't see anything special about it. And just who was going to be playing it? She wondered. There wasn't a bench or chair for the player to sit on.

Soon a woman entered the room and went to greet several of the guests.

"That's Mrs. Augustus Smith," Margaret whispered to Brideen. "She's the wife of the Mayor of Cedar Falls. This is their house." She was on the verge of telling Brideen more about them when their hostess broke in, announcing with a flourish

"And now, ladies and gentlemen, I present to you.... The Pianola!"

The room quickly filled with some spirited, fast-paced music. Brideen looked around in utter confusion. Where was the music coming from? Then she noticed that the keys on the piano were moving up and down on their own. No human hand was in sight.

The piano was *playing itself!*

"See why I wanted you to come?" Margaret said. "It's called a Pianola. It's the newest thing."

"But... But how?" Brideen sputtered.

Margaret explained that air pressure was driving a paper roll with small holes punched into it that directed the hammers to strike the keys. Brideen had no idea what she was talking about, and her attention wandered back to the music itself.

"And what is that song it's playing? It reminds me of a jig."

"It's a type of dance music, called "Ragtime". The young people love it. But that reminds me..."

As the Pianola wound down to silence, the audience clapped. Margaret went over to confer with the hostess, who directed a servant to replace the paper roll with another one. As he did so, Margaret went back beside Brideen.

"I put in a special request for you."

"You shouldn't have," Brideen protested. "I don't want a fuss. I'll enjoy anything it plays."

Margaret smiled.

"Just you wait."

The Pianola geared up again, and a tune burst forth. Brideen looked at Margaret in wonder. She knew the tune, but couldn't quite name it, hearing it played on this unfamiliar instrument. Then it came to her.

"It's *Sí Bheag, Sí Mhór*!"

Brideen was overcome. It had been so long since the *ceili* days in Buchanan County, so long since she'd played or even heard the old Irish music she loved so much. When the tune was over, she turned to Margaret, eyes brimming with tears.

"I don't understand. How could you possibly find it....?"

"It was easy, Mother. On the invitation, Mrs. Smith said we should each ask for a piece of music we'd like to hear, and she would send away to the Pianola company for it. They turned out to have lots of the old Irish tunes."

Later, on the way home, Brideen asked a question.

"If I move to your house, will I be allowed to play my whistle?"

"Why, of course, Mother. You shouldn't even ask."

"It doesn't sound as pretty as it used to. My fingers have gotten so arthritic. When I'm by myself, I've been singing some of the old ballads. I'm trying to remember the ones your Great-Aunt Mary used to sing at booleying time. She was a wonderful singer, Aunt Mary.

"I'd love to hear them, Mama. So would the rest of the family."

"That's good. This music shouldn't be forgotten."

"So you'll move to Waterloo?" Margaret asked excitedly.

"I'm still thinking about it."

* * *

What is the best gift which can be given to a community? A free library occupies the first place, provided the community will accept and maintain it as a public institution, as much a part of the city property as its public schools, and, indeed, an adjunct to these.

-- from The Gospel of Wealth by Andrew Carnegie, Steel
magnate and philanthropist, 1889

It turned out that there really were things Brideen liked about living in town. The main one was the fact that she could read the newspaper every day. At the farm she'd only seen a newspaper when John or one of the boys went to Independence on errands and brought the latest issue of the *Bulletin-Journal* home. It contained mostly local news, but occasionally there were short pieces about events in Ireland, which John had followed avidly. But here in Waterloo you didn't have to go out and buy the newspaper—it came to you! There was daily delivery to households who paid a subscription fee.

Reading the newspaper made her feel like she was part of the wider world, that she knew enough to form opinions about what was going on. She followed all the discussions about the approaching turn of the century. There were endless debates over when the twentieth century would begin: At the stroke of midnight on the first of January, 1900, or on the first day of the year 1901.

There were learned arguments on both sides, but she decided it was a big fuss over nothing. What did it matter, in the face of such a momentous occasion as the dawn of a new century?

"It's all nonsense, this arguing about when the new century will start," she told Margaret and John. "I'm just glad I'm still around to see it."

Some months later she read a piece that caught her attention. It was a report about a smallpox outbreak in the Midwestern states that had hit the Meskwaki settlement particularly hard. A vaccine against smallpox had been developed and made available, but the Meskwaki had been reluctant to get it. They'd been subject to an enforced quarantine to contain the spread of the epidemic. There were even threats that anyone trying to leave the Settlement would be shot. The article was harshly critical, quoting whites who used the same disdainful language she recalled from the campaign to remove them decades ago. So her Meskwaki friends were still suffering the same kind of prejudice and abuse. But she was glad to know that they were still living on their own land.

One day she saw a piece in the Waterloo *Courier* about a new library in Fairfield, down in Jefferson County. The article said that the money for the new library came from Mr. Andrew Carnegie, who was described as the "richest man in the world". He was a Scottish immigrant to the United States who had made his wealth in the steel industry and was a leading "philanthropist", a word Brideen hadn't encountered before. She looked it up and learned that it meant a person who donated money to causes for the benefit of the community. Carnegie's newest cause was building libraries in cities across the United States, and the article contained information on how to apply for funds for a library.

She remembered how exhilarating it felt when she finally learned to read. It was a skill that children nowadays learned in school, but that she had only acquired in adulthood. There were many books that she wished she could read but it was a lot of trouble to get them. There were a few stationers' shops in town that sold books, but the selection was very small. What if Waterloo had its own library where she could browse and borrow the books she wanted to read—for free?

She told Margaret and John about the article. "Imagine. They're getting a library in Fairfield, and all they had to do was ask Mr. Carnegie for the money. We should do that here in Waterloo, too!"

They both responded enthusiastically, and Margaret suggested it might be a project that the Women's Club could take on. But Brideen was on fire with the idea, and wanted to get started on it right away.

"What's the phrase you use? 'Get the ball rolling'? The article says that the first thing they did in Fairfield was write to a Mr. James Bertram, Mr. Carnegie's assistant, and ask if they could get money for a library. Then he wrote back with a bunch of questions. I'll go to the Women's Club once I hear back from Mr. Bertram, so they can help me with the answers."

Brideen composed the letter.

"Mr. James Bertram Esq.

Dear Mr. Bertram. I am a resident of Waterloo, Iowa. We want to have a library in our town and hope that you and Mr. Andrew Carnegie can help us achieve that goal. Many thanks for any help you can offer us. Sincerely, Mrs. Bridget McDonnell."

Less than a week later, an envelope arrived from the Andrew Carnegie foundation. The return address was New York City— Brideen was surprised that the U.S. Mail could move that quickly. The letter was from James Bertram and contained a long list of questions that needed to be answered before Waterloo's request for a library could even be considered. What was the population of Waterloo? Did it already have a library, and if so, how many books did it have? Was an appropriate site available for the library? Was the town willing to pledge funds for the library's annual maintenance? So many questions, and she didn't know the answers to any of them. Margaret was sure that the ladies of the

Women's Club would be able to get all the necessary information. They were good at getting things done, she said.

Brideen was a bit nervous at her first meeting of the Women's Club. They were nice city ladies, mostly younger than she was. But there were no Irish or Catholics among them, and certainly no farm women. But they praised Brideen for taking the initiative, and were eager to offer their help, which she knew she was going to need. It took several of their weekly meetings to get through the list of questions. There were endless discussions about even the most minor points. To Brideen, it seemed like each of the members had to express an opinion on every subject, even if they simply repeated what another member had just said.

Finally they'd gathered the information needed and Brideen was ready to compose a reply to James Bertram, but there was still one outstanding issue: the location of the new library. It turned out that temporary libraries had been operating out of two rented rooms—one on each side of the Cedar River, which cut through town. A rupture developed among the members of the Women's Club, between those who wanted the new library on the east side of the river and those who said it should be on the west side. Through two meetings the factions argued and debated. Brideen was appalled that this simple matter should be so contentious. She tried to reason with them.

"Does it really matter which side of the river? It's all the same city, and it's no bother to go from one side to the other. You just walk over one of the bridges."

Her argument fell on deaf ears. Neither side was willing to give an inch. Brideen was at her wit's end.

"It's like talking to a wall," she told Margaret. "At this rate I won't live long enough to see the ribbon-cutting."

"Oh, Mama, don't talk like that."

As the stalemate wore on, Brideen decided she had waited long enough to reply to Mr. Bertram. It was difficult to know what to say. She decided to explain the problem, and be prepared for the consequences, which would, she was sure, result in Waterloo forfeiting the chance for a new library.

"Dear Mr. Bertram. I apologize for the long delay in replying. I have answered all the questions on the paper that accompanies this letter, except for the one about the location of the library. The truth is, the members of the Women's Club cannot agree on a location. Our town has a river, known as the Cedar, that runs through it. Some members want the library on the East side of the river, while others feel just as strongly it should be on the West side. I have been trying to bring both sides together in our discussions, but I have not succeeded, and I'm not sure I ever will, even if you extend more time to resolve the question. Thanks to you and the foundation for considering our request. As Mr. Carnegie himself has said, there is nothing more important to a community than a library. Yours very truly, Mrs. Bridget McDonnell"

The reply arrived as swiftly as had Mr. Bertram's previous letter.

"Dear Mrs. McDonnell. I see that this process has taken a toll on you, a problem that was certainly never intended by Mr. Carnegie. I have explained your situation to him, and he has suggested a possible solution: The foundation is prepared to increase the total grant by an amount that, divided in two, will be enough to fund the construction of two libraries, one on either side of the Cedar River. Each of the two libraries would of necessity be smaller than the one originally contemplated. But Mr. Carnegie points out that, if the collection of each avoids duplication with the other, the best books will be available to all residents of Waterloo. For both buildings, all other conditions must still be met. Please let me know if this proposal meets with your group's approval. Yours very truly, James Bertram, Esq."

Brideen was utterly flabbergasted. She had to read the letter several times to make sure she had it right. Two libraries were an outcome she could never have imagined! First she said a prayer of thanks to God, to the Virgin Mary, and to St. Jerome, the patron saint of libraries. Then she imagined herself reading Mr. Bertram's letter to the members of the Women's Club, adding the comment "even though—after all you ladies have put me through—I believe that you don't *deserve* two libraries...". Of course she would say nothing of the sort when she conveyed the news of Mr. Carnegie's decision. But it gave her a wicked kind of pleasure to imagine the looks on the ladies' faces if she did.

Chapter 16: FOUR GREEN FIELDS

I, John Berne, do solemnly swear that I am acquainted with James McDonnell of Independence, Iowa, that he is at least 37 years of age; and that I am acquainted with Sarah Burns of Independence, Iowa, that she is at least 20 years of age; that neither party is married at the present time, that both parties are legally competent to enter into the marriage contract, that I believe there are no legal objections to their marriage, and that I am a disinterested witness in this application for license. Subscribed and sworn to before me this 3d day of June A.D. 1902, M.O. Fouts, Clerk
-- from Marriage Record No. 11, Buchanan County, Iowa

Brideen was glad she didn't have to handle all the arrangements, as she had for her two daughters. These days she tired easily. But she was thrilled at the prospect of James marrying Sarah Burns. It had taken him long enough to get around to proposing! But that he fell in love with one of John Burns' own daughters was proof, if any was needed, that her fifth son had the soul of a farmer. The farms of two families connected by their Irish descent, and now by marriage, would occupy a wide swath of Washington township, Buchanan County.

The wedding mass was at St. John's in Independence, and a huge celebration with a *ceili* was held in the Burns' barn, with a band that included her own Thomas on fiddle. Brideen was overjoyed to hear the traditional tunes after so long, and wished she could join in on her whistle, but her elderly fingers would no longer cooperate. Her grandchildren were all there, dancing up a storm along with the rest of the guests. She was grateful that so many of her children still lived close by. Even Johnny had travelled all the way from Arizona for the nuptials.

James and Sarah got started right away on having a family. They had two babies in quick succession, and were already expecting a third. And though the final arrangements had taken some time, Waterloo's two libraries were finally under construction. Now it was a race to see which would be completed first, and of course the ladies of the Women's Club were cheering on their preferred candidates. Brideen's life was full, but it was plain to everyone around her that she was growing weaker. Margaret made an appointment for her to see an esteemed doctor in Waterloo. To her surprise, Brideen didn't immediately dismiss the idea, which showed that she herself had concerns about her health.

"Dr. McGee thinks it's her heart," she told Annie. "He says there's nothing for it, she just has to take it easy."

"What did he tell her?" Annie asked.

"Not much," Margaret replied. "But I can tell she knows that it's serious, that her time might not be long. She told me, 'I'm not going anywhere just yet. Not until I meet your little one, and hold a book from the new library in my hand'."

"Neither of them are ready to open, are they?"

"Not 'till the new year. And earlier she made that joke about not living to see the ribbon-cutting."

"They must already have some of the books in stock. Maybe if you tell them how instrumental she was in getting the library built, they'll let you borrow one early."

"That's a good idea, Annie," said Margaret. "I'll ask."

The head librarian was receptive to the idea. She told Margaret to find out what her mother might like to read, and she'd see if she can find something.

"See if there's anything by that young poet everyone's talking about," Brideen told her daughter. "I can't recall the name, but he's from Sligo and he writes about the old ways."

When Margaret went back and gave her mother's description, the librarian knew just who she was talking about: William Butler Yeats.

"I'm sure we'll be getting a book of his poetry soon. We just got this in, though—a new play he wrote with Lady Gregory, called *Cathleen Ni Houlihan.* It was performed at the Abbey Theatre in Dublin just last year."

Margaret took it home to show to her mother. Brideen took the slim book in her hands and opened it.

"It's not very long, is it?"

"It's a one-act play, Mama. I'm sorry I couldn't get some of Yeats' poetry, this is the only book of his they have right now. Would you like me to read some of it to you?"

Brideen nodded. Margaret turned to the first page. "Interior of a cottage close to Killala, in 1798."

"Oh, it's set in Mayo! And in the Year of the French!"

Margaret knew that her mother was born in County Mayo, and that the Year of the French was important in Irish history. She had no idea what had happened in that year, or why it was called that. But she was glad to see Brideen excited about the book.

As she continued reading, Margaret admired the play's language, but had trouble following the story. At first it seemed to be a happy account of a family engaged in preparations for a wedding later that day. But they keep getting distracted by sounds coming from outside. Something big is happening in the town, but they're not sure what it is. In the midst of all this, a mysterious character appears, an old woman named Cathleen Ni Houlihan, who speaks in strange, cryptic declarations. When asked why she wanders the roads, she replies, "My Land was taken from me. My four beautiful green fields." The family members don't quite know what to make of her, and speculate that she might be a "woman beyond the world". They mostly ignore her, except for the groom, who acts oddly solicitous toward her.

Well along in the story, Margaret stopped reading, thinking she heard her mother speak. But after listening a moment, she realized that Brideen was singing to herself in a quiet, almost ethereal voice.

"Oh, the French are on the sea, says the *Sean-Bhean bhocht*
They'll be here without delay, says the *Sean-Bhean bhocht*
The French are on the sea, they'll be here without delay
And the Orange will decay, says the *Sean-Bhean bhocht*"

Margaret was not familiar with the song, and she had no idea what it was about, especially the refrain, which was in Irish. From the look on Brideen's face, it seemed to call up feelings of deep contentment in her. The passage Margaret had just read referred to the arrival of a ship from France carrying a regiment of soldiers, much like the words of the song. Maybe the play called to mind a song from her mother's childhood.

After a few verses, Brideen went quiet, and Margaret resumed reading. Toward the end, she was jolted again by another strange turn in the story. With the sounds of battle raging in the distance, Cathleen Ni Houlihan tells the groom he must go join the French soldiers. He appears to have forgotten about or lost interest in his impending wedding, and prepares to leave, despite the family's objections. Having gotten wind of his plans, the bride arrives and begs him not to join the soldiers. He goes out the door, leaving his intended bride in tears. The characters' final glimpse of Cathleen ni Houlihan suggests she is indeed from another realm: She has been transformed into a beautiful young woman.

The entire play had taken Margaret less than an hour to read. She closed the book and was about to ask her mother about the strange ending. But she noticed that Brideen was starting to nod off. She let her mother be, and slipped quietly out of the room.

That night Brideen had a dream. It was a dark night with great howling winds. She saw herself as a very young child, huddled inside some kind of tunnel. Over the roar of the wind, she heard voices outside, shouting things like, *Where is she? Do you have her?* The force of the wind was rolling the tunnel back and forth, until she realized it wasn't a tunnel at all—it was the barrel of a butter churn. She stretched out and wrapped her arms around the plunger, which lay beside her. Her own weight, spread horizontally, helped stabilize the barrel until it stopped rolling.

The storm abruptly died down. All was quiet. She wondered if it was safe to crawl outside. She could see bright sunlight pouring in through the opening of the barrel. She crawled toward the light, and when she emerged into the open air, she was standing on the spot where four fields met. Four beautiful green fields. She knew their names: Ulster, Munster, Leinster, Connaught.

The last was the one she knew best. Because it was her home.

* * *

The death of Mrs. Bridget McDonnell occurred on Saturday morning in this city. Her maiden name was Bridget Sweeney. She was born in County Mayo, Ireland on May 4, 1838. Mrs. McDonnell was a kind mother, friend and neighbor. All who knew her speak in the highest words of praise of her life and her good deeds. She was a devout Catholic, at all times upholding the principles of that faith. In 1871 Bridget and John McDonnell moved to Buchanan County, Iowa, locating on the farm on which they resided for so many years. Bridget was the mother of nine children, two dying in infancy. Those who survive her are John, William, Anna, Edward, Thomas, James and Margaret.

-- from the Waterloo, Iowa *Courier* January, 1906

AFTERWORD: THE STORY BEHIND THE STORY

You may be wondering: Is this book fact or fiction? In which section of a bookstore does it get shelved? It's a legitimate question. The entire field of literature in prose has long been organized around the distinction between fiction and nonfiction. It was a question I had to grapple with when I embarked on writing this book. One thing I knew for certain was that I didn't have (and couldn't find out) enough information about my great-grandmother's life to fill a book. Not even close. But I'm a writer and I wanted to write this book. In truth, I felt compelled to write this book.

Many stories have another story behind them. Let me tell you this one.

BRIDEEN is built on a scaffolding of the few known facts about the life of my ancestor, Bridget Sweeney. She was born in County Mayo, Ireland in 1838 and left Ireland in 1847. From there she went to Wednesbury, a town outside Birmingham, England, where she lived for more than ten years. In 1853 she married a fellow Irishman, John McDonnell, who also likely hailed from County Mayo. They came to the United States with their two children in 1858 and settled in Hagerstown, Maryland. There they had five more children, and in 1871 they acquired a farm near Independence, Iowa, where they lived out the rest of their lives. Bridget Sweeney McDonnell died in 1906 in the nearby city of Waterloo, Iowa, a few months before the birth of her grandson Alfred, who was my father.

There was nothing particularly notable about my great-grandmother's life. She didn't accomplish great things. She wasn't a trailblazer in any field of endeavor. In truth, she's a needle in the haystack of history, one in the great mass of humans whose lives go unrecorded, except in census records. Beyond my own family connection, there's no reason for her life story to arouse interest. So why write about it? I had my reasons.

Over the years I've read a good deal of Irish history. In particular I've been drawn again and again to stories about the Famine, the grim, often horrifying accounts of the year the Irish call "Black '47", the height of the Great Hunger when the potato crop failed, and the country lost almost half its population to starvation and emigration. I was vaguely aware that my great-grandmother's time in Ireland had overlapped the famine years, and for a long time I was reluctant to even *think* about the possibility that some of those terrible things could have happened to her. I knew of no famine stories in my family. If there were any, there's no one still living who could tell me about them.

But I couldn't leave it alone, and in recent years I began to put a few clues together. If Bridget Sweeney's family was reasonably well-off, they would have been insulated from the worst consequences of the famine. On an online Irish history site, I found a land registry from nineteenth-century County Mayo and checked it out. It showed no landowners named Sweeney. Her family could have been part of the small class of merchants and shopkeepers, people of modest means and some resources. I couldn't find any records of that, either. What is known is that the vast majority of people in Mayo were tenant farmers, living on small plots of leased land where they grew potatoes, a few other vegetables, kept a cow and perhaps a pig or two. These families were the poorest in the country, of the class most severely impacted by the famine. Putting all that together, combined with the fact that she left Ireland in "Black '47," I concluded that it was very likely that Bridget Sweeney was a famine survivor.

Around that time I became familiar with the theory of transgenerational trauma—the notion that traumatic experiences in the past can have effects on subsequent generations. There was a related idea, Blood Memory, the belief shared by many cultures, particularly Indigenous people, that we carry the experiences of our ancestors in our bodies. I began to wonder if these ideas could apply to me. What mark could my ancestors' famine experiences have left on my own psyche?

I thought back to an earlier period of my life, long before I'd ever heard the term Blood Memory. On my first trip to Ireland, in my late twenties, I experienced a kind of breakdown, a bout of severe emotional turmoil that lasted throughout the entire three weeks of the visit. I was riddled with anxiety and almost completely unable to sleep. And the worst part was that I had no idea what was causing it. I'd gone to therapy before and have since, but I couldn't relate what was happening to anything in my present-day life or my childhood. The problem faded away soon after I got back from the trip, but the memory of it, the agony I'd gone through, stayed with me. I feared a recurrence, and decades passed before I felt ready to go back to Ireland.

Eventually I did go back, making several trips in the years leading up to the Covid-19 pandemic. By then I knew something was calling me back to Ireland, and that it had to do with my great-grandmother. I had to go to research this book. But more than that, I felt a need to *be* there, on the patch of earth, air, and sea, where she'd lived her early life. I've never known enough to pinpoint exactly where in Mayo she'd come from. But I had some good hunches.

I didn't have a recurrence of what I'd experienced on my first visit. But at times in Mayo, I thought I felt inklings of what had happened there almost two centuries ago. Were these echoes of my great-grandmother's trauma? Sometimes it felt foolish to think I could channel a dead person's life experiences. Just who was I writing about, anyway? An ancestor who'd survived one of the great calamities of world history? Or myself, nestled in the comforts of twenty-first century life?

Unlike many in the Irish diaspora, I'd never been especially interested in tracing my lineage or building a family tree. But I was fortunate to have a first cousin on my father's side who had a genealogical bent. She'd done some of the initial legwork and gathered her findings into a spiral-bound book, gifting copies to every branch of the large McDonnell clan (which, true to Irish-Catholic form, then numbered around seventy adults and children). The book listed the seven sisters and six brothers of my father's generation, plus all their offspring. It also included several grainy turn-of-the-century photos, all group shots save one, a full-page formal portrait of a woman wearing a high-necked vintage dress. There she was, the matriarch, gazing out from across a gap of nearly two centuries: Bridget Sweeney McDonnell, the link between the home country of Ireland and the promised land of America.

There was one problem, however. Just *what* was I going to write? How to go about researching a life about which so little was known? On a visit to Iowa I stumbled upon a treasure trove of news I could use: A photocopy of her obituary, which ran in the local paper. It was several paragraphs long, much longer than the obits surrounding it, and contained information about the various places she'd lived and for how long. Could that have been her doing? I wondered. Did she take steps before her death to ensure that the basic facts of her life would make it into print? So that one day, someone would tell her story? Was that someone me?

The obituary certainly helped me cobble together a believable account of her life. Of course, there were huge gaps, and therein lay my fact-or-fiction dilemma. I considered writing the book as historical fiction. But I resisted going that route, because I wanted to honor the real-life roots of the story. I wanted to use my great-grandmother's real name. Fact vs. fiction: Did it really have to be one or the other? In the literary world itself, the sharp distinctions between fiction and nonfiction were fading. Maybe Bridget Sweeney's life story could be—had to be—both.

I wrote my way out of the dilemma. I decided there would be no flights of fancy. Every incident in the book would have to be grounded in fact, or in plausibility. I learned as much as I could about what was going on in those places during the times she lived there. To give readers some sense of those places and times, I included quotes from various historical periods throughout the text. These are not intended to be read as "footnotes" but as integral parts of Brideen's story. In essence, the book evolved into a blend of what *did* happen and what *could have* happened in the life of Bridget Sweeney.

Some examples: She's listed in the 1851 British census records as living at an address in Wednesbury, along with some apparently unrelated adults. Was it a nail cottage? Wednesbury was one of the main nail-making villages in the Black Country, so it could well have been. Hagerstown, Maryland, where she lived with her family in the 1860s, was close to Gettysburg and other Civil War battle sites. There was an infirmary there, on the estate of a wealthy widow named Frances Kennedy. Did my great-grandmother assist with the care of wounded soldiers? I don't know one way or the other. But she could have. Did she (almost) meet Frederick Douglass, the great abolitionist? I admit that one's a bit of a stretch. But Douglass did give a lecture at Bethel Church in Baltimore on November seventeenth, 1864. Was the McDonnell farm a couple of hours' buggy ride away from the "last tribe in Iowa"? Yes, and they're still there (the Meskwaki nation, not the McDonnells. The family farm was sold decades ago.).

"Brideen" is actually a name in my family. One of my father's sisters was named Lucille at birth and became a nun in adulthood. When she made her vows, she took that name, and thereafter was always referred to in the family as "Sister Brideen". I only met her once or twice, when I was very young, and she died when I was a teenager. I was always intrigued by her name, and years later I learned that Brideen is a pet name for Bridget ("little Bridget") in Ireland. So it's not out of the question that Bridget Sweeney could have taken that name for herself.

A closing note about the music (no pun intended). Long before I knew anything about Bridget Sweeney, the music of

Ireland had been a thread running through my life. Growing up in Chicago, I heard plenty of Irish-American music, a genre typified by comic numbers like "McNamara's Band," a late nineteenth-century music-hall song popularized in the 1940s by crooner Bing Crosby. There were maudlin ballads too, like "When Irish Eyes are Smiling", also recorded by Crosby. As I grew up I moved beyond that faux-Irish heritage and discovered the traditional music known as "trad", old ballads and dance tunes, some with dates as far back as the Middle Ages. Much of Ireland's history is told through their music, particularly the great wealth of emigration songs from the famine times, wrenching laments about the pain of leaving loved ones you will never see again.

In my teens I began to play and sing Irish trad, and it's been a constant in my life ever since. On my visits to Ireland I've taken part in their unique culture of "singing sessions", informal gatherings, usually in pubs, where non-professionals take turns singing the old songs, mostly solo and unaccompanied. I found that my years of huddling by our big mahogany radio listening to the Clancy Brothers and Tommy Makem stood me in good stead—I already knew dozens of trad songs by heart! Then came the pandemic, when even the Irish couldn't go out to the pubs, and the singing sessions moved online. During the period I was working on this book, I took part in a far-flung global community of trad singers. So the choice to make Brideen a musician and keeper of the tradition came naturally. The music sustains her, keeps alive her connection to the homeland and the loved ones she had to leave behind. The music feeds her soul.

That could have been true for my great-grandmother as well. It's certainly true for me.

ACKNOWLEDGEMENTS and SOURCES

First, I want to thank my dear friends Annie Szamosi, Ellen Murray and my life partner Alec Farquhar, who all stepped up to be early-draft readers. They didn't gush, but each of them helped bolster my belief that Brideen's story was compelling and that my manuscript had merit. They gave me exactly what I needed to keep going to the finish line.

I was fortunate that my cousins Kathy Schmidt, Joe Regan and Brian Regan had paved the way for me. They passed on their extensive knowledge of our family ancestry and I'm deeply grateful for their help. My sister Sheila McDonnell Mickus, our longtime family memory-keeper, also lent help and support along the way.

I was lucky in the "expert" department, too. The staff at Eneclann, the Irish Family History Centre at the Emigration Museum in Dublin, were always willing to go the extra mile to help in my search for Brideen's origins. Regarding her post-emigration life, I also received valuable help from Bob at the Buchanan County Genealogical Society in Independence, Iowa. Simon Briercliffe at the Black Country Living Museum was a great source of information about the Irish who emigrated to the Birmingham area. Stephen Bockmiller of Hagerstown, Maryland generously shared his extensive knowledge of the town's history.

I made some wonderful friends in Ireland over the course of my research and writing. Chief among them are Fiona Neary, who invited me to give a talk at the Linenhall Arts Centre in Castlebar (reproduced in the Appendix at the back of this book) and Mayo historian Michael O'Connor, who met me for a pint at Westport's distinctive Octagon. Others in Ireland who helped (even when they weren't aware they were doing so) are David Larkin, Seamus Dooley, Des Geraghty, Margaret O'Connell and Jerry O'Reilly.

I'm grateful to Michael Occhionero and the staff at AOS Publishing in Montreal for embracing this book, and I appreciate their skill and dedication to high standards in getting it ready to send out to the world.

For the whole of my writing life, I've been held in a loving circle consisting of my partner Alec, our daughters Martha and Ivy, their partners Tyler and Eliot, my grandson Ciaran, and the extraordinary community on Toronto Island, where I live.

NOTES ON SOURCES

The Great Hunger: Ireland 1845–1849 by Cecil Woodham-Smith. First published in 1962, this book is one of the earliest and most influential examinations of the famine and its causes.

The Great Calamity: The Irish Famine 1845-1849 by Christine Kinealy

The Graves are Walking: The Great Famine and the Saga of the Irish People by John Kelly

Ireland's Welcome to the Stranger: An excursion through Ireland in 1844 & 1845, for the purpose of personally investigating the condition of the poor by Asenath Nicholson

Annals of the Famine in Ireland in 1847, 1848 and 1849 by Asenath Nicholson

Dozens of books have been published about the famine, but two by Asenath Nicholson merit special mention. Most famine accounts are written with historical hindsight, but Nicholson was an eyewitness to the events she wrote about. She was an American woman travelling solo, mostly on foot, through some of the most remote areas of Ireland. As a Protestant missionary, she didn't hide her animus for Catholicism, but her compassion and fierce determination to help the Irish people shine through nonetheless. Both books are in the Public Domain and available through various websites. *Ireland's Welcome to the Stranger* is also available in a contemporary version, edited and annotated by Maureen Murphy.

Emigrants and Exiles: Ireland and the Irish Exodus to North America by Kerby A. Miller

The Preacher and the Prelate by Patricia Byrne is a fascinating account of the controversial mission school run by Edward Nangle on Achill Island.

My Father's Wake by Kevin Toolis is a portrait of life on remote Achill Island.

A Damn Yankee, am I? Thanks!: Portraits of the Irish in the era of the American Civil War by

Aidan O'Hara

Follow the Money: The 1864 Confederate Ransom of Hagerstown, Maryland by Stephen R. Bockmiller

Hagerstown in the Civil War by Stephen R. Bockmiller

Lincoln and the Irish by Niall O'Dowd

Irish Iowa by Timothy Walch

The Irish Americans: A History by Jay P. Dolan

When the Irish Invaded Canada by Christopher Klein

Two online sources about the Black Country, both drawing on the work of Simon Briercliffe:

https://www.irishinbritain.org/news/researching-the-irish-in-britain-simon-briercliffe-on-the-irish-in-the-black-country

https://simonbriercliffe.com/2016/09/05/black-country-irish-walsall-in-the-1850s/

APPENDIX

THE NEEDLE AND THE HAYSTACK: Searching for Bridget Sweeney McDonnell
A talk presented at the Linenhall Arts Centre in June, 2022

From the Waterloo, Iowa *Courier* January, 1906:
The death of Mrs. Bridget McDonnell occurred on Saturday morning in this city. Her maiden name was Bridget Sweeney. She was born in County Mayo, Ireland on May 4, 1838.
I am a child of the Mayo diaspora. Bridget Sweeney McDonnell was my great-grandmother. There's no one alive now who knew her. Even my own father never knew his grandmother. She died the same year he was born.
The obituary in the Iowa paper gives a few details about her:
Mrs. McDonnell was a kind mother, friend and neighbor. All who knew her speak in the highest words of praise of her life and her good deeds. She was a devout Catholic, at all times upholding the principles of that faith.
Pretty much the standard language you find in obituaries. But it doesn't tell you a whole lot about who she was as a person.
Like many Irish-Americans, I grew up with pride in my Irish heritage. I play and sing traditional Irish music, I've read and learned a lot about the country's history. But for most of my life, I wasn't terribly curious about my own family roots. I knew that my ancestors came from Ireland to America back in the 19th century. But that was all.
One day I was looking at an album compiled by a cousin on my father's side, full of grainy old photos of various family groupings. I'd paged through it many times before. But this time one of the photos leapt out at me. It was a posed, formal portrait of a woman. The caption underneath read "Bridget Sweeney

McDonnell." I knew that she was a great-grandmother on my father's side. But I felt an odd sense of kinship I hadn't felt before. Just who was this woman staring out at me from more than a century ago?

I decided to share the photo with a County Mayo History group on Facebook, and I was taken aback by some of the emotional responses: "She looks kind." "A Great Lady." "Such an Irish face." "She is lovely and emanates strength and kindness" What was it about this woman that caused complete strangers to read so much into her face? I set out on a journey to find out more about this relative I never knew.

I wrote to the Buchanan County Genealogical Society in Iowa. A helpful fellow named Bob kindly sent me the little information they had about her, which included her obituary. I was glad to have it, but it left so many questions unanswered. Just where in County Mayo had Bridget Sweeney come from? In an effort to find out, I ventured down a rabbit hole of online Irish genealogy websites, entering her name and year of birth into their search records. But I kept coming up empty. I shouldn't have been surprised that there were literally hundreds of Bridget Sweeneys in the 19th century records in Ireland, especially in County Mayo. But nothing really matched. I couldn't determine the parish or townland she came from.

Over time it dawned on me that searching for my great grandmother was the equivalent of looking for a needle in a haystack. I realized that if I wanted to learn what I could about Bridget Sweeney's life, instead of a vain search for the needle, I'd be better off learning more about the haystack. So I set out to learn what I could about life in Mayo in the early nineteenth century.

On the geneaology sites, there are lists of the names of landowners in the county prior to 1850. I checked, and there were no Sweeneys among them. Her family could have been shopkeepers or tradespeople. Possibly they could have worked in the linen trade, in this very building we're in now. But more likely, like most people in Mayo, Bridget Sweeney's parents worked the land, spoke the Irish language and, with any luck, owned a cow and maybe a pig. So my great-grandmother likely came from poor farming people, who left Ireland more than 150 years ago. Why did they leave?

There was a big clue in her obituary, staring me in the face:

When a young girl of 9 years she moved with her parents to England. Her young girlhood was spent in Birmingham.

Bridget Sweeney was nine years old when she left Ireland. She was born in 1838. 1838 + 9 = 1847, aka "Black 47." My great grandmother was a survivor of the Great Famine.

Bridget Sweeney knew what it was to be hungry.

I was born in the United States, and so was my father and his siblings. How did the family get to the U.S. from England? And why did they go first to Birmingham? What was that about? Once again, the likely explanation lies in Mayo history: People left Ireland in droves in the year 1847, and Mayo was one of the hardest-hit, losing a third of its population to a combination of death and emigration. But many of those poor farmers couldn't afford the passage across the Atlantic to America. So whole families went to England instead, where they hoped to earn money for the voyage by working in the factories around Birmingham.

For a good part of her girlhood and teenage years, Bridget Sweeney was probably a factory girl. But unlike the lass in the folk song with that title, Bridget did not have a wealthy gentleman offer to rescue her from a hard life. She got married at the age of seventeen to a young man named John McDonnell, who likely also came from County Mayo.

Her marriage to John McDonnell occurred at Walsall, England in 1855. Three years later they removed to America, locating in Hagerstown, Maryland.

Bridget Sweeney McDonnell finally made it to America in 1858, more than 10 years after she fled the famine in Ireland. Though a lot of Irish immigrants ended up in New York, she went to Hagerstown, Maryland. Where was that? I figured it was probably some nondescript town near Baltimore. Until I looked for it on a map and noticed some of the nearby towns and cities had names like Antietam. Fredericksburg. Gettysburg. Sites of the bloodiest battles of the American Civil War. In the thick of those battles, thousands of Irish soldiers fought on side of the Union. They became famous as the Fighting Sixty-Ninth regiment

I don't really know if any of my ancestors fought in that regiment. But I do know that my great-grandmother and her family lived right in the midst of where the war was raging in 1861 – 1865. Did it affect their lives? How could it not? Bridget Sweeney McDonnell lived through two of the signature historical events of the 19th century: the great Famine in Ireland, and the American Civil War.

For the remainder of her life, Bridget returned to her rural roots.

In 1871 they moved to Buchanan County, Iowa, locating on the farm on which they resided for so many years. Bridget McDonnell was the mother of nine children, two dying in infancy. Those who survive her are John, William, Anna, Edward, Thomas, James and Margaret.

James, the second-youngest child, was my grandfather. His son, my father Alfred, grew up on that farm in Iowa.

So that's pretty much the extent of what I know about Bridget Sweeney McDonnell. Well, not entirely. Like I said about the needle and haystack, the big events, the common things that happen to everyone, contain the individual stories too. There are many dozens of songs about the sad farewells and wrenching departures of the famine years. What songs like "Thousands are Sailing" tell us is that, like so many others, Bridget Sweeney's family did not want to leave Ireland.

Brideen

Ye brave Irish heroes, wherever you be
I pray stand a moment and listen to me.
Your sons and your daughters are going away
And thousands are sailing to Amerikay

On the morning of leaving, they move to and fro
Till the trunks are all packed up and ready to go
O their hearts will be breaking as the ship leaves the shore
Fare thee well, dear old Ireland, we may ne'er see you more

So good luck to those people and safe may they land
They are leaving their country for a far distant strand
They are leaving old Ireland, no longer can stay
And thousands are sailing to Amerikay